*Memoirs of a
Mother-in-Law*

*Memoirs of a
Mother-in-Law*

George R. Sims

ALMA CLASSICS

ALMA CLASSICS
London House
243-253 Lower Mortlake Road
Richmond
Surrey TW9 2LL
United Kingdom
www.almaclassics.com

Memoirs of a Mother-in-Law first published in 1892
This edition first published by Alma Classics Ltd in 2014

Printed and bound by CPI Group (UK) Ltd, Croydon, CR0 4YY

ISBN: 978-1-84749-341-5

Contents

*Memoirs of a
Mother-in-Law*

Memoir I

Myself

F ROM TIME IMMEMORIAL it has been the fashion for mothers-in-law to be held up to ridicule and contempt. I am not quite sure about the use of the word immemorial, because I am not a professional author, and when I was a girl young women were not so highly educated as they are now, and plain writing, plain sewing and plain cooking were what I was brought up to – and, I may as well add at once, plain speaking, which I inherited from my dear mother.

My dear mother always spoke her mind. Many a time have I heard her say to my dear father when he remonstrated with her about something she had said in company, "I can't help it, Zachariah; I always did speak my mind, and I always will, no matter whether it offends people or not."

As a girl I spoke my mind, as a young woman I spoke my mind, and, though I am a middle-aged woman now, I speak it still, and I intend to speak it in these memoirs. I know that I have occasionally given offence by so doing. A woman with four married daughters and three married sons, a single daughter, who lives at home, a dear, clever little mischievous boy of eleven for her youngest, and a husband who can't say "boh" to a goose, unless the goose is his wife, and who has for the whole thirty-five years of our married life left me not only to say all the unpleasant things, but to do them also, while he keeps out of the way, can't help giving offence occasionally if she is honest and plain-spoken.

Of course, if my husband – not that, as a man, I wish to say a word against him – had done his duty as a husband and a father, I should not in certain quarters bear the reputation of being "a Tartar". That is the elegant expression I once heard applied to me by a young man from an ironmonger's shop in my own house to my own servant.

Tartar or no Tartar, I didn't allow his master to impose upon my husband, who really has no more idea of the value of things than a child, and ought never to be trusted in a shop alone. He believes everything the shopmen tell him, and hates what he calls haggling over the price of anything. I once let him go with me to buy a bonnet because he said he had seen one in a window that he thought would suit me, and I declare he made quite a scene. Directly I had tried on about half a dozen he began to fidget with his stick and shuffle his feet, and he wanted me to have a hideous thing that made me look a perfect fright. Of course I saw what was the matter. He thought I was giving the young woman in the shop a little trouble. "Oh, of course," I said to him, "you don't mind what sort of a fright I look, you only think of other people."

I said it out loud, and he went as red as a turkey cock, which is a painful habit he has when I speak to him before people.

"I don't want you to look a fright, my dear," he stammered, "but you don't want to try on every bonnet in the shop and then walk out without buying one."

I have never been able to understand why men have such a horror of walking out of a shop without buying anything. Of course the assistants would like it if you bought the entire contents of the shop, but you don't go into a shop to please the assistants – you go to please yourself, and if you are not pleased with anything you see, or if it is too dear, why should you buy it?

Two of my daughters take after their father in this respect. I have known my eldest, Sabina, after we have spent a morning at Shoolbred's, or Whiteley's, or Marshall & Snelgrove's,* and not found exactly what we wanted, rush back just as we were going out of the shop and buy some absurd and utterly useless bit of trumpery for sixpence, and when I have remonstrated with her for wasting her money, reply: "Oh, Mamma, we have given such a lot of trouble, I was obliged to buy something."

It was the absurd idea of buying something, I am sure, which led my husband to buy the cruet stand at the ironmonger's in the Tottenham Court Road, which caused the young man to tell my own housemaid that I was a Tartar. And the hussy had the impudence – she didn't know that I was looking over the banisters – to say that I was that, and no mistake, and poor master would never hear the last of the cruet stand. Poor master, indeed. I poor-mastered her, and she left that day month, and but for her mother calling and appealing to me as a mother myself she'd have had no character from me. There's a good deal too much "poor master" about the giggling, flighty servant girl of today.

I daresay I did say some very unpleasant things to the ironmonger, but I only spoke my mind, and I would have done it under the circumstances if he had been twenty ironmongers.

I happened to say one day at dinner that we had never had a decent cruet stand; of course we had cruet stands, flimsy, silly, tottery-overy modern things, but I always remembered dear mother's best cruet stand (which was my admiration when I was a little girl, and an ornament to any dining table), and my two boys trying to reach the pepper at lunch knocked the one we had over and saturated the clean tablecloth (and one of my best ones) with vinegar and Worcester sauce, not to mention mustard. I spoke my mind, and said that it was not the sort of cruet stand I expected when I married a man of means.

The very next day my poor, foolish husband – as good-hearted a man as ever breathed – must march off to an ironmonger's in Tottenham Court Road, and go in and ask to see some first-class cruet stands. Why he went to an ironmonger's I don't know, especially to a cheap, advertising ironmonger, with fire irons and dustpans and things hanging up outside to attract attention; but he did, and the proprietor soon saw the sort of man he had got hold of, and persuaded him to buy a big, vulgar, wretched thing, and charged him six guineas for it. Directly it came home I saw what it was at a glance; and when John – that's my husband – told me what he'd paid for it I was horrified, and I said, "If you think I'm going to allow you to be swindled like that you're mistaken. I'll send it back at once and demand the money."

Then he began to argue, and said that he'd bought it and paid for it, and I was prejudiced. We argued the matter over for an hour, but he was obstinate, and said I couldn't expect him to go into the shop and tell the man that his wife said he was a fool. I don't think this sentence is quite clear. Those his and hims always did bother me, but then I'm not a professional writer. It is much easier to say what you mean than to write what you mean. I made my husband understand me, for I said: "Then if you don't go back with the cruet stand *I* will" – and I wrapped it up in the flimsy pink tissue paper that they had sent it home in, and took it by the handle, and I went off with it then and there, and I walked into the shop and put it down on the counter, and I said to the proprietor, who was staring at me as if he'd never seen an indignant wife before, "You'll be good enough to give me back six guineas, which my husband, Mr Tressider, paid you for this trumpery thing yesterday." There were several customers in the shop, and the proprietor was evidently taken aback for he gasped before he could speak. "I don't understand what you mean, madam." "Oh, I will make my meaning plain," I said. "My husband doesn't know what cruet stands are, and he paid you six guineas for *this*. I *do* know what cruet stands are, so I'll trouble you for the money back again."

"If you are dissatisfied with the cruet, madam, I'll change it – but we never return money." "Then," said I, "you'll have to begin the practice now."

He gurgled in his throat and glared at me, but I wasn't frightened. I knew I had the best of it. He couldn't turn me out of the shop, and the other customers had left off buying and were listening, and the assistant couldn't attract their attention. I found out afterwards one lady was giving a large wedding order for a young couple going to be married, and she was quite close and could hear every word. I think the proprietor thought she might be alarmed and think she had come to what my eldest son John called "the wrong shop", and not give the order. At any rate, he saw that he had a determined woman to deal with, and he altered his tone and said in a loud voice, "Madam, it is not my desire that any article which does not give satisfaction should be forced on a customer. I will give you the money back rather than have any unpleasantness." And he did, and I went back in triumph, and I put down the money on the table under my husband's nose, and I said, "There, if people can take the coat off *your* back they can't off *mine*," and then I put the money back into my pocket and gave him a look and left him, and it was a very long time after that before he went shopping on his own account for the house again – and I made the old cruet stand do.

I have narrated this little incident because it gives some slight idea of the responsibilities which have fallen to my lot as the practical head of the family. A better husband than mine in many ways no woman could desire, and I can honestly say that I wish in some things all my daughters had been as fortunate, but when everything disagreeable that has to be said or done is left to the wife to say or do, you cannot wonder that she gets a reputation for being what that impertinent ironmonger's man – he only came to bring a coal scuttle home which had been repaired, and it would never have gone to his master's shop if I had known it – called a Tartar. Goodness knows I have had enough to make me a Tartar. You don't bring up nine children and see seven of them married without having something to try your temper and make you occasionally distrustful of human nature, not to speak of servants and a husband who, though a clever man in business, is utterly helpless when it comes to a bother at home, and yet so devoted to his domestic hearth that it was with the greatest difficulty that I could persuade him to go into society now and then for the sake of the girls. Nice marriages they would have made if it hadn't been for me, and even as it is, I am really very anxious about two of their husbands. My girls – God bless them – have always been the best of daughters to me, and they are now wives that any man might be proud of; but I have never been able to induce my husband to take the position he should do as a father-in-law. If a foot has had to be put down, it has always been mine, and I say that it is a father's place to look after his sons-in-law.

They say that your son is your son till he gets himself a wife, but your daughter is your daughter all the days of your life, and I always made up my mind that my daughters should not be absolutely removed from my influence, or deprived of my advice when they married and had homes of their own. As to my sons – well, I cannot say that their choice would have been mine. I know where John Tressider would have been had I been like my second son William's wife. She is a very lovely girl, and her manners are charming. It is really very hard to find fault with her, but her views are not mine. Indeed, I doubt if she has any views at all. When people say to me, "What a lovely girl your second son's wife is," I can't help shaking my head. Her beauty, her sweetness – for she really has a sweet temper – have completely blinded William to her utter lack of household management. I was horrified when I learnt from William what his household bills came to, and the money he allowed her for dress. I tried to reason with him, and told him I should talk seriously to Marion – that is his wife – and all the thanks I got was, "Oh, Mother, for goodness' sake don't find fault with Marion, she's so sensitive; she'll take it to heart. She's been crying over her butcher's book ever since you found out that mistake of ninepence in the addition. I'm sure you didn't mean any harm, my dear mother, but that and your asking what she paid a pound for lamb at our little dinner party has preyed upon her mind. She's always saying to me that she is afraid you don't think she's a fit wife for me."

Of course I said it was very hard that I couldn't make a simple remark without being accused of trying to ruin my son's domestic happiness, and I felt hurt. I certainly did speak my mind on the occasion referred to, and I shouldn't have been doing my duty as a mother if I had not done so.

It was the most natural thing in the world. William gave a little dinner party – quite a family affair, his friends and dear Marion's, for she is really a dear girl – and quite innocently in the middle of dinner, having been discussing the terrible price of everything in London nowadays with a lady who was talking about the Stores,* I said to my daughter-in-law, "What do you pay in this neighbourhood, my dear, for lamb?"

Could a mother-in-law ask a more harmless question, and yet will you believe it, the silly girl turned crimson to the roots of her hair, and stammered and said, "she didn't know."

"Not know, my dear," I said. "Don't you check your butcher's book? Do you allow him to charge you what he chooses?"

I am sure I spoke most kindly but Mr Tressider, my husband, began to wink violently at me, and William, my son, glared at me. He has a terrible habit of glaring which I tried in vain to wean him off when he was a child. I can't think where he got it, because his father doesn't do it and there never was a glare in my family.

"What *is* the matter?" I said, and then I noticed that the silly girl's eyes were full of tears.

That annoyed me, and I spoke my mind, not unkindly but firmly. I said: "My child, I'm sorry if I have in any way hurt your feelings, but it was only my mother's love which spoke. If William doesn't mind what you pay for your lamb, of course it is no business of mine."

There was silence for a moment, and then Mr Tressider began to tell one of his absurd stories about when we first set up housekeeping. Of course, he did it to turn the conversation. He has told the story a hundred times, and everybody always laughs, and I suppose that's why he is so fond of telling it, but I never could see the humour of it.

The story, which he generally exaggerates, is this. When we were first married I found a cigar bill of my husband's lying about, and wishing to know the price of everything, I asked him how many cigars he got for all that money, and he told me. I forget how many now, but I know they came out at about sixpence each.

I thought it a great deal of money for a wretched little thing that a man puffs away in half an hour, and so one day, happening to be in a grocer's shop, and seeing some boxes of cigars labelled "a bargain", I thought I would see if I couldn't save John a little money in cigars, so I asked the price, and the grocer told me they were ten-and-sixpence a box of a hundred. I bought a box and took them home, and I said to my husband: "John, dear, you had better let me buy your cigars in future. Look, I can get them for ten-and-six a hundred, and you have been paying fifty shillings." My husband took a cigar out and looked at it, and then he burst out laughing, and said that he was very much obliged to me, but he wanted to live a little longer for my sake, and I believe he gave those cigars to the gardener, who came in once a week at that time, until I discovered that for his entire year's wages we only got four gcraniums and his dirty boots tramping in and out of the hall, and then I stopped it and looked after the garden myself, and made the servants help me.

I have never understood to this day why John wouldn't smoke those cigars because I paid less than the usual price for them. A cigar is a cigar, and I'm sure those smoked beautifully, for I met the gardener out with one one Sunday, and it smelt quite as strong as any my husband smokes. But everybody laughed at the story as if it was something out of *Punch*,* and I made no further remark. But after dinner William came to me, and he said: "Mother, I know you meant it kindly, but Marion is very sensitive, and no young wife likes to be made to appear ignorant before her own guests. Please don't do it again."

"Oh, very well, William," I said. "If your wife objects to my making a remark at my own son's table…"

He saw that I was hurt, and so he took my face between his hands and kissed me. "There, there, mother," he said, "don't get angry, you old dear; let us say no more about it. You know Marion thinks you the most wonderful woman that ever lived, and so do I."

William was always a good son, and his heart is as soft and gentle now as it was when he was a boy. I can't be angry with him, and I never could, but all the same, I do not think that a young woman who doesn't know what she pays the butcher for lamb is the wife for a young man who has his way to make in the world.

Mothers-in-law always have been misunderstood, and I suppose they always will be. No one has ever put *their* side of the question properly. That is what I intend to do here, and that is why, now that all my children but two are married, and I have more time on my hands, I have determined to take up the cause of the most maligned race on the face of the earth. I am quite sure when I have related my experiences I shall have put quite a different complexion on the matter. I daresay I shall offend some of my sons-in-law, and some of my daughters-in-law will feel aggrieved, but I can't help that – I always did speak my mind, and I certainly am not going to mince matters now.

It is time that someone said a good word for mothers-in-law. In most books that I have read they are grossly misrepresented, and on the stage they are always held up to ridicule and, I might say, contempt. I have never been able to understand why there is such an absurd prejudice against them. Of course, I can understand a man when he marries a young, confiding girl, who knows nothing of life, not caring for her mother – an experienced woman of the world – to know or to see too much. But it is a mother's duty to point out to her daughter the proper way to manage a husband, and to give her the benefit of that knowledge which the poor thing (the mother-in-law) has often acquired by painful personal experience.

I have always intended to write my own personal experience, and with that end in view I have made notes of many things as they occurred, and I have kept a diary. I have always kept it under lock and key, for Mr Tressider has a most irritating habit of picking up any little scrap of writing that may be left about on my table, and reading it – and there are many things one writes in one's diary which one doesn't care for everyone to see. Talk about curiosity being a female failing! I never yet met the woman who was half as inquisitive as some men I've known. But John Tressider has never seen my diary, and I have kept him in absolute ignorance of my intention to make public my experiences as a mother-in-law. If I had only hinted it to him it would have been all over the place in no time, and I have no doubt that he, in his foolish, soft-hearted way, would have made no end of objection to it, and would have pretended that my sons-in-law and daughters-in-law might not like it.

As I am going to tell nothing but the truth, I cannot see how they can possibly object. At any rate, I shall not ask their permission first. What I am doing I am doing in the interest of a very large and a very badly used class, and though the sons- and daughters-in-law may occasionally wince – there are very few people who can stand plain speaking – I am perfectly certain that before I've finished I shall have earned the gratitude of every mother-in-law in the United Kingdom. So much for myself by way of introduction. It was necessary that I should say something, though I was never one to talk much about myself. But I do not wish to be misunderstood, although for the matter of that I ought to be used to it by this time. My husband never understood me, and my children have not always shown that appreciation of my motherly care and foresight for their welfare which I could have desired. But I have never been deterred from doing my duty, and I shall continue to do it unflinchingly as long as my name is Jane Tressider.

I shall now proceed to my first experience as a mother-in-law, or, rather, as a prospective mother-in-law – the painful moment when I learnt for the first time that my eldest daughter, Sabina, had conceived an affection for someone outside her own domestic circle, and that a young man was anxious to remove her from the bosom of her family and take her from her devoted mother! It is naturally a blow to an affectionate mother when the first of her children shows symptoms of a desire to quit the shelter of the maternal wing. I am not ashamed to say that my first feelings when I heard that a young man had fallen in love with my daughter were those of indignation. There was a reason for my indignation, and that reason was the gentleman himself. I consider his behaviour... But that young man will have to be my second memoir.

Memoir II

"Miss Sabina's Young Man"

"MISS SABINA'S YOUNG MAN!"
Those were the words that struck my horrified ear one morning when, absolutely without the slightest idea of listening, I accidentally overheard a conversation between the housemaid and the cook in the housemaid's pantry. I had gone downstairs into the kitchen to see the oven, cook always complaining that it was the oven's fault when the pies and cakes, etc., were sent up to table either half baked or burnt to a cinder.

I have had a good many years' experience of housekeeping now, and I have never yet found an oven and a cook that exactly suited each other. My oven is too slow for some cooks and too quick for others.

I know what the cooks say about the oven, but I wonder what the oven would say about the cooks if it could speak.

And it is not only with regard to the cooking that the oven has to bear all the blame – it is the same with the coals. The way the coals are used in the kitchen is something too terrible. No sooner is the cellar full than it is empty, and if I complain and point out to the servants that coals are a small fortune per ton, and that I do not wish my husband to spend his old age

in the workhouse through the wilful extravagance of his servants, I am always met with the statement that it is all the fault
of the grate. It is a wasteful grate; with such a grate the coals
are gone in no time – it is impossible to keep a small fire with
such a grate, and all the heat goes up the chimney.

I am sure I have spent a small fortune and tried no end of
things to try and get that oven and that grate right so that the
servants could not possibly make them an excuse for their own
laziness and their own extravagance.

I have had bricks put in the back of the grate and things done
to the chimney, and my husband even once went so far as to
consult a scientific gentleman, who charged a guinea to come
and look at the fireplace, and came on a dirty day, and never
wiped his boots, and put his wet umbrella down in the dining
room and let it trickle all over the carpet, and then walked away
and wrote to my husband, enclosing him a design for some
newfangled affair which would cost about seventy pounds, and
looked to me like having the house half pulled down to fit it up.

When my husband showed me the man's letter I spoke my
mind pretty plainly, and I would have written a reply, only
my husband, who is a most nervous man, begged me not to,
saying that the law of libel was a very peculiar one in this
country, and it was always more dangerous to call a man a
swindler who really was a swindler than one who was not. I
said if that was the law more shame for those who made it, and
if women had more to do with making the laws they would
prevent men making such foolish ones. It has always seemed

to me so utterly absurd to pretend that women cannot go into Parliament because they are not logical, with the laws made by men in Parliament staring us in the face. I defy women to make Acts of Parliament more illogical than those the men have been making for centuries.

But that has nothing to do with the oven and the kitchen, though if I have time some day I should very much like to make my views public upon the present position of women in connection with politics.

My husband and my sons and daughters have never appreciated my views on the subject, and begged me, with tears in their eyes, not to join a women's league which was started some years ago, because they pretended to be afraid of what I should say if I once got up on the platform. I should have spoken my mind whether there were any reporters present or not, but I am sure I should not have said anything which my husband and children need have been ashamed of.

My son William really was quite upset when I mentioned that several ladies had asked me to join and be the secretary for our neighbourhood. "For goodness' sake, Mother," he said, "don't think of such a thing; you are too honest, too plain spoken, to take an active part in public affairs. I am sure you wouldn't like to be called to order by the chair or to be made to leave off before you had finished." "I should like to see anybody making me leave off till I'd said what I had to say," I replied.

"They would do it, Mother, I know that," said William, "and then there'd be a scene, or perhaps in the excitement of the moment you might tell the chair what you thought of her, and it really wouldn't be nice, you know, Mother, for the *Daily Telegraph* to come out one morning with 'Scene at the Women's League – Extraordinary Speech by Mrs Tressider' – would it, mother?"

I thought the matter over, and I agreed not to join; but really I cannot understand why my children should always try to make out that I am such a gorgon. Some day, when I am gone, they will appreciate me, but, as I say to them often when they annoy me and upset me, it will be too late then. I will not deny that I am quick-tempered, but then I have had a great deal to try my nerves and make them what they are, and I soon forget and am very easily mollified.

I certainly flew into what my husband calls one of my "rages" when I heard the cook and housemaid talking about my eldest daughter in that unbecoming manner in the housemaid's pantry. They evidently had not heard me come down into the kitchen to see about the oven, for they were giggling and talking at the top of their voices. I heard something about a fine-looking young fellow and a dark moustache, and then I heard the words which for a moment paralysed me and rooted me to the spot: "Miss Sabina's young man!"

I ask you, dear readers, that is those of you who are mothers and have had daughters to bring up, if it would not have given you a shock to hear two giggling hussies of servants discussing your eldest daughter's "young man" when you hadn't the slightest idea of the existence of such a person.

When I heard that, I felt the hot blood rush to my cheeks, and I was inclined to walk straight into the pantry and ask the hussies how they dared talk of their young mistress in such a way, but by a great effort I managed to control myself. I felt that I really might say too much, and if — which I hardly thought possible — my Sabina had really given those girls any reason to link her name with that of a young man, the information had better come to me from my daughter herself.

Sabina was upstairs playing the piano in the morning room, and singing some absurd thing in Italian or German — both languages are the same to me, for I am not ashamed to say that in my younger days girls were not expected to know more than their own language and a little French, but my eldest daughter, Sabina, and my second daughter, Maud, "the beauty of the family", as her brothers and sisters call her, are really very clever linguists, reading Italian and German, and speaking it remarkably well, though up to the present it has not been of much use to them, except to enable them to talk together occasionally without letting me know what they are saying.

I have frequently told them that young girls have no business to converse together in a language which their mother does not understand, but they always say if they don't practise how are they to keep up their knowledge, which certainly is a fair argument, but I very much prefer them to talk their German and Italian when they are alone, and not before me.

I have always been proud of my daughter Sabina's many accomplishments, and I am not ashamed to confess that

I always looked forward to her making a good marriage. At the time I received my terrible shock from the housemaid's pantry, Sabina was just eighteen, and though her father would sometimes say "I suppose we shall be having Sabina engaged presently", I had not seriously thought of her being sought in marriage by anyone.

None of my girls have ever been what the world calls "flirty", and in this they take after me. John Tressider was the first young man who ever paid me marked attention, and as soon as I felt that I loved him I made no concealment of the fact, and from the hour we first understood each other's feelings I can conscientiously say I never caused him a pang of jealousy.

I did not conceal the fact that I was in love from my parents. I took my dear mother into my confidence at once, and my dear father immediately began to make enquiries as to John's worldly circumstances, and as soon as we were satisfied that they were such as would enable him to maintain a wife in comfort, if not in luxury, I delicately hinted to John that an interview with my father would be desirable if he really wished that we should be engaged to each other.

Brought up in those strict principles, which I understand are now sneered at as old-fashioned, I could not understand any child of mine having an affair of the heart without the cognisance and approbation of her mother and father.

I remembered, then, with something like apprehension, a circumstance which I had long since forgotten. When Sabina was at a boarding school at Clapham, being then about fifteen years of age, a young gentleman at a boys' school, which sat opposite to the young ladies' school in church, had had the audacity to tell her in the deaf-and-dumb alphabet, during the singing of the last hymn, that he was in love with her, and asked her what her name was. The little imp was only fourteen, so, of course, it was mere childish mischief; but on that occasion, instead of reporting the affair to the headmistress, Sabina, I regret to say, replied with her fingers and gave him her name. And this terrible boy – he was the son of a baronet in India, and the climate and living among barbarians may have had something to do with it – had the impertinence to send her a letter a few days afterwards to the school, couched in most romantic language.

It was through that letter it all came out, for my daughter was showing it to her bosom friend, the niece of Lady Smith, whose husband was formerly Lord Mayor of London, when the French governess fortunately observed the guilty appearance of the girls, and, thinking something was wrong, kept her eyes open, as only a French governess can, and pounced down upon the letter and confiscated it, and brought the matter before the headmistress. Then of course it all came out, and Sabina, brought up like all my children to be truthful, confessed everything, and, it being close upon breaking-up time, brought home a holiday task as a punishment, and a letter from the headmistress explaining the circumstances.

I was very angry indeed, and but for her father I should have gone over to Clapham, and called upon the principal of that young gentleman's school, and have told him what I thought of the supervision which allowed his pupils to converse in the deaf-and-dumb language with young ladies in church. But my husband as usual made absurd objections, and so after lecturing Sabina seriously the matter was allowed to drop.

I ought to say that the child – for she was only a child – was sincerely penitent, and declared that she would never do such a thing again, and she didn't think she would have done it then only the girls were used to talking to each other in the deaf-and-dumb alphabet, and she answered the boy without thinking she was doing any harm.

Since that time she had never given me a moment's uneasiness, and really had, as I thought, attracted very little attention at balls and parties – not half so much as Maud, her junior by a year, and, as I have explained previously, "the beauty of the family".

Poor Maud had really been very much worried, and had to endure no end of chaff from her brothers owing to the number of young fellows who had been supposed to have fallen head over ears in love with her. Certainly several young men of our acquaintance were assiduous callers before Maud became engaged, and left off calling so often directly afterwards; and, when I come to deal with that portion of my experiences, you will understand what a nuisance it was to me – one gentleman in particular, who was much too old for her, being thirty, and having a huge red moustache, the brother of a Miss Mosenthal, a great friend of Sabina's, always calling to fetch his sister with a huge bassoon outside a four-wheel cab, which was a source of considerable merriment to my boys.

Of course, when the boys chaffed their sister about him, as boys will, she was most indignant, and I heartily sympathized with her, for though young Mosenthal had money, I never could take kindly to the idea of my beautiful, graceful Maud marrying a man with a red moustache and a big bassoon. It was bad enough to have it waiting outside our front door for hours on a four-wheel cab, but a big bassoon always in the house would have been a fearful thing to go through life with, especially if he played on it at all.

If John Tressider had been afflicted with a big bassoon, or any huge musical instrument of that sort, I should have said, "If it comes to the big bassoon and myself, John, you can take your choice, but one roof does not shelter us both." Thank goodness my husband is not musical. What with the girls at the piano and Tommy, my youngest, who is really a remarkable musical genius and can play anything, and from a child had a nursery full of drums and penny whistles and concertinas and Jew's harps,* and a dreadful arrangement of pipes which he used to go up- and downstairs with, blowing and pretending to be a Punch and Judy man, and generally selecting the morning when I had a bad headache to come and play God Save the Queen outside my bedroom door, there is quite enough music in the family without my having a big bassoon for a son-in-law.

My youngest son was christened Thomas, but everybody calls him "Tommy Tressider", and I have fallen into the habit myself. A brilliant career lies before that boy, I am sure, and I shall never be satisfied until I have persuaded his father to send him to Eton or Harrow, and to one of the universities afterwards. There is really nothing he cannot do, and though now only eleven years old he has taken more prizes than any other boy in the day school he attends, for I cannot as yet bring myself to part with him and let him go to a boarding school. He *is* mischievous, but there, all boys of his age are, and I tell his sisters they ought to be proud of him. I once had severely to reprimand my third daughter Jane for saying that Tommy could do anything because he was my favourite. I have no favourites. All my children, married and single, are as dear to me as each other, but Tommy is the youngest, the child still, and I think as we grow older we cling to the child that is still a child, though, for the matter of that, our children are always children to us.

I have a dear old aunt who is now nearly ninety years of age, healthy and hearty still, though occasionally her memory is a little weak. She plays whist every night, living with her married son, as she has done for many, many years, and her grandchildren are all young men and women now, but often at night she will suddenly drop her cards and say, "Hush! I think I heard one of the children cry." Poor dear, the youngest of those children is two-and-twenty now, but she still fancies that they are in the nursery upstairs, and in her loving old heart they will never grow to men and women.

Of course, that is a case of the mind wandering and old age, but to a great many of us our children never grow up. When your son is fifty he is still "your boy", when your daughter is forty she is still "your girl", and this is, I fancy sometimes, where a mother-in-law is misunderstood. Her children marry, but they are still children to her, and she is too apt perhaps to think of them as children, and as children to behave towards them as a watchful mother.

"Mother," your boy will cry when he is a man and married, perhaps with children of his own, "I am no longer a child." Not in his own eyes perhaps – not in the eyes of the world, but in his mother's eyes, yes. A child he is, a child he always will be.

I am not a sentimental woman, I hope, but there is one thing I never think of without the tears coming into my eyes – the story of the dear old mother who sat by the deathbed of her son, a man of sixty, wrinkled and aged with a wild life, and lifting the grey head gently from the pillow, let it lean against her breast, while she prayed that God would spare "her child – her little one".

It would have been easy, perhaps, for some people to laugh at the old woman calling that old grey-haired man "her little one", but to me it has always been a beautiful poem – tender and true – for to the mother's loving heart time tells no tale. Her children are her children always – old and bent and grey, they are still her "little ones".

And that, perhaps, is why sometimes, too, a mother clings to the youngest – the one who has not grown up and begun to resent being looked upon as a child. I am quite sure I always try to be perfectly just, but I will not let my poor Tommy always be made out to be in the wrong; and his sisters, though not spiteful or unkind girls, do really sometimes give him a worse character than he deserves.

I have had to mention Tommy before I intended to, because he considerably smoothed the way for me towards an elucidation of the mystery of – to use the language of the servants – "Miss Sabina's young man".

When I entered the morning room and saw Sabina seated at the piano, my mind had, for a moment, reverted to her early school escapades, and I had a momentary idea – absurd, of course – that perhaps some deaf-and-dumb-alphabet business had been going on.

I hesitated to ask Sabina about it. I didn't like to say to my child that I had heard the servants talking about her, and so I stood in the doorway hesitating. Sabina evidently did not notice me, for she went on singing, when all of a sudden I saw Tommy crawl out quietly from under the table with a horrible thing they call a scratchback – where the boy got it from goodness knows – and, before I could utter a sound, he was behind her and scraped the thing right down her back. Sabina gave a shriek and almost leapt into the air – I'm sure I should have shrieked, too – then turning round she caught sight of Tommy.

"Oh, you little wretch," she shrieked, and in her temper she gave him a tremendous box on the ear.

Tommy is a brave boy, but the tears came into his eyes and he clenched his fist.

"You coward!" he cried. "You know you're a girl and a man can't hit a woman, but I'll pay you out for it. The first time I meet your lamp post in the street I'll hit him, and then he'll have to fight me."

"You little wretch; who do you mean by my lamp post?"

"Oh, yes, just as if you didn't know. I saw him walking up and down in front of the house yesterday, looking up at the window and grinning. Yes – and you waved your hand to him. Ah, you think I don't know. Wait till Ma finds it out, that's all. She'll lamp-post him. She'll give him a bit of her mind."

That was more than I could stand, so I hurried into the room and I said, "Sabina, what is the meaning of all this? What on earth does Tommy mean about a lamp post?"

Sabina turned the colour of a peony, and Tommy gave a little whistle.

"Now, Tommy," I said, "be good enough to explain. Who is Sabina's lamp post?"

"Excuse me, Ma," said Master Tom, drawing himself up, "but a fellow never splits on a girl – it isn't cricket."

"I don't care," I said, "whether it's cricket or football, or marbles, or only battledore and shuttlecock;* I mean to know. Perhaps, Sabina, you will be good enough to explain."

"Oh, Mamma, it's – it's only Tommy's nonsense," exclaimed my daughter half sobbing. "Let me go to my room, please, Ma. That bad boy frightened me so, and I feel faint."

29

"Very well, my dear, go to your room by all means," I said, calmly, "but when you feel better I shall expect you to come down with a full explanation of who the lamp post is who looks up at your window, and to whom you wave your hand. I may tell you, I have heard something of this before."

"Oh, Mamma, dear Mamma, don't be angry, and I – I'll tell you everything presently; but let me go now, please."

"Sabina, my child," I said kindly, drawing her to me, and laying her head on my shoulder, "don't distress yourself. I am not cross – only there must be no secrets between us, my child, especially in a matter of this sort, for I presume the lamp post your brother refers to is a young man. There, my dear, go to your room now; calm yourself, and when you feel better come to me, and we'll have a quiet chat in my own little room."

Sabina, who was always a most tender-hearted girl, fairly broke down when I spoke so quietly, having, I suppose, expected a storm – though why my children always expect I am going to fly out I can't imagine – and, putting her handkerchief to her eyes, went out of the room.

Tommy followed her, looking very crestfallen, and outside I heard him say to her, "Sabby, I am so sorry; upon my honour I am. I didn't know the mater was there, or I'd have bitten my tongue out sooner than have blabbed. Don't cry, Sabby, and when you come down you shall punch me as hard as ever you like, and I'll never call Gus Walkinshaw lamp post again!"

"Gus Walkinshaw!" I stood rooted to the spot with horror. Gus Walkinshaw, the son of our vicar, a young man without the slightest expectation in the world, for he had several elder brothers, and six feet two high in his stockings, not, of course, that I ever saw him in them, but my boys have told me that was his height – and he was the being alluded to by my son Tommy as "the lamp post" and by my cook and housemaid as "Miss Sabina's young man".

Six feet two and no expectations, and my daughter Sabina was the shortest of all my family – being barely five feet.

No wonder I shuddered. If there was one thing which I had *not* contemplated it was being the mother-in-law of a giant.

Memoir III

My First Son-in-Law

"G US WALKINSHAW!"

At the words which my son Tommy uttered – I am quite sure in his excitement he forgot that I could overhear him – the scales fell from my eyes, as they say, and everything was clear as noonday to me.

Never for one moment imagining that a daughter of mine would think anything of Augustus Walkinshaw, I had spoken my mind about him pretty freely on several occasions, not perhaps particularly of him, but of the whole family, Mrs Walkinshaw, the vicar's wife, having on one occasion in my presence made a remark about young men of good birth marrying into trade, which I considered very narrow-minded, and, seeing that it was made in general company, very uncalled for.

It was at Mrs Jones's "at home". Mrs Jones was our doctor's wife, and the conversation had turned on the capital marriage Miss Grantham, the Bond Street hosier's daughter, had made. Living in our terrace, and the marriage having taken place at our church, we were all of course rather interested in it, especially as young Larkaway, the bridegroom, would be a baronet when his father died, so that Miss Grantham would be Lady

Larkaway. I ventured to say, when one lady said she couldn't see what young Larkaway saw in her, that perhaps he saw her money, and then Mrs Walkinshaw rolled up her eyes and said it was a very dreadful thing to think that so many eligible young men were now marrying tradesmen's daughters.

I bridled up a bit at that, and said that I supposed I might consider my girls as tradesmen's daughters, as my husband had a wholesale business in the City, and I begged to assure Mrs Walkinshaw that, as a tradesman's wife, I didn't want any penniless young fellows coming after my girls, and I shouldn't think such an alliance an honour at all.

Of course, Mrs Walkinshaw tried to get out of it, and pretended that there was a difference between retail and wholesale, and Mr Grantham was retail.

"I can't see the difference," I said. "If it's a degradation for a young man to marry into a family that sells *one* shirt, it must be more of a degradation for him to marry into a family that sells a *gross* of shirts."

"I don't think we need discuss shirts!" exclaimed Mrs Walkinshaw haughtily.

"Oh, certainly not, madam, if you object," I said. Then all the ladies began to talk at once, and looked at me as if I had said something dreadful, and I got up and went. I daresay everybody condoled with the vicar's wife after I had gone, and assured her that I was a dreadful person. Vicar's wife or no vicar's wife, it wouldn't have been me if I hadn't spoken my mind. Her husband doesn't despise the money that is made in trade, and I don't think his living would be such a good one if his congregation was composed of the "nobility and gentry" of the neighbourhood.

There *is* a prejudice against trade in certain quarters, I know, but it is dying out a good deal, and it is only old-fashioned people like Mrs Walkinshaw and a few stuck-up nobodies who run it down nowadays, and generally those whose relations have been in it and got out. At any rate, my husband is engaged in business, and, I am glad to say, very successfully engaged, and has been able to give his daughters, when they have married, a very comfortable allowance, and I naturally resented business being sneered at in my presence, though, of course, then none of my daughters were married.

When I got home that day from Mrs Jones's, I gave my opinion pretty freely about Mrs Walkinshaw, and I can't say why it was, but from that time I took an intense dislike to her, and I believe that she returned the compliment. I told my husband about it, and he said it was a pity I had taken any notice of the matter. "Oh, of course," I said, "I didn't expect you would appreciate my defending you in your absence, but if you like to lie down and let people walk over you I'm not going to. I never did, and I'm too old to begin now. I should think it would be a very good thing for Mrs Walkinshaw if those great hulking sons of hers married daughters of men in business themselves, for they are never likely to make much by their own exertions."

"They're very fine young men, my dear," said my husband. "One of them is in the army, and another is studying for the Bar."

"Fine young men indeed," I said. "I call them giants. Why, there isn't one of the five of them who is not over six feet. Tall men are always lazy, and they're never good for much except playing billiards, and flirting and lolling about. No daughter of mine should marry a Walkinshaw if I had my way."

Remembering that I had always freely expressed my views about the Walkinshaws, I understood at once why my Sabina had concealed from me the fact that she and Gus Walkinshaw, the youngest of the family, had fallen in love with each other.

I made no doubt that it was so, though how it had happened I was at a loss to understand, as beyond meeting at balls and parties in the neighbourhood, and seeing each other in church on Sunday, they had had no opportunities of being in each other's society. Then I suddenly remembered that my Sabina had for the last six months taken great interest in what she called "church work", and that she had assisted in decorating the church on several occasions, and had sung at the penny readings and entertainments which the vicar had organized at the parish schools.

It was all clear to me then, and I had no necessity to question my daughter very closely, when, an hour later, she came to my little room and we had a tête-à-tête.

The poor girl was still very nervous I could see, her cheeks were flushed, and she looked as if she would cry at the very first opportunity, so I said to her, "Sabina, my dear, I have been thinking things over, and I understand it all now. It was the church work."

"No, Mamma, not exactly."

"Well, at any rate I suppose you have met Gus Walkinshaw a good deal, as he is his father's right hand and goes with him everywhere?"

"Yes, Mamma."

"And… and… you are really in love with him?"

"Ye-es, Mamma."

"And is he in love with you? Has he… er… said anything?"

Sabina bent her head.

"Come, my child, don't be foolish. There is nothing to be ashamed of, though it's all very odd, and the last thing I should have expected. Has… Mr Walkinshaw given you in any way to understand that he is in love with you?"

"Ye-es, Mamma, and he… he would have come to you and Papa long ago, only…"

"Only what, my dear?"

"Only we were both afraid you wouldn't like him, because, Mamma, you've always said so. Oh, Mamma, he *is* tall, but he can't help it. He's tried everything to look shorter, even to having no heels to his boots and stooping when he walks: tallness runs in his family."

We had a long and quiet little talk over matters, and though I told my daughter, as I was bound to do, I did not think it a good match, I said I would talk the matter over with her papa that evening, and let her know the result, and she left me quite radiant with happiness.

I didn't expect much assistance from John Tressider – never, surely, did a poor woman have such a helpless creature for a husband when it came to domestic difficulties and responsibilities, but I did at least hope that he would take the matter up in a manner worthy of a businessman and the father of a family.

Not he! He listened to what I had to say, said that he wasn't at all surprised, and then coolly left everything to me, saying that he was sure that if I were satisfied it would be all right.

"What!" I exclaimed indignantly. "Do you expect me to interview the young man and his father? Surely that is not the mother's place, John Tressider."

"I don't know, my dear, I... er... I haven't had much experience in such matters."

"And pray where do you think I got my experience from?"

"Well, my dear, women naturally understand these things much better than men."

"Understand or not," I said, "the happiness of your child is at stake, John Tressider, and you will have to ascertain from Mr Walkinshaw, senior, as soon as his son has made a formal proposal, what he is going to do for him. I presume you will give your daughter something."

"You may be sure I shall do what is right."

"Very well then, do it the right way," I said, "that's all I ask. We won't have words about it, but I shall expect you for once in your life to do your duty as Sabina's father, and not leave all the responsibility to me."

I am bound to say that my husband behaved very well in the matter eventually, actually summoning up courage enough to call on the Revd Mr Walkinshaw, and smoke a cigar with him, and point out to him that it was only right, as Sabina would have a good income secured to her by him (my husband), that he (Mr Walkinshaw) should make a proper provision for his son.

I told my husband what to say and how to put the matter plainly, but I have no doubt he did it in a much more roundabout fashion than I should have done.

However, all was arranged satisfactorily, even my first interview with Mrs Walkinshaw after it was known that her son was going to "marry into trade". It was rather a triumph to me after what she had said, but I don't think I showed it – at least I tried not to, though it was on the tip of my tongue to say, "My dear lady, how painful it must be, with your ideas of trade, to think that your son is going to marry the daughter of a man engaged in business."

But I didn't, and must acknowledge that Mrs Walkinshaw was very nice, and I couldn't help feeling that, after all, except for the fact that young Walkinshaw would not have so large a sum as I could have desired, it was not a bad marriage. Sabina would have a fair income of her own, her father behaving very generously in the matter, and the Walkinshaws are a really *good* family – a Walkinshaw having been beheaded or something by Oliver Cromwell, and lost his estates, and there having been a

Lord Walkinshaw in the reign of James I, and later, I think, but history is not my strong point. All I know is, the title was lost through a Lord Walkinshaw mixing himself up with a person called the Pretender,* and now all that the family has left are some portraits of their ancestors, which my son-in-law, Gus Walkinshaw, scoffs at most irreverently, though they hang in his own dining room.

Well, everything was satisfactorily arranged after Gus had duly called on my husband and had obtained our consent to the engagement, which I stipulated should not be too short a one, as I have always considered it very much better that young people should learn as much of each other's ways as possible before marriage.

I don't think my sons took to Gus Walkinshaw all at once. William, especially, rather resented his sister being married, though I don't know why he should, but being short himself, as all our family are, he declared he had an objection to tall men. Tommy, also, was at times very troublesome, plaguing his sister considerably, but Gus soon found a way to get over him, and Tommy had what the boys call "a good time".

I am sure that boy's pockets were always filled with sweets and things, and the strawberry ices that Mr Walkinshaw treated him to at the confectioner's! Really, I wonder the boy's inside wasn't frozen.

Boys will be boys, but I certainly think girls have a higher sense of honour. No girl would keep on going into the room when her sister and her lover were there to be bribed to leave off playing their tricks with sweets and strawberry ices. But girls always sympathize with love affairs and boys don't – that is, boys of a certain age – Tommy's age.

The first visit that Gus paid us – that is to say, the first visit after he had been formally accepted as my future son-in-law – was to luncheon. I thought it would be nicer for him to come when only the girls were at home at first – dear Sabina being naturally a little nervous of her elder brothers, who were severely critical, and, as she said, watched every movement of poor Gus, as though they expected him to do something awkward or peculiar every moment.

So I thought it would suit her better if we asked Gus to luncheon with the girls and myself, and on that occasion, by special request, we gave Tommy two shillings and packed him off with another boy, a great friend of his, to an afternoon performance of a circus.

I like Gus Walkinshaw very much, in fact, he is my favourite son-in-law now, but he really was a little awkward at first. He felt his height, poor fellow, and he was broad built and heavy as well, and that made him perhaps try to appear to be lighter and more graceful than he was. When he came into the drawing room, before luncheon was served, he sat down, most unfortunately, on a little gilt chair, which was much lower than he thought it was, and I, seeing what would happen, couldn't help exclaiming, "No, no, not there," and I think that confused him, for he tried to get up before he got down and must have lost his balance, for he came down on the chair with all his weight, and the crash was terrible as the poor young man went down on the floor almost full length and my poor chair went to pieces, for all the world as if it had been an eggshell that he had sat upon.

Of course I said that it didn't matter, but Sabina went quite crimson, and all the girls rushed to Mr Walkinshaw's assistance, and really he was so helpless I think he was bewildered, and the perspiration stood on his brow in great drops, that they could hardly get him up, and I feared he was hurt.

"I... I hope you are not hurt," I exclaimed, really half laughing myself, and he said, "No-o-o," and then, seeing Maud and Jane trying not to laugh, he burst out laughing himself, and I was very glad, for it was quite a relief, as it induced us all to laugh too, and he got up by degrees – in sections William declared it must have been, but I don't know what he meant.

Gus told me afterwards that for the few seconds he lay there his feelings were terrible. He knew the girls couldn't get him up, and he was considering how he could get up most gracefully by himself without rolling over and getting up that way.

He said he was quite relieved when we all laughed, but I was sorry for my poor chair, and I began to wonder if it would not be as well to have the furniture all seen to and specially strengthened for the occasion. As it was to be rather a long engagement, I feared if something were not done we should not have a chair left by the time my daughter was married.

I must say that of all my sons-in-law Gus Walkinshaw has proved himself the gentlest (not with the furniture, perhaps) and the most considerate. I have come to the conclusion that big men and big women are often very much more tender-hearted and gentle than small people. I have a son-in-law who is short, and I consider him decidedly bumptious and self-assertive. Little people always are self-assertive – that is to say, little men are. Little women are not. I am a little woman myself, and my fault has always been not asserting myself sufficiently.

It seemed strange, of course, to me at first to have this great big fellow so often in the house. It was just as if a big Newfoundland dog had been added to the establishment. He was devoted to Sabina, and they seemed to understand each other thoroughly; but, somehow or other, he never seemed able quite to get on with William, my second son.

William resented his presence in the house – though being away all day at business with his father he didn't see very much of him.

"I can't imagine, Mother," he would say, "whatever Sabina can see in Gus Walkinshaw."

"I am sure he is very nice," I said, "and shows a great deal more consideration for me than my own sons do sometimes."

My son William has not the best of tempers, and he flew out at that and muttered something about an "outsider", but I put my foot down at once.

"William," I said, "if I and your father are satisfied with Mr Walkinshaw as a husband for your sister that is quite sufficient; your approbation is not necessary."

I have heard a good deal about the jealousy of women, but my experience is that men are quite as jealous of each other, and certainly more small-minded. Certainly my second son was jealous of the regard I and his sisters had for Gus Walkinshaw, and this foolish jealousy made him absolutely blind to the young man's merits, and caused considerable annoyance to his sister.

In a spirit of mischief, he would tell his sister the most absurd tales about Mr Walkinshaw. Of course he only did it out of mischief, but it was very foolish, and not what I should have expected from my son. He would come home sometimes and declare that he had seen Gus Walkinshaw flirting desperately with a girl in a flower shop in Regent Street, and he quite alarmed me by saying that one bank holiday when he had been to Kingsbury Races he had seen Mr Walkinshaw betting heavily.

I have always had a horror of young men who bet or play billiards, and, as a careful mother, I naturally determined to know the truth of the matter, and I asked Mr Walkinshaw himself if he was in the habit of backing horses, as I had heard he had been seen at Kingsbury Races.

He laughed and said, "Dear me! Whoever told you that I was there? I certainly was, and I had five shillings on a horse, because it belonged to a brother officer of Lawrence's" (Lawrence was his brother in the army) "but, I assure you, I don't bet as a rule."

I was very much relieved, and immediately revealed the fact that William had told me. I saw that he was hurt, and he said something to Sabina, and she made quite a scene with William about it, and then William – he always was terribly impetuous, though as good-hearted a boy as ever breathed – flew in a rage, and said that he wasn't going to be insulted in his own home by an "interloper", and he'd give Walkinshaw a bit of his mind.

When words began to get rather high, I said I would have no more of it, and William got up and put on his hat and said he would go and take lodgings, as home was home to him no more, and with that he went out and banged the door, and Sabina began to cry.

"Good gracious me," I said, "am I to be plagued out of my life like this? Haven't I worries enough without my children quarrelling?"

Sabina said, "Oh, of course, Mamma, I know it's all my fault. I'll tell Gus tomorrow, and he shall never come to the house again. Perhaps you'd like me to break it all off and go into a convent? I don't want to sow discord in the family." And she went upstairs to bed, crying.

Maud and Jane were very indignant with William, and, of course, took Sabina's part, and I said to my husband:

"This is a nice state of affairs. There is a family quarrel, and all absolutely about nothing at all. But what can you expect when the father is not the head of his own house?"

"Well, my dear," he replied, "I don't think any man would have much chance of being the head of the house while you were in it."

I hadn't been feeling well all day – in fact, to tell the truth, I was a little irritable, having one of my nervous headaches, and having had a lot of trouble with a new housemaid who had very nearly spoilt one of my beautiful steel fenders by giving it what she called "a polish up", and I suppose this, and the upset with William and Sabina, and William marching off out in a temper, made me a little tetchy, and when Mr Tressider said that, one of the servants just having come into the room at the time (to do him justice, I don't think he knew it), I lost my temper, and burst into tears, and went off to my own room and had a good cry.

Really I don't think any poor woman ever had so much to put up with as I had. There must *be* a head of the house, and it is very hard to blame me for doing my own duty, and someone else's as well. But it is the way of the world. Never mind, they'll all miss me when I am gone.

As soon as I had had a good cry (I am not ashamed to confess that I indulge in that feminine weakness) I felt better, and I went to Sabina's room to see how she was, and found the silly girl quite hysterical, and Maud and Jane, her sisters, sitting with her. She was writing a letter in lead pencil, reading it out loud and sniffing and sobbing between each line. Sabina is very romantic, which she doesn't get from me, though I believe a cousin of Mr Tressider's was once on the stage, which may account for it.

Really it was a most absurd letter she was writing to Gus Walkinshaw, and when I read it I was very angry and spoke my mind.

It was bidding him farewell for ever, and saying that as their engagement had caused family dissensions on *both sides*, perhaps it was better she should go and nurse the wounded on the field of battle and he should try to forget her.

"Both sides!" I exclaimed. "Why, what does that mean?"

And then I got it all out, and Sabina told me that old Mrs Walkinshaw had been saying something to Gus about John, my eldest son, and she said she had heard things, and it seems there were words then and Gus was a little short in his answers, and then Mrs Walkinshaw told him that it was only what she expected when he wanted to marry into a tradesman's family.

It was only because dear Sabina was indignant about it herself that she let it out, but I was glad to hear it, for I knew what I had to do.

"I shall call on Mrs Walkinshaw tomorrow," I said, "and tell her what I think of her."

For some absurd reason Sabina was terribly alarmed at that, and so were Maud and Jane, and they all began to implore me not to, but I declared that, whether the marriage was broken off or not, I would, and then Sabina had hysterics, and I was obliged to promise that I would let the insult pass unnoticed.

It was most trying coming altogether, and I thought to myself, I really shall be glad when the girls are all married and settled, and I can have a little peace.

I went up to John's room to see if he had come in, because I wanted to ask him what Mrs Walkinshaw could have been saying about him, and found he had not, and then looking about the room I saw an envelope, which had evidently fallen from his pocket and was lying on the floor.

I picked it up, and found that it contained a photograph. I took it out to look at it. It was the portrait of a young woman, and underneath it was written "Your loving Lottie".

It was the last straw that broke the camel's back.

Absolutely without my having the slightest suspicion of it, my son John had "a loving Lottie".

Memoir IV

My Eldest Son John

"**Y**OUR LOVING LOTTIE."

The photograph nearly dropped from my hands as those words caught my motherly eye.

My eldest son John had already caused me and his father considerable anxiety, owing to his erratic ways, and so it naturally gave me a turn when, going into his room, I accidentally found the photograph of a young woman with those words written in a female hand underneath it.

You may be sure that when I had recovered my composure I scanned that young woman's face eagerly. My first impression, great as the shock had been to me, was not altogether unfavourable. It was a kind, honest-looking face, and there was a very gentle look in the eyes. So far as I could judge from a photograph, the girl also appeared neatly dressed, and was decidedly ladylike.

You will, perhaps, understand my anxiety about the young lady better when I tell you that John had always been what may be called eccentric in his views and careless in his habits, and I had always said that he would be a great responsibility to the woman who married him. John never appreciated the value of money, and always had the most extravagant ideas and dreadfully trying ways, which I believe are called bohemian.

When he left college, where, although a clever and intelligent lad, he really seemed to do nothing but get into trouble, for his pranks and practical jokes, it was decided, after a very anxious consideration, that he should go into his father's business, and he did. But he didn't stop in the office long. His father complained that he wouldn't take his proper position or settle down seriously to work, and declared that he was absolutely demoralizing the office.

My husband told me that over and over again from his private office he would suddenly hear roars of laughter in the counting house, and, when he hurried out to enquire the meaning of such an unbusinesslike disturbance, he found that "Mr John", as he was called, had been telling the clerks funny stories and making them shriek.

Of course, that sort of thing could not go on, but his father talked to him severely and determined to give him another chance.

He was a little better afterwards, and managed to keep his strong animal spirits in check, at any rate while his father was about the place, but at the end of twelve months it was found that he really would never be any good at the business.

One day there was quite a scene between him and his father at the office. It seems John, after having failed at nearly everything entrusted to him, was given the correspondence to attend to. He could write an excellent letter, was a good French and German scholar, and his father thought that he could not very well get up to mischief in writing letters. But after about a fortnight there was terrible trouble. One of the most important firms with which my husband did business wrote and complained of the manner in which its letters were answered, and enclosed a specimen.

Master John had been at his tricks again, and had replied to a business communication with a *comic letter*. My husband told me there were actually *puns* in it.

My husband said when he read the letter he almost had a fit, the head of the firm to whom it was addressed being a most strict man and the elder of a chapel, and naturally looking upon such proceedings in business as most disgraceful, not to say wicked. He wrote off at once a personal apology, and then he called Master John into his private room and told him that he was hopeless, and that he had much better stay away, for if he came there and didn't reform he would end by bringing the house of Tressider, which had been established nearly a hundred years, to ruin.

John declared he couldn't see that there was any harm done, but he supposed people in business had no sense of humour, and he promised to adopt a more serious tone in his correspondence for the future.

Perhaps you will hardly believe it when I tell you what that bad boy did. The very next day he wrote a letter in answer to an enquiry about some goods and he began, "Friend," and filled it with "thees" and "thous", just as if he was a Quaker, and he signed himself "Your fellow sinner", and the letter would have gone to the customer, had not my husband providentially come into the office at the time it was being copied in the letter book and seen the office boy roaring over it.

That was too much of a good thing, and, as he said, utterly impossible for him to look over, so he reprimanded John most severely before all the clerks, tore up the letter, dismissed the office boy (he took him on again afterwards), and told the cashier that he was to stop Master John's salary for the next month as a punishment.

The cashier, a weak, nervous little man, was evidently upset about something when my husband said that, and my husband, who is very much smarter in his business than he is at home, instantly suspected something, so he called the cashier into his private office.

"You understand me," he said, "Mr John does not have his salary next month. You stop it."

"I beg your pardon, sir," replied the cashier, going very red, "but I cannot stop it."

"And pray why not, sir?"

"Because Mr John has had it already – he's drawn it in advance."

My husband was extremely annoyed you may be sure, because a young man who draws his salary in advance is evidently living beyond his means.

"Oh," said my husband, "and pray, what right have you to pay anyone in advance? But I'll look into the matter at once. Did you take his IOU for it?"

"Yes, sir."

"Bring me your cash box."

The cashier brought the cash box, and my husband looked in it, and there he found John's IOU not only for one month's salary, but for more money than three months' salary would cover.

He gave the cashier a severe lecture, and told him that if ever such a thing occurred again, it would subject him to instant dismissal; then he looked round for John, and found that John had put on his hat and walked out of the office.

When my husband came home to dinner that evening he was in a greater state of excitement than I have ever seen him before. He told me what had happened, and I was naturally very much worried, for I could not conceal from myself the fact that my eldest son was not going on in the way to grow up into a sound businessman like his father.

"I'll never have him in the place again," my husband said. "He's demoralizing the entire concern, and he must shift for himself."

"Don't be hasty," I said. "Remember, he's only a boy. Let me talk to him."

"Talking is no good," said my husband. "I have talked to him. He's incorrigible, and he'll never be worth his salt. When he comes home tonight, I shall tell him plainly that I wash my hands of him."

I knew that, angry as my husband was then, he would soon be calmer, so I was not seriously alarmed, and I determined to catch John before he saw his father, and speak plainly to him myself.

But before dinner was over the servant came in with a letter, which she said a hansom cabman had left.

It was addressed to my husband, who opened it, read it, uttered an exclamation of surprise, and then handed it over to me, saying:

"What do you think of that?"

The letter was from John, and, as nearly as I can remember it, this was the way it ran:

Dear Father – I have made up my mind that I shall never be any good in the business, and I hate it; but I don't want to be a burthen on you, so I am going to be independent and shift for myself. I don't know yet whether I shall drive a hansom or get a job as a 'bus conductor, or go on the stage, but I'll let you know soon. I have taken a cheap lodging, and will send for my things tomorrow. Tell the mater not to fidget; I am all right. I am sure you will all get on a good deal better without me. If I get a chance on the omnibuses, will you be my reference? I think you know the chairman of the London General Omnibus Company. A word from you would go a long way.

Always your affectionate son,

John Tressider.

That was a nice letter for an affectionate father and mother to receive in the middle of dinner – and it naturally upset us terribly.

"Oh, my poor boy," I cried.

"It will do him good," growled my husband.

"Do him good," I exclaimed, a vision of my poor boy standing all day long shivering in the pouring rain on the steps of an omnibus and shouting, "Bank – Mother Red Cap* – Old Kent Road – and Highgate Archway," and all that sort of thing. "Do him good! How can you be so inhuman, when you know how subject John is to rheumatism, and how he inherits his bronchial tubes from you? If you were a father with a father's heart you would go and find him at once and bring him home. Goodness only knows what epidemic he may catch if he stops in a cheap lodging."

"Oh, nonsense! He will most likely go to a good hotel. John Tressider is not the young man to put up with any hardships. Let him come to his senses."

"What's the good of his coming to his senses if he comes to his death?" I said. "You know how reckless he is. It's your duty to go out at once and find and bring him home."

"Certainly not; he knows where his home is, and he can come to it when he likes."

"Then if you don't I shall!" I exclaimed indignantly, and I went upstairs and put on my bonnet.

My husband came upstairs after me.

"Jane," he said, "don't make yourself ridiculous. You can't go and wander about the streets shouting 'John, John', and as you don't know where to look for him, you cannot do anything else."

"I shall go to the police station," I said. "I shall have bills printed offering a reward. I shall advertise in *The Times*."

"Hadn't you better have the canals dragged and the steamers searched at all the ports of embarkation, and the trains watched while you are about it?" said my husband, and then, seeing how distressed and upset I really was, his manner altered, and he said, quite kindly: "Come, come, my dear. Don't worry yourself. John's quite old enough and quite clever enough to take care of himself, and if he doesn't come home tonight, I'll find a means of bringing him back tomorrow. We mustn't let him think he has frightened us, or he'll be always playing us pranks of this sort."

I allowed myself to be persuaded that there was no danger, and I took my bonnet off, but I sat up and listened to the door till nearly two o'clock in the morning, and when at last I went to bed I never closed my eyes all night. I was too ill in the morning to get up, but I made my husband promise to go and find John and bring him home at once. Soon after my husband had gone to business, the servant came up to my room with a letter. I knew at once it was from my boy.

"Please, ma'am, a cabman brought this, and I was to give it to you at once."

I snatched the letter and tore it open. It was from my boy.

"Dear mother," it said, "will you meet me at twelve o'clock at the Marble Arch? I want to explain things. Please bring a fiver with you. Your loving son, John."

As soon as I knew my son was safe, I had a revulsion of feeling, and I felt angry with him for the grief and distress he had caused me.

"Things have come to a pretty pass," I said, "when a respectable mother has to go loitering about the Marble Arch to meet her son. Bring a 'fiver' with you, indeed! Where does the boy think I can get five-pound notes from, with the housekeeping expenses running away with every shilling of my allowance?"

However, I put five pounds in my purse before I went out and then I took the omnibus (I have never yet been able to bring myself to hansom cabs, and Mr Tressider had taken the carriage to the City) and I went to the Marble Arch.

And there was my unhappy son, as bold as brass, and actually with a flower in his buttonhole, and he came up to me quite jauntily and said:

"I hope you haven't been worried, Mater, but things were desperate and I had to do something."

"Worried," I exclaimed. "You'll break my heart, John, that's what you'll do. I never closed my eyes all night. What do you mean by such conduct after the careful way in which you've been brought up?"

"Don't bully me, Mater," the boy said, "I'm really in an awful fix."

Something in his tone alarmed me.

"What do you mean?" I cried. "Don't torture me, John. Tell me at once."

"Well, the fact is, Mother, I knew there'd be a row when the governor found out I'd borrowed that money from the cashier, and so I thought I'd better get away and let him know the worst at a safe distance. The fact is, I'm awfully in debt, and those beastly creditors won't be put off any longer, and they are going to send the bills in to the governor, and I thought I'd better be out of the way."

"How much do you owe, John?" I said with a trembling voice. "Twenty pounds?"

"Twenty pounds! Good gracious, mother, you don't think I'd run away from home for twenty pounds. I'm afraid it's about two hundred."

I was horrified, as any mother would have been, at such a confession.

"Whatever have you done with all that money, John?" I exclaimed.

"I haven't had the money, Mother. I owe it. You see, it's this way. The allowance the governor makes me is awfully small for a fellow, and so instead of paying for my clothes and things out of it, I've been letting the accounts run on, and I owe a bit of money as well in one way and another, and I've stalled it off as long as I can, but now one or two of 'em won't wait any longer, and I expect the bills will be sent in to the governor. I'd made up my mind to make a clean breast of it yesterday, only he got in such a rage over that letter, and told the cashier not to give me any more money; and so I thought, as the storm had burst, it would be just as well for me to keep out of the way till it was over."

"I don't know whatever your father will say when he hears it. There's sure to be a scene," I said. "How could you have been so extravagant, John? It's dreadful in a boy of your age; it's absolutely wicked."

"I am not a boy, Mother," he replied haughtily, "and that's where you and the governor make a mistake. I'm twenty, and that's a young man."

"I'm afraid, John," I said, "that you are not steady. I'm afraid you picked up bad companions in that horrid billiard room you go to of a night. No good ever did come of young men going to billiard rooms. It leads to betting, and gambling, and drinking, and all manner of dreadful things. Do you owe any money at the Wellington?"

The Wellington was an hotel in our neighbourhood where there was a billiard room, and I had heard that many young men went there of an evening.

"Well, Mother," John said, "it's no good disguising it, I do owe a bit there. One or two of the chaps have won a bit of me, and, like good fellows, they let it stand over because I was hard up."

"Oh, they have won money of you at the Wellington, have they?" I said. "I thought as much. I'll go round this afternoon to the landlord and tell him what I think of him encouraging a lot of boys to gamble and drink at his place."

John went red up to the roots of his hair. "For goodness' sake, Mother," he said, "don't go and make a scene at the

Wellington. It's nothing to do with the landlord, who is a very respectable man."

"Oh, very respectable, I've no doubt. If I had my way all such places should be shut up by the police."

"Oh, very well, Mother, if you are going to turn against me I haven't a friend left in the world, and I'd better work my passage out to America."

"Don't talk such nonsense," I said, but more kindly, for I was afraid that perhaps he might really do something of the sort. "What can I do to help you? I have not got two hundred pounds."

"No, but I thought if I had a fiver to go on with I could stay away a day or two, and you could break it presently to the governor and get him to help me out of the mess."

Well, the long and short of it was, I agreed to speak to his father, but only on condition that he returned home at once. I think he would sooner have had the five pounds and stayed away a little, but I wouldn't hear of it.

That evening I broke it as gently as I could to his father, who, of course, was very worried, because, he said, what with his unbusinesslike habits and his extravagances, what in the world would he ever do except grow up to bring our grey hairs with sorrow to the grave?

However, I pleaded very hard for the boy, and his father consented to pay his debts and give him one more trial in the City, and he did. But John never took to it, and just as I had begun to despair of his ever doing anything at all, he came to me one day and told me that he had written a story and sent it to the *Family Herald*, and it had been accepted, and he had received five pounds for it.

I knew he'd always had a ready pen, and had "scribbled" verses to amuse himself, and all that sort of thing, but I never expected that John would blossom out into an author. Naturally, I felt very proud, and when I told his father, I said: "There's a good deal more in John than we think. He may be a credit to the family after all."

But that story being accepted quite ruined him for business life. After that he hated his office more than ever, and was always sitting up in his bedroom late at night and writing, and he declared that he should never settle down to anything but authorship. And he took to wearing a velvet coat and smoking a horrid black clay pipe, much to the horror of his sisters, who said it was disgraceful for him to go out of the house in that state. But he said he was a born bohemian, whatever that might mean, and hated society, and wasn't going to be a slave to conventionality any longer.

At last his father made up his mind it was no good trying to make a businessman of him, so he told him he had better strike out a career for himself, and he would let him live at home and allow him a hundred a year till he had done so. He wrote at home a good deal, and he went out a good deal, and frequented a bohemian club, and had odd-looking men to see him now and then, and he made a little by writing, but I didn't see any career coming, and he was a great trouble to me because I had hoped to see him take his father's position one day when his father retired. But William stuck to the business, and was quite different to John, and it was when things were like this, and John was living at home, and doing nothing but be a bohemian, that I went into his room and discovered the photograph of his loving Lottie.

Now you can understand my feelings, and the terrible anxiety it was to me.

What happened afterwards I shall have to tell you by and by, when I come to it. At present I must get back to my eldest daughter Sabina and Mr Augustus Walkinshaw.

It was about John that Augustus and his mother had had words, and I don't wonder at her, with her peculiar and narrow-minded notions, and John's velvet coat and clay pipe.

It seems he had been pointed out to her one day as Miss Tressider's eldest brother, and the lady who pointed him out to her said, "Surely, you know your future daughter-in-law's own brother?"

She was very indignant at being linked with John and his clay pipe, and she told Augustus about it, and evidently said something which he considered degrading to our family, for he fired up and told Sabina all about it, and that he and his mother had had a quarrel through John's clay pipe.

And Sabina, who is a very high-spirited girl, although she felt that John was not a credit to the family, yet took the part of her own people to Augustus, and they had a few words, and these caused her to write that absurd letter which she was crying over when I went into the room.

It came all right very soon, being only a lovers' quarrel, but it was not pleasant for me to know that Augustus's mother made remarks about us, and in a way looked down upon us. I have never allowed anybody to look down upon me, and it was very hard to have to begin it through the obstinacy of my children – especially after the sums that had been spent upon their education.

However, rather than make any unpleasantness, I swallowed my pride, and did not call on Mrs Walkinshaw, but began to make preparations for the wedding.

It was decided that when Sabina and Augustus were married Augustus should invest his money in some land in the country and be a gentleman farmer, he having had some training for that sort of thing, and when he had found a place he thought would do, I went down with Sabina to look at it.

Augustus had decided on a farm which was about five miles from anywhere, and though we had a few words about it, as I didn't want to drive five miles from a station whenever I wanted to see my daughter, I ultimately gave way, as Augustus assured me, from a commercial point of view, the place was a great bargain.

When they had settled there, and my poor Sabina, accustomed to society and next-door neighbours and civilized life, found out what it was like to live in a desolate part of the country – with her husband gone off in the middle of the night three miles in a thunderstorm on horseback to fetch a veterinary surgeon to a prize pig that had over-eaten itself or something of that sort – she often remembered her mother's words.

But of my maternal anxieties and my poor child's experiences in her fresh home (five miles from anywhere), you will hear on a future occasion.

Memoir V

Five Miles from Anywhere

WHEN I CONSENTED to Augustus Walkinshaw taking the farm (five miles from anywhere), which he had taken us down to see, as my dear Sabina's future home, I certainly allowed myself to be over-persuaded. But poor Augustus had had so much trouble to find a suitable one, having been sent all over the country by his agent, and he had seen such dreadful places, that really I was quite sorry for the boy, and I allowed my sympathy to get the better of my judgement.

He was naturally hopeful and sanguine, and inclined to look at the bright side of things. He was in love, you see, and when a young man is in love he thinks the stony desert would become a Garden of Eden if only his particular Eve was to share it with him. But I am afraid a good many more Gardens of Eden become stony deserts after we are married than stony deserts become Gardens of Eden.

Still, it is only natural that young folks should look at things through rose-coloured spectacles. I always admire the young fellow who, in so many melodramas, laughs away every difficulty, and says to the girl of his heart (generally to the gallery as well): "Never mind the loss of your father's wealth, my darling; we've youth and health, and, hand in hand, we can face the future bravely."

It is a noble sentiment, and one which always gets a round of applause, but I notice that the hero and the heroine generally have a very bad time before they come to the fifth act.

After all, it is as well that we should have our little troubles and difficulties at the outset. It is in times of trial and anxiety and worry that the great lessons of life are learnt. I couldn't help feeling that Augustus and Sabina were risking a good deal in taking that lonely farm. I should much have preferred their living nearer home, where I could have seen more of them; but, as Augustus explained, farms are not found every day within the four-mile radius, and so reluctantly – most reluctantly – I gave way, and the purchase of the farm was completed.

The house was charming, and there was no doubt about the situation being a good one, but the roads were simply awful. I never was so jolted and banged about in my life as I was in the fly that took us there from the station. The last mile was up a road like a ploughed field, and at the finish the driver had to keep getting down and opening gates. The agent met us at the station, and went with us, and he kept making the best of it, saying that the weather had been bad, and that a new road was going to be made, and all that sort of thing, but I had a fearful headache for days afterwards.

If ever I have anything to do with taking a farm for any child of mine again I shall take care that the agent does *not* meet us. It was he who told the flyman where to drive to, evidently before we came down. It was this artfulness on his part that prevented us finding out until too late what the name of the farm was. When I heard it I felt most indignant. The farm was known in the neighbourhood by the dreadful name of "Gallows Tree Farm".

There had, it seems, once been a gibbet on the hill near it, and that gave the name of the farm. "Augustus," I said to my future son-in-law, when the truth leaked out, "never will I consent to a child of mine living at such an address. You will have to alter it. I can never put a gallows outside a letter addressed to my own daughter." He promised he would, and I know that he tried, but it was no good. The name stuck to it. Everybody called it by that name, and Gallows Tree Farm it remains to this day, though, thank goodness, they have left it long ago.

Do what I would, I could not banish the name of Sabina's future home from my mind, and it weighed on me during all the preparations for the wedding. The dear girl herself bore up wonderfully, and begged me not to distress myself, as it would never be known by that name after they got in it. I suggested they should call it "Wild Rose Farm" or "Honeysuckle Farm", and Augustus said he would try and get something of that sort in the county directory and at the post office. John, my eldest son, said, "Why not call it Walkinshaw Hall or Tressider Castle!" but that was absurd, and, as Sabina said, would look like presumption, seeing that nothing would make it a hall or a castle.

Augustus had some correspondence on the subject with the local authorities, I know, but the result was anything but reassuring, for he found out that the full and only legal address was Gallows Tree Farm, Great Puddlebury, Warwickshire. This was the first time he had heard of the parish of Great Puddlebury, and it was another blow. That artful agent had never even hinted at Great Puddlebury, but in all his correspondence had described the farm as "near ——", which was an important, not to say aristocratic, town, and was five miles away, as we found out to our cost, when we got out at the railway station.

I didn't blame Augustus, who was young and naturally imprudent, and in love, which blinds a man to so much he would see if he had his eyes open. I blamed my husband. If he had done his duty as a father, he would have gone down himself and seen the farm, and have made proper enquiries, but of course, as usual, everything was left to me, and what could I be expected to know about farms?

"John Tressider," I said to him, when we were alone the night I made the discovery, "I hope this will be a warning to you. Your first married daughter is going from her mother's arms to a Gallows Tree, and her young married life is to be spent at Great Puddlebury."

All he did was to make some absurd remark about Shakespeare and "What's in a name?"* but I am not a woman to be put down with Shakespeare, and so I said: "It is not Shakespeare's daughter who will have to live at Gallows Tree Farm, but mine; and, as to there being nothing in names, I don't suppose even you would have liked it if I had suggested that our eldest son should be christened Judas, and our eldest daughter Jezebel – certain names are associated with certain things, and you cannot deny it."

He couldn't, and so he didn't try, but declared he had come to bed to sleep and not to argue, and in five minutes he was snoring, though whenever I wake him up he declares he doesn't, and that it is the railway train which runs at the back of the garden. I don't pretend to be infallible, but I do know a snore from a railway train – but it is no good arguing with a man who is a heavy sleeper, and if you dig him with your elbow only grunts and turns over on his other side, dragging half the clothes with him.

Though Sabina's father made light of the matter, it was on my mind for days, but at last, on the distinct understanding that the name was to be changed, I allowed myself to be pacified, and certainly I had plenty to engage my attention with the trousseau and the wedding preparations generally.

Sorry as I was to part with my child, it really was a relief when the wedding day came, for I had been worried nearly out of my mind, especially by the dressmakers and the servants, and that discovery about John didn't tend to make matters better, and when the very evening before the wedding I discovered that Mr Tressider, to whom the ordering of the carriages had been left – that was all we had asked him to do – had forgotten all about it, I could have cried with vexation.

"Of course," I said, "it does not matter to you if we have to go in four-wheel cabs. Sabina will have our own brougham, poor child, and she will be all right; but what about the rest of us?"

"Oh, that will be all right. I'll send Jones" (our coachman) "to see about it at once."

It was eight o'clock then, and I felt there would very likely be some trouble, and there was.

Jones, instead of going to the proper people, went off to a little man who had just started (an acquaintance of his own, of course), and the result was that when I saw the carriages I nearly fainted, but not wishing to have any unpleasantness on my daughter's wedding day, I had to keep my feelings to myself.

Where the man got the horses from I can't think, unless he went to a veterinary hospital and hired all the horses under treatment for the day.

We were late starting as it was, and when we did start it was at a pace that was simply dreadful. I controlled myself as long as I could, but at last I was obliged to put my head out of the window, and say to our driver, "My good man, this is not a funeral, it is supposed to be a wedding."

"Oh, it's all right, mum," he said, "these 'ere 'osses is a bit hock'ard at first, but they'll be all right directly," and then he said, "Clk, get up," and began to flog them, and that made one of them kick, and the other hung back in the collar – jibbed I think they call it – and wouldn't move an inch.

And then a lot of butchers' boys and greengrocers' boys who had been hanging about outside to see us start, and had followed, began to jeer and to make impertinent remarks.

"This is more than human flesh and blood can endure," I said. "I'll get out."

I put my head out of the window to tell the man to let me set out, and at that moment he flourished the whip, and it caught me on the face, which was a nice thing for a mother on her daughter's wedding day, and all through leaving such a trifling matter as ordering the carriages to her husband – and then people wonder that sometimes I lose my temper.

Fortunately, though the blow stung me for a minute, it did not draw blood or leave a mark, and at that moment the horses gave a violent plunge and started off at a gallop, nearly frightening me out of my life, which, though it made me tremble all through the ceremony, was fortunate, for we just arrived at the church in time. Fortunately, too, the other horses, though they looked poor creatures, had not jibbed, and so the brides-maids and all the people who had come from our house were there, and I had only just time to be bustled – I cannot say I was shown – into my place when the ceremony commenced.

After that, thank goodness, everything went off beautifully, and I got over my natural indignation and was quite happy till the time came to bid my dear child goodbye and hand her over to the care of another.

I cried – how could I help it? – and my dear Sabina – God bless her! – cried too; and when we came down, I had a brief interview with Augustus, and made him promise me that he would be careful with my child and not run any risks, and to be sure never to let her drink the water in the foreign hotels (they were going abroad for their honeymoon), and to make strict enquiries if there had been any fevers in the towns they stopped at, and always to choose a carriage in the middle of the train in case of collision, and then I gave my daughter one more long, loving embrace, and hurriedly reminded her that I had put several prescriptions into her dressing bag in case of her not feeling well in any of those horrid Continental towns, and then I had to let her go, and everybody crowded out after the happy pair, and, amid a shower of rice and old slippers, they drove away.

One thing I will say, and I ought to say it now, and that is that Augustus Walkinshaw has never caused me a moment's anxiety (except about the farm and things that he couldn't help), and my daughter has a husband in a thousand. A more tender, devoted, gentle husband no woman could desire, and on many occasions he has been a great comfort to me. Of all my sons-in-law... But I will not be invidious.

My dear child wrote me many times while on her honeymoon, and I felt sure that she was perfectly happy. She spoke in the highest terms of Augustus's gentleness and thoughtfulness, so only one thing caused me any anxiety at all, and that was the farm.

They were going there directly they returned from their honeymoon; an old servant of the Walkinshaw family had been engaged as bailiff, and with his wife had gone down and had begun to get things straight. Sabina wrote me that Mrs Jolly (the bailiff's wife) had written her that all the furniture was in, and the house looked lovely, and the servants were engaged, and that Jolly had got the farmhands together and bought some stock, and that all was going on well.

She seemed quite easy about the farm, and I tried to assure myself that, in spite of its awful name, and its being five miles from anywhere, it would be all right.

But it was with grave misgivings that as soon as they had returned and settled down there I addressed my first letter to

Mrs Walkinshaw,
Gallows Tree Farm,
Great Puddlebury.

I looked at the envelope a long time before I let it go. It was not the sort of address I had imagined for my eldest daughter.

Sabina wrote me back and assured me she was very comfortable and very happy, and that she and Augustus hoped soon to have me with them for a short time, and directly they were settled I went.

I was delighted to find my dear child looking very well and happy, and certainly the home itself was charming and beautifully fitted up and furnished, but not being a young bride myself, I noticed many drawbacks that Gus and Sabina were much too wrapped up in each other to perceive.

It was very lonely, the nearest house, except the bailiff's, being quite a mile away, and when I saw the roads, and the pond, and the quagmires, I couldn't help saying, "Whatever will be the use of those lovely dresses of yours? They are not at all the things to feed the pigs and chickens in; and gracious goodness, child, whatever will you do when you want a doctor? Where is the nearest?"

"Well," said Augustus, "there is a veterinary surgeon three miles off, that's the nearest!"

"Augustus," I said, "I trust you don't think of sending for a veterinary surgeon to my child if she should be ill."

He laughed, and said it was only a joke. I always like to be near a doctor, and to have a good chemist where you can rely on prescriptions being properly made up within easy distance, and I felt really very uneasy when I found that they would have to send quite five miles for a medical man.

I talked very seriously to Augustus on the subject.

"Suppose," I said, "Sabina were taken suddenly ill, or got frightened by a beast, or got her leg entangled in some of the horrid machinery that I see whirling about, or caught a chill through getting her feet wet in that dreadful farmyard, which, by the by, I should strongly advise you to cover with carbolic powder every day; and be sure and have plenty of Condy's Fluid* about the house, because there is a good deal of fever about, I've heard, and see that all your farm labourers are vaccinated; and if ever you hear of measles or anything of that sort in any of the villages round here, never go near them without having plenty of camphor about you; and above all things be sure the drinking water is all right – and never touch a drop unless you have had it filtered first and then boiled."

Augustus laughed and Sabina smiled, but I said, "Yes, my dears, I daresay you think me very foolish, but it is only my motherly love..." They laughed then, but they lived to see how wise some of my warnings were, especially about the water, which got contaminated in some way, and then they had to send four miles for every drop they drank.

And though naturally anxious at such a time, I really was relieved in my mind when my first little grandchild came upon the scene (and five miles from a doctor, too!), and then there wasn't much hesitation about giving up the farm, and moving nearer to civilization. As I said to Augustus, "If you stop at that place, it will simply be infanticide," and Sabina saw it with my eyes then, and, thank goodness, I had them very soon after that under my own maternal eye, with a doctor next door to them, which was a great comfort to me, and a respectable chemist only just round the corner.

Ah, you young people, you think mothers and fathers such fidgety, troublesome, worrying people, but when you are fathers and mothers yourselves, you begin to understand what it means.

I am sure when I turn back to the letters my dear child wrote me from Gallows Tree Farm, and look them over, I wonder they ever stayed so long, but Augustus was a most loving and devoted husband and that will prevent even a gallows tree casting a shadow over one's pathway.

He just got out, I am happy to say, without any loss of capital, but much worried with sitting up all night with cows and horses occasionally, and having illness among the sheep, and such queer people to do with.

Their head man was as good as gold, but an old man and obstinate, and would have his way, and Mrs Jolly, his wife, worried poor Sabina's life out of her, being given to superstition and moaning, always hearing death-watches* and seeing omens, and declaring something was going to happen; and one night, actually when Augustus was up in London, with Mr Jolly, on business, and Sabina alone, coming rushing into the house, and begging her mistress to prepare for the Judgement Day, as the comet had touched the earth, and the end of the world had come, and then she went off into a kind of catalepsy, and my poor, delicately nurtured child had to sit up with her all night, and slap her hands and give her whisky, while the waggoner went off on horseback to fetch the doctor.

That waggoner, too, was a great trial to Sabina, because of her tender heart. He was in love with the cook, who would not have anything to say to him, and he was always going about with tears trickling down his cheeks, and sighing. As Sabina said, "it was quite painful to have a man about the place with a broken heart," and she spoke to the cook and told her that she ought to marry him, but the cook wouldn't, and so at last Augustus gave the poor fellow two months' wages, and told him to take his broken heart and his tears somewhere else because they upset Mrs Walkinshaw so much, and it was at

a time when Augustus was most anxious that his wife's sur-
roundings should be, as they say in the cocoa advertisements,
"grateful and comforting".*

And what my poor child had to put up with from their servants, not having much firmness (in which she takes after her
father), and, of course, no experience, was something terrible.
The cook and the housemaid were local girls and had a great
idea of the London fashions, and very soon after Sabina came
home they took to copying her dresses and mantles and bonnets and hats as near as they could.

The first Sunday Sabina saw them driving off to church (the
waggoner drove them in a light cart) she was horrified. They
had both bonnets exactly like hers, or as near as the local (five
miles off) milliner could make them.

She could not have that, and she told them so, and after that she
was always careful to watch them off every Sunday; and she was
glad to notice that they had plain, modest servants' bonnets on.

But one Sunday afternoon, after they had gone, Augustus
said, "Let us go to church ourselves this afternoon." And he
had his fast mare put in the dogcart, and they went. And, lo
and behold, when Sabina got to church she discovered the cook
and the housemaid in their pew, as bold as brass (the waggoner
was weeping outside on a tombstone), and they had on bonnets
exactly like Sabina's!

And she had seen them go away with plain ones on that very
afternoon with her own eyes. She discovered it all that evening,
by making them confess. What do you think the artful hussies

used to do? They used to go out early on Sunday morning before Sabina was up, and hide their best bonnets in a hedge a little way down the road, and change them again coming back. And these are your simple, old-fashioned country servants!

Another thing that upset her, too, was the local butcher, who bought Augustus's cattle from him. He was a very respectable man, but he had once seen a man killed in a quarrel, and it had affected his nerves, and all of a sudden, when he was discussing prices with Augustus, he would start, and begin to tremble and cry, "Keep him off! Keep him off! There is blood upon his hands!" and then Sabina had to rush and get whisky for him, while Augustus walked him up and down and tried to soothe him, and took any price for his pigs to get rid of him. He could not afford to quarrel with him, because he was his best customer and the only big buyer in the neighbourhood.

I think the finishing touch was put to the matter by an awful fright that she had one night late, when Augustus had gone to town and was not expected home till the next day. My daughter had always had one great fear at Gallows Tree Farm, and that was burglars. They had all their plate and her jewels there, and the place was unprotected, the men engaged on the farm living a long distance away.

And that night, after she had gone to bed, they heard noises down below, and the servants came in to her terrified and said, "Oh, ma'am, it's burglars, and we shall all be murdered in our beds," and began to shriek. Sabina was frightened, for the noise was quite like men tramping about below in big boots.

But she summoned up her courage and got Augustus's gun and went downstairs, but stopped at the kitchen door, with curdled blood, as a great crash came, and fainted, the gun going off and hitting the big grandfather's clock in the hall full in the face and smashing it, and when she came to herself there was the weeping waggoner with the cook fainting in his arms and the housemaid like a gibbering idiot, and it seems the waggoner had found out what it was and had not told before because he did not want the cook to get better and spurn him again.

And it was the pony who had got loose through one of the men's carelessness, and had got into the outhouse next the kitchen and was having a game to himself there with the tubs and the tins.

After Augustus junior was born, it was not possible for that sort of thing to go on, and so the farm was sold, and now I have them all near me, and am able to see them, which is a great comfort to me.

I cannot say it is such a comfort to me to have my eldest son, John, near me, for his poor wife is always sending round to me to know what can be done with him. He is certainly a great trial, and I say sometimes he cannot be quite right, seeing the way that he goes on. Why, only the other day I had a note from dear Lottie: "Dear Mother, Do come at once. John is making his will and going about and kneeling down and biting the chairs, and he says it's all his liver."

But I shall have to devote a special memoir to my eldest son, John, and his patient, long-suffering wife – poor girl!

Memoir VI

Some of My Worries

R EALLY I DON'T BELIEVE that any poor woman ever was so constantly harassed as I am. Not only have I all the cares of my own household on my shoulders, but I am continually having to worry about my married sons and daughters. My husband says that I worry myself unnecessarily, and put myself in a fever (that is his elegant way of expressing it) about nothing.

It is all very well for him to take things so calmly, but I can't. I believe that John Tressider wouldn't put himself out if the house was on fire, and I am sure it is a mercy it hasn't been many times with his horrible habit of sitting up late downstairs reading *The Times*, and then coming up to bed half asleep, and over and over again leaving the gas on the stairs turned on full.

I have endeavoured to make my daughters profit by my experience, and have always specially warned them against the fatal weakness of letting their husbands get into the habit of sitting up after everybody has gone to bed, reading and smoking, and the gas at their mercy.

I have remonstrated with Mr Tressider again and again, but he always says that he enjoys his newspaper and his cigar and his glass of whisky and water after everybody's gone to bed more than at any other time, and he'll sit down in the smoking room and read *The Times* often till one o'clock. Why can't he read *The Times* like other men do, in the morning, or when he's at business, instead of sitting up at all hours of the night to do it, and letting the fire out and coming to bed as cold as a frog?

It has always been the same thing with him. Nothing could induce him to retire to rest at a Christian hour. When the children were younger he would spend the entire evening with them till they went to bed, and then there was some excuse perhaps for him having a quiet hour or so afterwards.

He used to keep the children up late, too, and it was no good my saying anything, though often and often I have had one of my nervous headaches, and had to lock myself in my room to escape from the noise they made playing a dreadful game they called "Tom", and rushing round one after the other, knocking the tables and chairs over, and he used to make more noise than any of them.

Of course, it is a very nice thing for a father when he comes home from business to romp with his children, but with seven of them all romping at once, and a heavy man crawling about on all fours and pretending to be a bear, you can imagine the pandemonium it used to be.

An excellent father in many ways, to give him his due, is John Tressider, but most injudicious. I never left the children to him but something went wrong.

Never shall I forget my horror when one morning at the seaside my sweet little Jane, when only five years old, was brought to me by the nurse with her head swollen the size of a pumpkin.

"Good heavens, nurse!" I exclaimed. "Whatever is the matter with the child?"

"I don't know, ma'am," she said, "but master let her paddle in the sea for over an hour yesterday, and I expect she's got water on the brain."

I sent off for a doctor at once – Mr Tressider had gone to town – and when he came, he said there was no doubt it *was* the paddle in the sea had done it, and it was a mercy the poor mite didn't have erysipelas.* Fancy any father in his senses allowing his child to keep her feet in cold water for an hour without wetting her head! But men are always so injudicious with children.

I often say that my eldest son, John, ought not to be blamed for his wild goings-on, for very likely it is all his father's fault. When he was a little boy his father used to let him stoop down and put his hands between his legs, and then his father would take his hands and turn him head over heels, and I think John has been head over heels ever since. It is against human nature for a child to be continually turned head over heels. It must upset the mental balance.

When I sit calmly down now and recall the terrible frights that I had with my children through their father's injudiciousness, I wonder that my nerves are not more utterly shattered than they are, and I could never say much to him, for he was always quite as distressed as I was, and much more helpless.

I shall never forget the day he came into my room just as I was dressing, having had my breakfast in bed for a bad headache. His face was as white as a ghost, and he dropped down into a chair, and exclaimed in a sepulchral voice, "I am... I, er... I'm afraid Sabina's swallowed a farthing."

"Where is she?" I exclaimed, starting up.

"I've left her in the nursery. She's black in the face. I've held her upside down and shaken her, but it was no good. Oh, dear, oh, dear! Whatever shall I do?"

I didn't wait to hear any more. I was up the stairs in a moment, and there was my poor little lamb (she was only four then) almost choking, and the great idiot of a nurse, her eyes almost starting out of her head, slapping the child on the back, and yelling, "Spit it out, Miss Sabby, oh, do spit it out or it'll kill you!"

I snatched the child up, and I was so terrified to see her gurgling and choking that for a moment I lost my own presence of mind, and could only tremble in every limb.

"How did it happen?" I gasped.

"Oh, please, ma'am, it wasn't me – it was the master. He gave her a farthing, and she put it in her mouth, and he was riding her to Banbury Cross* and the farthing must have gone down her throat."

Fancy the father of a family riding his child to Banbury Cross with a farthing in its mouth!

It was Sunday morning and the people were just going to church, but I didn't think of that. I only knew that my child had a farthing in her throat, and I thought of her swallowing it and the verdigris* in her dear little stomach, which would be deadly poison; so just as I was, in my loose dressing gown and my hair down my back, I dashed down the stairs, the poor mite in my arms, and I flew down the street and across the road, and round the corner to where our doctor lived.

I daresay the neighbours thought I was mad. One or two of them stood with their church services under their arms looking after me as if they were petrified. But I couldn't help what they thought, and I couldn't yell out to everybody as I passed, "My child's swallowed a farthing."

I thought of it all afterwards, and what a sight I must have looked, but at the time I thought of nothing but my poor little girl.

I rang the doctor's bell violently, then I ran up the steps and banged away with the knocker so furiously that the people who hadn't gone to church all threw up their windows and put their heads out. The servant answered the door at once, and I made one rush across the hall and burst into the doctor's consulting room so out of breath that when I saw him there all I could gasp out was "Farthing – throat – quick!"

The doctor took the child, who was screaming violently, and looked down her throat.

"There's nothing there," he said.

"Then she's swallowed it," I said. "Oh, doctor, whatever shall I do? My poor child is poisoned – the verdigris will kill her."

I don't know what would have happened to me, for I felt my brain giving way with horror, but at that moment there came a loud knock at the front door, and I heard my husband's voice asking for me. In another minute he was in the room.

"It's all right, my dear," he exclaimed, "we've found the farthing!"

"What!" I exclaimed. "The child hasn't swallowed it, and you've let me… " And then, utterly overcome, I fell back on the sofa and had hysterics, and it was a quarter of an hour before I was well enough to go home again.

The doctor got a four-wheeler to the door for us. When the tension was removed I couldn't walk through the streets in a dressing gown, bareheaded, with my hair down my back, and in that cab I gave John Tressider a piece of my mind. The idea of letting a poor woman be terrified out of her senses believing that her child had swallowed a farthing, and allowing her to rush bareheaded through the streets on Sunday morning for nothing.

It seems that the nurse, after I had gone, had picked up the farthing on the floor. It had evidently slipped down the child's dress, and not down her throat, as her father supposed, and it had fallen on the floor when he turned her upside down and shook her, but in his terror he hadn't noticed it, and thought she'd swallowed it.

No wonder the poor mite screamed and went black in the face after that treatment, and being violently slapped on the back by the nurse, but that is the sort of thing I had to put up with during my early married life, and the only wonder is that it did not sour my temper.

My troubles were never over while my children were young, for if they hadn't the measles or the whooping cough, or some infantile complaint, they were always getting fish bones in their throats or tumbling down and cutting their knees, and John (my son, not my husband), not satisfied with catching everything that was to be caught – upon my word, if there was only a case of measles in the newspaper that was left lying about that boy would take it – actually got himself lost while out with the nurse and his little sister in the perambulator. When the girl came home and told me that she'd stopped to look in a shop window, and when she looked up the boy was gone – he was about six then – I wonder I didn't shake her.

I was most terribly anxious, as any mother would be whose child was lost in London, for the papers were full of cases of dear little children being enticed away with sweets, and their nice, good clothes taken off up a narrow alley and horrid rags put on them instead; and I made up my mind my boy was stolen and would, perhaps, be brought up as an acrobat or a Gypsy.

I put myself in a temper at first – I couldn't help it – but when an hour went by and the boy didn't come home, and night was coming on, I sent the servants all off to ask in all the shops and to give a description at the police station, and I could do nothing but walk up and down the hall and wring my hands, every now and then going to the front door and looking up and down to see if there were any signs of my boy.

And when he was brought home by a policeman, at seven o'clock in the evening, having been found at the Mother Red Cap crying and taken to the police station, I was so overjoyed that I gave the policeman five shillings and Johnny a whipping for getting himself lost and nearly driving me out of my mind.

When a mother has been through all this sort of thing the least she can expect is that when her children are grown up they will be a comfort to her, and that she will end her days in peace.

I don't know how it is with other mothers. Some of them may have been more fortunate than I have. All I know is that now most of my children are married and settled (unsettled would be a better word), I not only have to worry over them, but over their husbands or wives, as the case may be, as well. A mother's troubles are bad enough, goodness knows, but a mother-in-law's… Well, really I think they are worse, for you are not so young, and so strong, and so hopeful, when they come upon you, and then there are your grandchildren to worry about. They are a double worry, because if anything happens to them you are worried for their fathers and mothers as well, which is only natural.

There really never seems to be any end to my anxieties: no sooner is my mind at rest over my eldest daughter's little boy, who worried his poor mother to death by having water on the brain, than my second daughter's little girl has the measles, and you never know what that will leave; and when, thank goodness, it leaves nothing, and I begin to breathe again, my second son, William, gets terribly low-spirited and unhappy about his little boy, who is flung out of a perambulator on his head through a gawking nursemaid not looking where she is going and running into a pillar box, and the doctor is afraid it may have affected his intellect.

However, thank goodness, though, the children have all got well and there is nothing wrong with them up to now, but you never know what is going to happen, and I often open my letters with fear and trepidation.

That letter that dear Lottie sent me asking me to come round because my son John was behaving in such an extraordinary manner is a specimen of what I have to suffer.

I have told you what a trouble John was to me through his eccentric ways and not taking to his father's business, but being bohemian and turning an author – but I haven't told you about his marriage.

The first inkling I had of his ever being in love was that photograph I found in his room from his "loving Lottie".

When he came home that night I had gone to bed, but the next morning I said to him, "John, I went into your room last evening, and I found a photograph. Who is the young lady?"

He coloured up a little, but he laughed, and said, "Oh, that's a secret, Mater; don't you be so inquisitive."

I said I was not inquisitive, but I didn't think there ought to be any secret about a "loving Lottie", and then I begged him to be serious, and gave him a little motherly advice on the subject of female acquaintances, laying especial stress upon the fact that no man who has an honest regard for a girl need be ashamed of telling his mother all about her.

But John wouldn't be serious. He turned the conversation. He never would be talked to or take advice. Poor boy, it would have been much better for him if he hadn't been so sensitive and so ready to resent the very natural anxiety which I felt for his welfare.

I should have renewed the subject, because I am not a woman to be put off when I have made up my mind to find out anything, as my husband can testify, but unfortunately, about that time John, although his father had already most generously paid his debts, got under a cloud again, and finding, I suppose, that his creditors were coming to the house and worrying him, one day horrified me by saying that he was going to take "rooms" and live away from home.

Now if there is one thing that I have no faith in it is "rooms" for young men. I don't believe in young men going away from home influences until they go to a home of their own, where the wife's influence replaces that of the mother and the sisters.

I was very much upset, but what could I do? John was of age, and if he chose to go, there was nothing to prevent him. He pretended that it was necessary for him to have a place of his own for "professional" reasons, and, in spite of all I could urge, he went – which was a great blow to me – and took furnished apartments, right over the other side of the water, in Camberwell.

He came to see us, I will say, pretty often, and spoke very confidently of the way he was getting on, and there was no doubt that he had got onto the staff of a weekly newspaper, and was working for some of the provincial papers as well, so that he was making an income for himself.

That, at least, was something to be thankful for, so I gave up worrying myself about him and had almost forgotten about the photograph and the "loving Lottie", when, one day, I received a letter from him, and when I had read it I let it fall to the ground, and all I could say was, "Good gracious."

It was a very short, abrupt sort of letter, considering the nature of its contents, but that was John all over:

Dear Mother,

You will be surprised to hear that I am married. I'm sure you will like my wife, so I want to introduce you to her. Don't say anything to the governor yet, but come over yourself first. I want to break the family to Lottie by degrees. She's rather nervous about it, and she's afraid you'll all hate her, so I'm not going to spring you all on her at once. Will you come to dinner with us next Saturday at six? Put your best smile on, like a good old mater, for Lottie is very nervous about how you'll take it, and I want her to see what a jolly, nice, kind, sensible sort of a mother-in-law she's going to have.

Always your loving son,

John

After I had recovered from my astonishment, I couldn't help feeling angry. What on earth did John want to go and get married for, without letting anybody know? It was ridiculous – it was senseless – and what on earth was the girl about to allow such a thing, and what were her people about, and what did it all mean?

I was terribly afraid when I began to think it over that John had made a fool of himself and married a young woman who wouldn't be altogether a credit to the family. Young men are foolish sometimes, and are caught by a pretty face, and put their heads into a halter which makes them uncomfortable for the rest of their lives.

However, the mischief – if mischief it was – was done, and so all I could do was to wait and see. But I was very glad when Saturday came, and I should know the worst – or the best.

It was rather an awkward meeting, but the awkwardness didn't last long. Women know what women are at a glance, and one glance at my new daughter-in-law was sufficient to convince me that John's happiness was safe in her hands. After her first nervousness had worn off we very soon became good friends; and I could see that John was delighted at the good impression his wife had made.

Lottie was tall and graceful, and had a very sweet voice, and what I liked best about her was, she seemed so homely and such a thorough little housekeeper. Without appearing to be inquisitive, I soon managed to find out all about her. It seems that John had met her at the house of a newspaper friend of his, and it was there they had fallen in love. She was an orphan living with an uncle and aunt, but she wasn't happy at home. Perhaps it was not being happy at home made her consent to such a quiet marriage. At any rate, they were married, and they were very happy and comfortable. I could see that.

John was in high spirits all the evening, and before I left he reassured me on the subject of his position. I was naturally anxious now he was married that he should be free from any pecuniary trouble. There is nothing interferes with domestic happiness so much as unpaid butchers' bills.

He told me of his engagements, and of a very good one that had been offered him, and showed me that his income would be quite enough to keep them comfortably, even if his father didn't give him anything, and I left that evening quite happy in my mind about my eldest son, and very thankful that, after all, his "loving Lottie" had turned out to be a nice, sensible, homely girl, who would look after him and make him comfortable.

John had left it to me to break it to the rest of the family, and I did so, assuring his sisters that they would like their new sister-in-law very much.

Mr Tressider took it very quietly indeed. I never saw such a man in my life for taking things quietly.

When I got home I went straight downstairs to his den, and found him as usual smoking his pipe and reading *The Times*. I believe he thinks it is his duty to read his *Times* every evening, and that if he missed it something would go wrong with the British Empire directly.

I said to him, "John, be good enough to put down that paper and listen to me."

He looked up at me for a moment, but he didn't put *The Times* down. He only said, "Go on, my dear, I'm listening. What is it?"

I rose and quietly took the paper from him, and put it on the table.

"You can do without that paper for a moment, I suppose," I said. "You can't pay proper attention to your wife and your newspaper at the same time."

He looked at me in a blank, half-idiotic way that is particularly irritating, but I wouldn't be irritated, because I didn't want to have words with him on such an occasion as the announcement of his eldest son's marriage; so I said very quietly, "John is married!"

I expected he would have started up or betrayed some astonishment, but he merely lifted up his eyebrows and said, "Oh!"

"And I've been to see him, and his wife is a very nice girl."

Mr Tressider took his pipe out of his mouth, looked in the bowl, saw it was empty, filled it up again, struck a match, lit it, puffed three or four clouds of tobacco, and then, looking up at me again, said, "H'm!"

"John Tressider," I said, really beginning to be angry, "if that is all the interest you feel in your eldest son's marriage, you ought to be ashamed of yourself. If you had done your duty as a father..."

I hadn't time to finish the sentence, for the servant came in with Mr Tressider's bedroom candle, which, by my orders, was always put by him on the table, so that the gas on the stairs might be turned out without being left to his tender mercy.

When the servant had gone out, he picked up *The Times* again, and began to look for the place where he had left off reading.

"I'm glad she's a nice girl," he said, "and I'm glad he's married – perhaps he'll settle down now. I think he's done a very sensible thing."

"Not in getting married secretly – you don't approve of such marriages, I suppose?"

"Well, it saves a lot of fuss, doesn't it? There is no wedding breakfast, no speeches, no expense, no nonsense. I think if ever I were to marry again—"

That was more than I could stand, so I said, "You'll have the decency to wait till I'm dead first," and I marched out of the room and banged the door after me.

He didn't mean any harm, as he explained afterwards, but I don't know any man who can be so deliberately and calmly irritating as John Tressider when he chooses.

Now John does not take after his father in that. He is irritating, but not calmly irritating. He is absolutely exasperating. Even poor, dear, gentle Lottie... But you shall hear the way he was going on, and the absurd things he was doing when I went round to see what was the matter in answer to Lottie's letter.

I can't think how she puts up with it as quietly as she does. I should like to see *my* husband attempt anything of the sort. I am a long-suffering woman, *but*…

Memoir VII

The Apple Dumplings

WHEN I GOT ROUND to John's house, I naturally expected, from Lottie's letter, that I should find him seriously ill, though I was not so very much alarmed, for I knew by experience that his temper, though violent at the time, didn't last very long.

My eldest son John is one of those excitable people who are up one minute and down the next, and when they are up they *are* up, and when they are down they *are* down. I think I would sooner have people of that sort to deal with than your calm, quiet people who, when anything does go wrong with them, are generally sulky and silent. A man in a rage does silly things and says bitter things, but the things that he does are not so unforgivable, and the things that he says not so cruel as the things done and said by the self-possessed individual, who is always master of himself and thinks over his wrongs calmly and deliberately. Give me the people with tempers, I like them better. If Mr Tressider had only had a little more temper I am sure it would often have been much better for all of us.

But there are limits even to temper, and I must say that my son John was in the habit of throwing himself into such ungovernable rages all about nothing, that at times you would have thought he was a madman.

I have seen him dance about a room with passion and scream, and then go and kick the door or bang the wall with all his might.

He always declared that kicking the door or banging the wall was a relief to his pent-up feelings, and that if he didn't do something of the sort he should have a fit.

It doesn't so much matter now he kicks his own door and bangs his own walls, but when these performances took place under my roof I used to be exceedingly cross about it; especially one day when, because I said something he didn't like, he kicked the door of my little sitting room so violently that the panel flew out and his foot went right through and caught one of the servants, who was evidently listening outside, though she declared she was only passing. Having the tea tray in her hand, which she was bringing up for our five o'clock tea, John's boot, as it went through the panel, caught the tray and sent everything flying up in the air, and a nice mess there was with the carpet on the landing saturated with tea and milk, and bread and butter lying about all over the place, and, of course, as usual, the buttered side down.

The panel giving way, the crash of the crockery and the servant's shrieks sobered John considerably, and I believe he was heartily ashamed of himself, but I could have screamed myself with rage when I saw my door broken to bits like that, and my beautiful china tea service smashed to pieces.

I should not have alluded to this painful incident, but if I am to write the truth about my son John it is absolutely necessary that I should deal with his extraordinary paroxysms of temper. We did not think so much of them at home, as we had grown accustomed to them, these fits of sudden rage having been characteristic of him from his childhood.

The fact that he never did himself or anybody else any serious harm to a certain extent made us less alarmed than we should have been, but I often talked to him very seriously on the subject, urging him to control his temper, and his father did everything in his power to check him.

You never knew when he was going to have a violent outburst of rage. Some ordinary remark, some trifling thing would upset him, and then he would begin gradually to work himself up. I remember his father coming home one night as pale as a ghost, when John was at the office, and saying that really he thought he would wind up by killing somebody.

It seems his father had said something that offended John, or had upset him in some way, for all of a sudden, without a word of warning, he began to dance about the office, and presently he seized the poker out of the fender in the private office and flourished it over his head, and began to bang a small table with it and shriek, and when the top of the table was split in half he yelled, "So perish all my enemies." Then he hurled the poker away, burst into tears and fell on his knees, and taking up the end of the hearthrug began to bite bits out of it and growl like a wild animal.

This incident has always remained impressed upon my mind, because I and my husband had a few words about it. My husband, who, not being at home, had not seen so much of Master John's beautiful temper as I had, said he was seriously alarmed as to the state of John's mind, and I said, "Oh, he is sane enough; it is nothing but his uncontrollable temper." One thing led to another, and Mr Tressider, who never could argue sensibly, actually dared to hint that John took his violent temper from my side of the family. Naturally I resented such a suggestion, and spoke my mind plainly, and then he had the meanness to remind me of an incident which ought to have been forgotten long ago, seeing that I was really very ill at the time, and in a high state of nervous tension. And after all, I am not the first woman who has torn up her bonnet in a temper, and it wasn't a new bonnet, or one that I cared about, because I didn't look well in it. I thought of all that before I tore it up.

I wasn't going to be taunted with a bonnet that had been torn up twenty years ago for nothing, especially as it couldn't possibly have had anything to do with John's violence, so I reminded Mr Tressider of another incident which he had doubtless found it convenient to forget, and that was how the head of a certain house and the father of a certain family had one day taken up six boiled apple dumplings at the dinner table, and hurled them one after the other through the open window, to the astonishment of the passers-by, one of whom was a policeman; and I shall not forget it in a hurry, the sheepish expression on the face of that father of a family when the policeman rang the bell and demanded to see the master of the house. And when Mr Tressider went out there was the policeman standing in the hall with half a boiled apple dumpling in his right hand, and the other half smothering his face and completely blocking up one eye.

It was a very disgraceful scene, but, angry as I was, I really couldn't help laughing when the poor man, pointing to his face, and holding up all that was left of the apple dumpling in his right hand, exclaimed, "Look here, guv'nor, what's the meaning o' this? It come out of your window."

That policeman was taken down into the kitchen, and the dumpling removed from his features, and he was given a glass of brandy and five shillings, and when he was gone the housemaid went out with a broom and dustpan, and swept up the bits of apple dumpling from the pavement in front of the house, but it was a very long time before I ceased to remind Mr Tressider of the impropriety of such behaviour.

It was such a ridiculous thing of him to do, especially about a trifle. It arose in this way. Every mother of a family will sympathize with me on the great dinner question. There is nothing so difficult as always to have that which pleases City men who have a club and dine at the Mansion House* and with the City companies. You must change the menu sometimes. Now, my husband is passionately fond of boiled apple dumplings, but I couldn't have boiled apple dumplings every day that he was at home to dinner. One day when there was a blancmange and stewed fruit he grumbled, and said that he hated blancmange, and declared that he hardly ever had apple dumplings. "Oh! very well," I said. "I'll take care that you don't grumble again." And so I ordered the cook to send up boiled apple dumplings *every* day that Mr Tressider was at home to dinner.

I thought I would cure him of grumbling, and I did for a time. He liked the apple dumplings the first time, the second time he stared at them, but said nothing, the third time he frowned slightly when he saw them come on the table, the fourth time when they were laid before him he said to me, "Can I give you one?"

"No, thank you," I said. "I don't care for apple dumplings."

"Then take them away," he said, and they were taken from the table untouched.

But when the next time the cover was lifted, he saw apple dumplings again he flew into a rage.

"How much longer do you mean to insult me?" he exclaimed.

"Insult you, dear," I said, calmly. "I thought you preferred apple dumplings to anything else."

"Hang the apple dumplings," he said (only it wasn't "hang"), and then he suddenly seized the dish, dragged it towards him, and hurled dumpling after dumpling through the window, which was wide open, as it was a warm evening.

"There!" he cried, when he had finished. "That's what I think of apple dumplings, and if you put any more before me I shall serve them in the same way."

And then the policeman came in, and you know the rest.

It was this conduct I reminded Mr Tressider of when he had the audacity to suggest that John took his temper from my side of the family. He left off arguing directly. He always does when I remind him of those apple dumplings. But I had as much right to bring up his apple dumplings as he had to bring up my bonnet. Perhaps it would have been better to have mentioned neither, because, as John was in short frocks at the time, neither the apple dumplings nor the bonnet could possibly have had any influence on his nervous temperament.

You can easily understand that these things – not the dumplings, but John's youthful performance in the way of tantrums – made me very anxious about him when he married and settled down as a husband. I wanted him to be happy, but I also wanted him to make his wife happy, and it was not long after our first interview that I told the dear girl how odd John was at times, and begged her not be worried too much if he should break out.

"Don't argue with him, my dear, when he's like that," I said, "but just let him have his temper out. Arguing with him is only waste of breath, and with bad-tempered men every word you say they seize on to work themselves up with. It is merely adding fuel to the fire. It might have been once, when men *were* men, that a soft answer turned away wrath, but my experience is that if you give a soft answer they think they've frightened you, and they go on."

Lottie promised me she wouldn't be frightened, but the dear little goose was terrified out of her life the very first time she saw John in a temper. It was something in the paper that did it, some notice he read of a story he'd written in the magazines. Lottie told me that he hadn't been very well in the night, having had a bad attack of indigestion through eating mayonnaise of salmon and lobster at a supper party he'd been to, and then having tipsy cake,* of which he was passionately fond, after that.

When he woke in the morning, he said he had had dreadful dreams, and felt awfully bad, so dear, kind little Lottie got up and went downstairs, and made him a nice strong cup of tea herself, because he declared the servants couldn't make tea, never using boiling water (which is very often true, and I am sure the terrible trash that I have had when I have stayed at friends' houses which was supposed to be tea makes me think that very few people know what good tea is. To make tea properly it must be made with water which is just boiling, not hot water merely, and then it should stand for a few minutes with a cosy over it. You never get the full flavour of tea unless you cover the pot with a cosy for a short time. The real secrets of a good cup are the boiling water and the cosy). And when the tea was made, Lottie brought it up to him, but unfortunately brought him the newspaper as well as his letters, thinking that would keep him in bed, and do his head good.

He said she was a perfect angel, and she went downstairs to her own breakfast quite delighted, but when she came back again afterwards, she was horrified to find him dancing about the room in an awful rage, shaking his fist at some imaginary person in the corner, and calling the imaginary person the most dreadful names.

Then, when he had gone on for about ten minutes, making the most fearful faces, he rushed to the bed, seized the newspaper, threw it down and danced on it. Then he picked the paper up, tore it in pieces and threw it all over the room.

"Oh, dear, oh, dear!" cried poor Lottie, trembling in every limb. "Whatever is the matter?"

"Matter?" he shrieked. "Why, some villain, some wretch, some venomous ruffian has dared to say that my last story in the *Grasshopper* is a plagiarism. Oh, if I only had the scoundrel here who wrote the notice, I'd kill him, I'd dash him to bits, and jump on every separate bit. I'd take him by the throat and throw him out of the window onto the iron railings, and leave him there to die on the spikes, and when he was dying I'd hiss at him, like that: sss-sss-sss."

Poor Lottie declared that when she saw John stand and put out his tongue, and hiss like an idiot in a county lunatic asylum, she thought she should have fallen down on the floor with horror.

Fortunately he saw how frightened she was, and as she hadn't got used to his performances then, he checked himself and came to her and said, "There, don't be frightened. I've had my temper out, and I'm better now. I'm always like that when my liver's bad."

"Oh, dear," said Lottie, "then I hope it won't be bad often."

"It was that horrid mayonnaise of salmon," answered John, "and the tipsy cake last night, I expect. I was a fool to eat them, but I've no willpower. It's awful. Directly I see mayonnaise of salmon and tipsy cake my willpower is utterly destroyed. But I'll turn over a new leaf, I'll diet myself and give up smoking, and... There, don't you upset yourself, little woman, I'm all right now."

And he was, and for a week or two he went on all right, except for an occasional fit of depression, in which he said he wished he was dead, and asked Lottie if she should mind his being cremated, as there was no elbow room in a coffin, and he knew he should be restless and want to turn over, for he never could sleep on his back, and all that sort of wild nonsense, which we were quite used to at home, but which made Lottie (as she told me afterwards) feel as if she was in a padded room with a lunatic, and trying to keep him quiet till the keeper came.

The next time I saw John after that, I had a little quiet conversation with him, and begged him to try and exercise a little more self-control, pointing out to him how his extraordinary behaviour upset his wife, who wasn't used to it.

"Oh, it's all right, Mater," he said. "I know I'm a bit eccentric sometimes, but it's soon over. I've told Lottie not to take any notice, but just to let me have it out by myself. It's only when my liver's bad, and then I'm always better if I get in a bit of a paddy. It works the acidity out of me, I think."

"Still, my dear boy, it is very distressing to those who love you; come, try and remember when you feel inclined to give way that you cause a loving heart to ache, and loving hearts are much too scarce in this world not to be tenderly treated when they are found. I know I am a foolish old woman in your eyes sometimes, but if we don't think of others, if we only think of ourselves, depend upon it, my dear boy, we never get within measurable distance of human happiness."

"Why, Mater, you're getting quite a philosopher," he said. "But you don't surely imagine that I would worry Lottie purposely, do you?"

"No, not purposely, but remember what the poet says. I don't remember his name" (I never could remember poets' names):

Evil is wrought by want of thought
As well as want of heart.
Many a woman's gentle heart is broken without meaning it.*

"Oh, come, Mother, don't take it too seriously," said John. "One would think I was a sort of Bluebeard, and Henry the Eighth, and the King in the *Arabian Nights*,* three single ruffians rolled into one."

"You can't call *them* single men," I said.

John laughed and gradually turned the conversation, but I hoped that my words had not been thrown away.

Things went on pretty well, and Lottie was much more cheerful. She managed to keep John at home more of an evening, and so he didn't get staying late at the club and smoking, and she induced him to give up dining at foreign restaurants so much, and certainly his temper improved in consequence, and I began to think he was going to become an ordinary sensible human being, when one fine day I received the letter I told you about, and when I went off to Camberwell I found Lottie the picture of misery.

"Oh, my dear," I said, "I am so sorry. What has upset him this time?"

"I don't know, quite," she said, "but he's been queer ever since he went out, three nights ago, to the theatre with a friend. He told me that after the theatre they had lobsters and champagne, and he knew he should pay for it. I told him it was very foolish of him, and I couldn't think how he could do it, knowing what he would have to suffer afterwards."

Of course, directly Lottie told me about the lobsters and champagne I understood everything. He inherits a weak digestion from his father's side of the family, one of Mr Tressider's aunts having had to live on dry toast and boiled soles for over twenty years, and another relative, a cousin, always carrying a galvanic battery about with him and giving himself shocks at the dinner table between every course, which made me very chary of asking him to a dinner party, especially as he did nothing but talk about his ailments and groan all the time, and what with his battery under his chair and a bottle of some digestive wine in front of him and bismuth lozenges all round his plate, he wasn't exactly what you might call a cheerful guest.

I used to ask him out of politeness at first, especially as he was wealthy and unmarried, and had taken a great fancy to my youngest son Tommy, but after a time he presumed on his position as an invalid, and actually sent round one day to say *what he should like for dinner*, and as the principal dish he mentioned was Spanish onions boiled in milk, I thought it time to put my foot down and give Mr Tressider a bit of my mind on the subject of his dyspeptic relative. The idea of my having onions handed round at a dinner party!

John always was dyspeptic – John junior, I mean; Mr Tressider, himself, can eat anything, and I have known him have scallops for supper after the theatre, and even to eat cockles and winkles at the seaside, but it is from his family that John gets his dyspepsia.

When Lottie told me about the lobsters and champagne, I said, "Well, he has only himself to blame. Why on earth does he eat things that he knows will disagree with him?"

"He says it's lack of willpower – that in the presence of a lobster he is a child."

"Lack of willpower," I exclaimed angrily, "lack of rubbish. Where is he now?"

"Oh, I don't know, and it's that which makes me so unhappy. He found out that I'd written to you, and he flew into a terrible rage and said he would go out and look for a mad dog and get it to bite him, and then go and present his body to the Royal College of Surgeons so that he might be some good in the world when he was out of it."

I couldn't help smiling, it was so absurd.

"My dear child," I said, "you mustn't take any notice of him. He has talked in that wild way from a child. Has he been very bad this time?"

"Oh, dreadful! He got up yesterday at seven, and went out in the garden and dug up a worm, and when I came out he was patting its head and saying it was the only thing that loved him. Of course that made me cry, and then he said I needn't cry, because he'd made his will and left me everything except the dog kennel and the coal scuttle, and he wanted you to have the kennel and his father the coal scuttle, and always keep them in remembrance of him."

"Oh," I said, losing all patience, "he wants a good shaking. He is simply doing it to worry you."

"Oh, but that isn't the worst," said Lottie, the tears coming into her eyes again. "Do you know what he did yesterday?"

"I shouldn't be surprised at anything, when he's like this. What was it?"

"We were at dinner, and I got him some boiled apple dumplings because I know how he likes them."

"He takes after his father in that," I said. "Mr Tressider's favourite sweet is a boiled apple dumpling."

"Yes, I know, and so I made them myself, so that they should be nice and light, and would you believe it, when they came on the table he jumped up and shrieked.

"'What's the matter?' I said.

"'Matter?' he screamed. 'Murder's the matter. You evidently want to kill me, that you may marry somebody else – the idea of giving a man, who is in the agony that I am, an apple dumpling!'

"And before I knew what he was going to do he seized the apple dumplings and threw them out of the open window."

"Tell me," I exclaimed, starting up, "did he hit a policeman?"

"No, he threw them out of the back window, and the cook was in the garden and saw it, and had hysterics. She says she is sure the master is mad, and she won't live with a lunatic, and she has demanded a month's wages, and she's going to leave tonight. Oh, dear, oh, dear, whatever shall I do?"

I comforted my poor daughter-in-law as well as I could, and while I was trying to cheer her up the demon came in, and would you believe it, he was laughing – yes, absolutely laughing, and he said he'd had his temper out and now he felt better – he thought the dancing about had moved the lobster off his chest.

I stayed a little while, and left them with peace restored, and John and Lottie playing battledore and shuttlecock in the back garden; but that night, when Mr Tressider was smoking his cigar and reading his *Times* in his den, I went down to him and I said, "John Tressider, the sins of the father are visited on the children. Your eldest son has been flinging apple dumplings out of the window."

I never saw a man look so astonished in my life.

He gasped for a moment; then, recovering himself, he seemed suddenly struck with an idea.

Rising solemnly, he came across to me and took me gently by the shoulders, and looking me full in the face, he exclaimed: "Jane Tressider, let us be thankful that he hasn't also torn up his bonnet!"

Could anything have been more heartless than to remind a worried mother at such a moment of a thing which ought to have been forgotten years ago?

But men are not like women. They have no delicacy of feeling.

Memoir VIII

Outside the Omnibus

My second daughter, Maud, was, as I think I have previously stated, the beauty of the family. She inherited her good looks from my side of the house, and although I ought not perhaps to say it, she more closely resembles me than any of my children.

It is difficult for me sometimes when I catch sight of myself in the looking glass to believe that I was once the beautiful girl who attracted John Tressider's attention when he was riding past my father's house on the outside of an omnibus.

It seems – he told me all about it afterwards – that I was looking over the parlour blind at two dogs fighting in the street, and at that moment Mr Tressider, then a handsome young man of two-and-twenty, happened to look up from his newspaper, which he was reading on his way to the City on the knifeboard of a Favorite 'bus.*

It was with him a case of "love at first sight". "What a beautiful creature!" he exclaimed, and he dreamt about me all day, and that evening, instead of taking the omnibus, he walked home and walked down our terrace until he recognized the house, and as luck – or fate, perhaps, I should say under all the circumstances – would have it, I happened to come to the window and look over the blind again just as he was stopping to put the number of the house down on his shirt cuff.

Our eyes met, and I naturally, seeing a handsome young man regarding me fixedly – not to say staring at me – lowered mine and turned away.

Little did I dream that I had been gazing at my future husband, but so it was. Then Mr Tressider, having made a note of my address, went down the terrace to a fishmonger's shop which was just round the corner, and there purchased a pair of soles, which he told me afterwards he put in his overcoat pocket and forgot all about for several days, not wearing his overcoat again, but hanging it up in his wardrobe, the weather turning much warmer, and only remembered them when everybody began to go about the house and wonder where on earth the strong fishy smell came from. Poor fellow, he was in love, and that makes one forget even a pair of soles in one's pocket.

The reason he bought the soles was to have an excuse to enter into conversation with the fishmonger. He asked him if he knew who lived at No. 17 – our number – because of course he wanted to know my name, and when he had learnt it he went home and began to wonder how he could get an introduction.

It was very awkward his falling in love with a girl he didn't know at all, because real life isn't like it used to be in the old ballads and romances. In the nineteenth century a young man cannot come and play a guitar on a front doorstep, and there are no pretty pages by whom he can send billets-doux, and of course I shouldn't have thought of encouraging such a thing if there had been.

He felt it was necessary to get an introduction, but he couldn't find among all his acquaintances anybody who knew us, which wasn't very wonderful, as we had only recently come up to London from the country.

So all he could do was to ride by every day on the omnibus and gaze at our window, and hope I should be looking over the parlour blind, which was one of those short wire-gauze things which were fashionable in my young days, but which are quite gone out now except in old cathedral towns.

Sometimes I was there and sometimes I wasn't. I don't suppose I should have noticed him, but one day he raised his hat and then blushed so tremendously, that though it was a foggy morning I could see that his face was red.

"Well, of all the impudence!" I said to myself, but after that somehow or other it generally happened that I was at the window when the 9.30 Favorite omnibus went by, and of course I couldn't help looking at the top of it when it did to see if the handsome young man was there as usual.

He didn't raise his hat again, because I had only given him a stony stare when he did it, but he always blushed, and at last, when he saw that I saw him, I found that I was blushing, too.

You may imagine my astonishment and embarrassment when, about a fortnight after, at a small dance that we went to over at Peckham, the first person I saw when I entered the room was the handsome young gentleman from the top of the omnibus.

It is many a year ago now, and my children have grown up around me, and most of them have married, and little children climb about my knee and call me "Grandmamma", but as I sit and write these memoirs in the fading glow of a summer's evening, my eyes look out through the gathering haze, and I see myself once more a happy blushing girl. Oh, those dear old days, when everything seemed so bright and beautiful; when the world lay all before us and the black ox had not trodden on our feet. I can see myself as I was that evening, in my short-waisted muslin frock, and my pretty pink sash, and my dancing shoes with the elastic crossings, and my long mittens halfway up my arms. Oh, dear, oh, dear, whoever would have thought that one day I should be a poor worried mother-in-law, with rheumatism and gouty acidity and bad headaches, and children taking after me and worrying me nearly out of my life, some of them being so delicate, and whoever would have thought that the handsome young gentleman on the top of the omnibus, who used to blush when his eyes met mine, would one day come home and throw apple dumplings out of the window?

I never looked forward to anything of the kind when, blushing and trembling, I found the young gentleman from the top of the omnibus standing bowing and smiling in front of me, and being introduced to me by the son of the house as Mr John Tressider, and asking if he might have the pleasure of the next dance with me.

I don't know what I said, I was so confused, but I suppose it must have sounded like yes, for when the young lady at the piano began to play a set of quadrilles I found myself standing up by the side of Mr Tressider, and when it came to the time when your partner puts his arm round your waist I suddenly thought how he had seen me looking at him over the parlour blind every morning, and I went scarlet.

We got on very nicely, however, in spite of my natural confusion. He was very nice, and never even referred to our having set eyes on each other before – which was a great relief to me. He told me that the people of the house were very, very old friends of his, and after the dance was over he introduced me to his sister, who was in the room, and my mamma came up and sat down beside us and began to talk, and then we discovered that our dearest friends in London – the Smiths – were also friends of his family.

We had one or two more dances together that evening, and he took me down to supper; and as I was a country girl and had not seen much gaiety, it all seemed like fairyland to me, and I thought he was delightful. I kept stealing sidelong glances at him when he wasn't looking, and every time I looked I thought him handsomer than before.

We pulled crackers together, and he was very wicked, for he would read out loud the motto that was in our crackers, and one was, "Who ever loved that loved not at first sight?"* which I found out afterwards was from Marlowe, a playwriter who lived before Shakespeare, but at the time I thought it was the confectioner who wrote it, and I said it was a pretty sentiment.

Then Mr Tressider said, looking at me with a wicked look in his eyes, "Do you believe it?" and I said, "Really, I don't know anything about it." Then he asked me if I would not take a little champagne, and beckoned to the waiter, and I had my glass only half filled, saying that I was not used to champagne. In those days at little parties like the one at which I met John Tressider the champagne used to be either pink or straw, and had no name like it has now. And I can remember as if it was yesterday the waiter coming up with a bottle in each hand, and saying, "Pink or straw, miss?"

Five-and-thirty years ago is that evening, but I can see it still, and my old heart almost leaps again now as I think of John Tressider as he stood at the door, the lamplight shining on his wavy brown hair, and he saw Mamma and myself into a four-wheel cab, and stood bowing and looking after us on the kerb as we drove off.

"What a very nice young man," said my dear mother.

"Do you think so?" I said, as if I had really hardly troubled to look at him.

Wasn't it wicked of me?

Ah, love's young dream! Why do we ever awake from you to find that you were a dream? Well, I must not complain: I have had many blessings and, though a little trying at times, John Tressider has not been a bad husband and father, as husbands and fathers go nowadays, and my dear, loving children have been a great comfort to me, in spite of the many anxieties they have caused me; and now I have my grandchildren to think of, dear little mites, and when baby arms are once more round my neck, and soft baby lips are pressed to my cheeks, I feel that I have not lived and suffered in vain.

But I really do think that almost the happiest time of my life was after the party, when I knew that John Tressider was in love with me. Of course, now that we had been introduced to each other, I could smile and bow when he passed our window outside the Favorite omnibus, and there was no harm in it. It was not long before we met again at the Smiths', and then John's mother was introduced to my mother, and our families became friendly and visited each other, and one day John told me that he had loved me ever since the first moment that he caught sight of me when he was sitting outside the omnibus and I was looking over the parlour blind; and when he asked me if I hated him, what could I say? I referred him to my dear mamma at once, and my papa enquired into his circumstances, and as soon as my parents were satisfied we were engaged.

And it's all so long – so long ago, and here I sit today an old woman (though actually I don't look it and am not at all old in my ways), and John Tressider, who has also worn remarkably well and kept his complexion and his hair, though it is not so brown as it used to be, sits up into the small hours smoking and reading *The Times*, and comes to bed as cold as a frog, and goes through life in his easy, unconcerned sort of way, leaving all the worries of the house, and the servants, and the family, and our sons-in-law and daughters-in-law to me.

Sometimes when I have one of my bad headaches, and things have upset me, I say to my children, "Ah, my dears, wait till you've been through what I have. It's all very well to say don't worry yourself and don't fidget, but my nerves have been shattered, and I'm getting an old woman now." Sometimes I think they don't believe I ever was a bright, merry, jolly girl, and considered very beautiful, but there is a portrait of me in the dining room painted when little John was three years old, and they can see by that I do not boast when I say that Maud inherits her beauty from my side of the family.

I am painted as a young mother, with a white rose in my luxuriant black hair, which is rolled back after the manner of the time, and my little John, in a short frock, is lying in my lap and holding up a bunch of cherries.

Frequently people have said who have seen it, "What a beautiful woman," and when I have said, "It's a portrait of me when I was young," they have said, "Really, how very lovely you must have been," in a tone of voice that implied they never would have believed it to look at me now. But it was, and my second daughter Maud resembles me to a great extent, though her profile is more like that of the Empress Eugénie* when young.

Maud was always extremely pretty as a child, and everybody said she would grow up into a beautiful girl, but we had to be careful not to let her be admired too much, for fear it should make her vain.

As children my two eldest girls always had the grandest ideas. Many a time have I listened to them when, having made themselves long trains by tying a tablecloth round their waists, they would walk up and down the garden with their arms round each others' waists, calling each other Lady Eveline and Lady Araminta.

Goodness only knows where children get such ideas from, or where they hear such names, unless it is from the servants reading the *London Journal*, and talking before them. If you listen to children's conversation when they are playing you cannot help being struck with astonishment at the odd ideas they have managed to pick up, and the odd notions they have as to what they will be when they grow up. All my boys had made up their minds very early in life that they would be either omnibus conductors or railway guards, except Tommy, who was going to be an artist, and chalk lovely pictures on the pavement, like the old man who used to exhibit specimens of his skill near the railings of Mornington Crescent, in the Hampstead Road. He commenced his artistic career at the age of seven with a shilling box of paints given him on his birthday, and I shall never forget my horror when I came home from a visit and found that he had got into the drawing room unperceived with his paints and had commenced to decorate the drawing-room door with his idea of a country cottage, in green and blue, with black smoke coming out of three bright vermilion chimney pots.

Through playing so often at the game of being grand ladies, the boys began to chaff their sisters and called Maud "Lady Araminta", and the name stuck to her, and among her brothers and sisters she was always called Lady Araminta.

She really was not a vain or conceited girl at all, but very sensitive and rather a nervous child; but her troubles didn't begin until she grew up, and then, poor girl, she was plagued and worried out of her life by her brothers about her sweethearts.

I told you about the gentleman with the red moustache and the big bassoon. He was followed by a widower, a gentleman whom we had known for a great many years, and he was very attentive to Maud, but, of course, we never imagined that he was falling in love with her, though her brothers chaffed her about him, and began to call her Mrs No. 2, making her go quite hot sometimes at the dinner table, though she kept her temper admirably.

But one day my husband came to me and he said that Mr Briggs had spoken to him on the subject, and had asked him if he might pay his addresses to Maud, and if he thought that Maud cared for him sufficiently to marry him.

I threw up my hands when I heard of it, and said, "Why, the man must be mad to think we would allow such a thing." He was very wealthy, but he was at least fifty, and he had a grown-up son and daughter, both of them as old as Maud herself.

I called Maud into my room that evening, and I said to her, "My dear child, you don't care for Mr Briggs, do you? I mean, you wouldn't like to marry him."

The dear girl put on a most comical look for a moment and then she burst out laughing, and said, "Oh, Mamma, you… you don't mean to say that he has told you that he is in love with me, do you?"

I told her that he had had an interview with her father on the subject, and she seemed quite astonished – she had evidently never suspected anything of the sort.

We gave Mr Briggs a polite negative and the matter dropped, and for some time he ceased his visits to our house, not coming again until he came to introduce his second wife, a lady considerably nearer his own age, and much more suitable for him than our beautiful Maud.

The next suitor for her hand was an old gentleman also. Really it was absurd how she seemed to attract old gentlemen; and he was a widower as well.

His name was Johnson, and his daughters had been schoolfellows of Sabina's and Maud's, and became great friends, so that they visited at each other's houses. Old Mr Johnson used to do the most extraordinary things, the girls told me, sometimes coming into the drawing room dressed up as an admiral, and sometimes as a general, and once even bobbing in suddenly on the girls made up as a clown, and exclaiming, "Here we are again," and nearly frightening them out of their wits. His sons and daughters were very fond of private theatricals, and had a lot of dresses about the place, and that is where he got them from to dress himself up. But no man in his senses would have done such things, surely.

One day that the girls went to lunch with the Miss Johnsons, Mr Johnson suddenly took a bagful of sovereigns from his pocket and threw them all into the soup tureen, and then began to serve the soup and put the sovereigns in the girls' plates. Of course they left theirs at the bottom of the plates, but they were awfully worried by his odd goings-on. When the servant came to take the plates away, Mr Johnson made her put them under the sofa and put the tureen there as well, which showed that there was method in his madness. He didn't mean the servants to help themselves to any of his sovereigns.

Although we knew how odd Mr Johnson was at times, you can still imagine my astonishment, not to say horror, when one day my dear Maud came home very flushed, and said, "Oh, Mamma, that horrid Mr Johnson; I'll never go there again. He actually went down on his knees to me in his own garden, where the girls were playing croquet, and asked me if I would marry him."

"My dear!" I said. "You mustn't take it seriously. It was one of his extraordinary jokes, I expect."

But the next day, when Maud and her sister were out walking, Mr Johnson followed them, and, coming up to Maud, told her that he was a millionaire, and if she would marry him he would buy a foreign title and she should be a countess, and he went on with such an extraordinary rigmarole that the girls grew quite frightened, and Sabina said, "If you have anything to say to Maud you had better say it at our house. My papa will be at home at eight o'clock," and then they tried to walk away, but old Mr Johnson walked after them, making dreadful faces, and exclaimed, loud enough for people who were passing to hear him, that if Maud did not have him he should enlist as a private soldier and go and get killed at the Battle of Waterloo.

My poor child was terribly upset, and trembled like an aspen leaf when she told me of this terrible adventure, and I said it was clear that the poor old gentleman had gone thoroughly mad, and he ought to have a keeper, and I promised Maud that I would talk to her papa, and ask him to go round to Mr Johnson and demand that this persecution should cease.

But at seven o'clock that evening, while we were at dinner, Mr Tressider not having come home, we suddenly heard an extraordinary sound outside in our front garden, and there was old Mr Johnson standing bareheaded with a banjo and singing:

> Come into the garden, Maud,
> For the black bat night has flown;
> Come into the garden, Maud,
> I am here at the gate alone.*

Maud began to cry, and I was afraid she would have hysterics, and my son William jumped up and said he would go and punch the old scoundrel's head, but I said, "No, no, for goodness' sake don't let us have a scene and make it public. The poor old man must have gone out of his mind."

"I don't care if he has gone out of his mind," said William, "he's no business to come into our garden. I'm not going to have my sister insulted."

I don't know whatever would have happened, but at that minute one of the young Mr Johnsons came up out of breath, evidently having heard what his father was doing – they lived in our terrace, a little higher up – and took his father by the arm, and managed to get him away before a crowd got round.

And later on that evening he called on us to apologize for the annoyance, and he told us that the poor old gentleman's mind had undoubtedly been giving way for some time, but that now he was hopelessly mad, and the family had determined to put him in a private lunatic asylum.

Which they did to my intense relief, for if they had not I don't believe Maud would ever have ventured outside the door again. Poor girl, it was a nice position to be made love to in the street by an elderly madman old enough to be her grandfather.

I couldn't help saying to my husband as soon as we had got over the worry and annoyance, and Maud had been sent away to a friend in the country for a time (for really her nerves were quite upset), that it seemed as if we were to have nothing but trouble with "Maud's lovers", as the boys called them. It was most absurd to think that with a lovely daughter like that I should be plagued with widowers and elderly madmen who wanted to be my sons-in-law. And when John Tressider said, "Fancy yourself, my dear, as mother-in-law to a madman," I felt so enraged I could have boxed his ears.

But, fortunately, we had no more terrible adventures of that sort, and soon afterwards a young gentleman – whom I had always thought a very charming young fellow – began to be a constant visitor to our house, where he came as a friend of my son William's, and from what I observed and hints that the boys dropped I began to fancy that he was sweet upon Maud, and I could see that he was by no means disagreeable to her.

But, unfortunately, though he was a very nice fellow and a perfect gentleman, and very well connected, he was not in the position I could have wished, for I will not hesitate to confess that I had always looked to Maud to make "the" marriage of the family.

However, we cannot have things in this world just as we want them, and so when later on Frank Leighton flung himself figuratively at my feet and besought me to use my influence with Mr Tressider to bring about the union of two loving hearts – his and Maud's – my woman's nature got the better of me, and forgetting my dreams and aspirations (unselfishness has always been my distinguishing characteristic), I remembered my own young dream of love (which I told you about at the beginning of this chapter), and promised the young couple my hearty assistance.

You have heard of Maud's lovers; in my next memoir I will tell you about Maud's husband.

Memoir IX

Maud's Husband

FRANK LEIGHTON, my son William's friend, who had fallen in love with Maud, "the beauty of the family", was a very good-looking young fellow, and a young man for whom I had the greatest respect, having known his family for many years, but, as I have told you, I had always expected Maud to get a better offer, though, perhaps, seeing how little Mr Tressider had done to advance his daughter's prospects, I was a little unreasonable.

Wealthy young men and heirs to vast estates are not met with every day, and unless you go out a great deal and get into what is called society it is difficult to meet them at all.

I always said that Maud had not had a fair chance, but when I pointed this out to Mr Tressider, he said: "What would you like me to do – would you like me to advertise in the *Daily Telegraph*? 'To dukes, earls and millionaires. A beautiful daughter of marriageable age. To be seen daily between 4 and 7. Apply to John Tressider, The Laurels, Maida Vale.'"

"Don't be ridiculous, John," I said. "It is all very well for you to turn the matter into a joke, but if you had done your duty as a father, Maud would probably by this time have had a chance of marrying exceedingly well."

"What could I have done?" he asked.

"Many things," I replied. "For instance, you are a City man, and although you always pretend that business is bad whenever I want an extra hundred or so for anything, yet I believe you are a wealthy man. Being a wealthy City man you might easily have become an alderman or a sheriff, and then you could have been a lord mayor, and we should have had an opportunity of bringing our daughters out at the Mansion House."

"Oh," he said in his irritating way, "I see what is the matter; you would have liked to have danced with the Prince of Wales."

I was not going to let myself be annoyed by Mr Tressider's absurd remarks, so I said, "No, John Tressider, I am not in the habit of thinking of myself. All my life long I have sacrificed myself to my husband and my children, and I suppose I shall have to do so to the end. Why I wish that you had gone in for a position in the City – civic honours I believe they call them – is that you would probably have been made a knight or a baronet."

"And you would have been Lady Tressider, eh, my dear, is that it?"

"Nothing of the kind. I am only thinking how much better it would have been for the girls. They might have made such excellent marriages. There is Maud, for instance…"

"Well, Maud has had plenty of offers. There was old Mr Johnson, for example, and he is tremendously rich. You had him put in a lunatic asylum – you can't expect suitors for your daughter's hand to come forward if it involves the risk of being put into a lunatic asylum."

It was with the greatest difficulty that I kept my temper at such a remark as that. If a man going on for sixty can't be serious when the future of his children is concerned, he is hopeless.

However, knowing that it was only a specimen of what Mr Tressider calls "chaff", I bit my lip and tapped my foot on the ground, and kept my opinion of his conduct to myself. But I gave him a look which said a good deal, and he understood it, for the exasperating grin which had up to then distorted his features suddenly disappeared, and he said, quite seriously: "Come, you haven't been talking like this for nothing. What is the matter now? Have you discovered another secret engagement in the family?"

"No," I replied, "I have not, I am glad to say; but Maud has had an offer of marriage, and as you are her father, it is your duty to consider the matter seriously."

Then I told him about Frank Leighton and Maud, and he said he wasn't altogether surprised, as he had rather suspected something of the sort. He thought that young Leighton was a very worthy young fellow, and that he would do well, though he wasn't in a particularly good position at present, being in the office of his uncle, who was an accountant in the City. But his father was in very comfortable circumstances, and he had a brother a solicitor, and his family was highly respected, and no doubt Frank, who was young and energetic and had plenty of common sense, would get on.

We had a very long talk that evening about it, and a day or two afterwards my husband had an interview with Frank's father as to his future prospects, and eventually we agreed to the engagement, but it was distinctly understood that the marriage was not to take place for some time, and that in the meantime Frank was to leave his uncle's office and establish himself as an accountant, for which he was fully qualified.

The courtship was an uneventful one, for Frank and Maud were very sensible over it, and did not – as some engaged couples do – make themselves a nuisance to other people. And they had no lovers' quarrels, and Frank, I was delighted to find, was very much liked by the boys, which saved me a good deal of worry and annoyance, as when boys take a dislike to their sister's sweetheart they can make things very unpleasant.

When they were married, they took a charming little house on the river, Frank being fond of boating, which caused me considerable alarm for a long time. I was always expecting that they would be upset, but Maud being fond of the water too, they had their own boat, and a very nice boat it was, though they never succeeded in getting me into it. I don't know, perhaps, that I should have minded so much if I could have got into it on dry land, but going down the steps at the bottom of their lawn, and stepping into a tittery-tottery thing, and having to step exactly in the middle and then settle yourself down, was more than I could summon up courage to attempt, especially as I am rather stout.

For a long time after they came back from their honeymoon and settled in their riverside villa, I never saw "Fatal Boating Accident" on the newspaper contents bills without a kind of wild fear that it was Frank and Maud, and once I had a shock that would have turned my hair grey if it had not already been that colour, and that was when I read in the *Daily Telegraph* that a boat had been found floating upside down, and it was supposed that a young lady and gentleman, who had been seen in it that evening, had been drowned. I was so upset that I telegraphed at once to Maud and asked her if she was alive and well.

But my dear Maud was very happy, and wrote me that they were leading quite an idyllic life, and that Frank was getting on capitally in the City as an accountant, and was very hopeful about his inventions. I will tell you about those inventions presently.

It was before I went to stay with them for a week that Maud wrote me about the idyllic character of Laburnam Cottage. I had not been there very long before I saw the side of it that was anything but idyllic, but of course I looked at things with different eyes to a young married couple in the first flush of their romance.

The cottage was close to the place where they hire out boats, and there was also a riverside public house close at hand, which caused a number of riverside loafers to be always hanging about, and their conversation was at times far from idyllic, I can assure you.

Some of them were the oddest characters, and sitting at the open window reading while Frank and Maud were on the river, I got in time to know their names. There was one man they called Prisoner Dick, because he had been in prison, and another was known as Soft Billy, and another was Lame Jack, because he had one leg shorter than the other, and another was Gypsy Sam, and from morning till night, while they were hanging about looking after the boats and waiting for a job, the neighbouring villa residents had the benefit of their conversation, which was on a variety of subjects, local, political, social and domestic, more especially domestic, with frequent references to "the old woman" and "the missus".

I said to Frank that I thought he might have chosen a villa which was not in quite such close proximity to the landing place and the loafers who congregated there, but he said it was all right and they weren't such bad fellows after all, and he had asked them not to swear more than they could help, and they had promised that they wouldn't. But I was not at all satisfied, and I said to my daughter, "Maud, my dear, mark my words, you'll have trouble one of these days with these people hanging about the place," and before I left there was very nearly a murder.

It happened in this way. A friend of Frank's had given Maud a beautiful little bird, which is called a Virginian nightingale, and the bird hung up outside the window facing the river, and as the lawn in front was only a very small one, all the loafers could see it. One day while I was sitting at the window, I heard the men beginning a dispute as to what this bird was, and presently they all went to the public house. When they came out they were having high words, and looking across towards the bird and the window where I was sitting, and I heard the one who was called Gypsy Sam say, "Look here, if there's much more of it I shall ring the bell and ask the lady what it is!"

And presently he came away from them and came up to the door. He didn't see me at the window, and he did ring the bell.

The servant was upstairs, so I went to the door, which was open, and I said, "What do you want?"

"Beg pardon, mum," he said, "but me and my mates has been havin' a argeyment as to what that there bird is, and we've got a bit o' money on it. Wot is it, mum?"

"It's a Virginian nightingale," I said.

"Oh, that's what it is, is it?" he said, looking very crestfallen. "Well, thankee, mum, all the same."

He went away, but he didn't go back to the men who were waiting, so presently another of them came, and seeing me in the garden shouted out, "Beg your pardon, marm, but what's the name o' that there bird?"

"It's a Virginian nightingale," I said, thinking it best to answer them civilly.

He went back to the others and yelled out, "He's lost. 'Tis a Wirginian nightingale."

Then they all went off into the public house and had more drinks.

I didn't see any more of Gypsy Sam that day, but next morning we heard there had been a fearful fight in the public house that night, Gypsy Sam having gone in, but refused to pay the bet he had lost, saying he hadn't got any money, and that led to words, and one of the men hit him over the head with a pewter pot and he had to be taken to the hospital.

"This is a nice place," I said to my son-in-law, "to bring Maud to! You'll have to have a policeman on the premises if something isn't done!"

He laughed, and said: "Oh, they won't hurt us." But he took the bird and hung it up on the other side of the house that it might not be the cause of any more bloodshed in that "idyllic" spot.

There was one old boatman there who was a great favourite of Maud's, and he always rowed her out when Frank was in town. One day it was so beautiful on the water that I could not resist her appeal to go out, especially as there was a very big family boat to be hired, and she promised to have that. So we took our books and some shawls, and, conquering my nervousness, I managed to get into the boat – four men holding it to keep it steady – and the old boatman rowed us up the river.

It was in the morning, and there were very few boats about, and I was just beginning to enjoy myself, when the boatman got up to shift something, and all of a sudden, without a word of warning, he began to wriggle about, and went flop over the side of the boat into the water.

In my horror I shrieked to my child to sit still. I was terrified lest she should rush to the side of the boat and tilt it over, and we should both be drowned.

It was a most awful situation, and I vowed never again to trust myself in a small boat on the water – and all the time the poor man was drowning. I was too paralysed with fear to do anything but tremble, but Maud rushed to the side of the boat, and leant over and caught the man by his hair as he came up, and held on and shrieked for help, and I shrieked too; and presently two gentlemen in a boat came up, and told us not to be frightened, and they dragged the poor man into their boat, and rowed off to the bank with him at once.

When they had gone, I should have had hysterics, only I was afraid to in a small boat. I said to Maud, "We shall be drowned, we shall drift over a weir and be dashed to pieces," but she said, "Don't be frightened, Mamma, I can row well enough to keep the boat straight," and she took the sculls and began to pull for the bank.

I said, "It's no good, Maud, I shall never be able to get out alone, and you'll run into the bank, and that will turn us over," and then I saw a steam launch coming, and I made sure we should be run down, and then I remembered that I had left no directions with regard to certain things which I wished to be done after I was dead, so I said to Maud, "If you are saved, Maud, remember that I wish your brother John to have the big punchbowl that was my dear father's, and there is fifty pounds in banknotes hidden away in the top left-hand drawer of the chest of drawers in the blue bedroom, saved out of my housekeeping money, let it be divided equally among all my children, and I wish to be buried at Kensal Green as near my dear father and mother as possible, and be sure that a needle is run into the ball of my eye to make certain that I am dead. Promise me that I shan't be buried alive."

"Oh, Mamma, don't talk like that," said Maud. "We're not going to be drowned."

I said, "It's no good waiting till we're in the water for me to give you my last instructions," and at that moment the steam launch came right up to us, and before I knew what had happened a gentleman had jumped into our boat, making it heel over nearly to the water's edge, at which I couldn't help shrieking, and he took the sculls from Maud and rowed us to the bank, where I was taken out more dead than alive.

I was so ill when I got home that I had to go to bed with one of my dreadful headaches, and I felt that my nerves were utterly shattered, but after I had had a strong cup of tea and a handkerchief saturated with eau de cologne on my head I was a little better, and when Maud came up to see me I asked at once if the poor boatman was dead.

To my intense relief, Maud informed me that he was not, for apart from my sympathy for the poor fellow, I had been picturing to myself the horror of having to appear at the inquest, and having my name in all the papers.

I was very sorry for the boatman until Maud told me that she had found out he was in the habit of having epileptic fits, and that he had fallen out of a boat once before, and then I was very indignant. The idea of a man with epileptic fits being allowed to go out in a boat with ladies!

"Maud, my dear," I said, "I trust you will never have that man again. He may be a very nice, civil old fellow, but you can't go rowing about the river with a man who tumbles into the water in a fit and has to be fished out again."

The dear girl promised me that she would not, but that evening, when I told Frank about our adventure, I made him give me his promise too that he wouldn't employ the man under any circumstances on the water, and it was only at his earnest request that I refrained from at once sending a letter to the editor of the *Daily Telegraph* on the subject and requesting him to warn all ladies from taking a boatman who was subject to fits.

When Frank came home of an evening he generally retired after dinner to a little room he had fitted up for himself, and which he called his workshop. Nobody was allowed to go in, and so I was naturally curious as to what he was doing there. Maud told me that he had some wonderful invention he was carrying out there, out of which he was going to make a fortune.

I knew a man once who had inventions, and I remembered what happened to him, so I told Maud I didn't like it – that no good ever came of inventions – but she said that Frank was very sanguine about his, and it was nearly finished.

One evening he came down about ten o'clock quite jubilant, and he said, "I've got it," and then he began to dance about the room. "Got what?" I said.

"The invention that I'm going to make a fortune out of," he said. "Come along, I want you to try it."

He took us upstairs into his workshop, and there was a basin of cold water on the table, and a jug of hot water and two bits of India-rubber tubing – each with an India-rubber ball in the middle, and onto the end of each tube he had fastened the rose of a watering can.

"Good gracious, me!" I exclaimed. "Whatever is it?"

"It's my grand new patent self-shampooer," he exclaimed triumphantly. "Everybody can shampoo themselves in their own bedroom with it. It will sell like wildfire."

I had never heard of wildfire being sold, but as I didn't wish to damp his enthusiasm I refrained from saying so.

"Come along, Maud," he said, "you must help me. I'm going to make my first grand experiment with it."

"I'm not going to be shampooed at ten o'clock at night," said Maud.

"Can't I have one of the servants up to try it on?" he said.

"No, my dear," replied Maud. "I think they would object. It isn't the cook's place to be shampooed, and it isn't the house-maid's. You had better try it on yourself."

He said he would, so he got hold of the machine and put one end of one tube in the cold water and one end of the other in the jug of hot water, and then he put his head down in the basin and held the rose of the water can over his head and began to squeeze.

Instantly a tremendous shower of water rushed out, but instead of going on his head, through some defect in the making the roses of the watering can dropped off into the basin and two cross streams of water flew across the room, and Maud and I, who were standing on either side of him, were drenched to the skin before we could utter a cry.

He said he was very sorry, but what was the use of that? I was absolutely drenched, and so was dear Maud, and my dress was completely spoilt. I couldn't help losing my temper, and I spoke my mind pretty plainly, and I went to my room and took off my saturated clothes and went to bed.

Maud came and knocked at my door soon afterwards, and said she hoped I should not be offended, as Frank was really very grieved, and it was quite an accident; but I said, "Look at my dress, it's ruined, and it is very likely I have caught cold, and taken my death. To have a stream of cold water running down the back of your neck at ten o'clock at night is enough to wreck the strongest constitution, and I am no longer young."

Maud seemed very much distressed at my being upset, so I told her that in the event of a fatal termination I acquitted her of all blame, but I besought her, in case she should be deprived of my motherly love and forethought at an early date, never to countenance any further inventions on her own domestic hearth.

"Let him invent at his office," I said, "as much as he likes, but a man's home should be sacred. He has drowned us this time, the next time he may set the house on fire. I knew a man once who was an inventor, and was going to make a fortune out of something that he did with chemicals and a fireplace. I daresay it was a very grand invention, but nobody ever knew properly what it was because before he had quite finished it the roof went suddenly off his house, and he was found in a garden two doors off, and his wife was discovered later on down the area of a house in another street, and that, my dear, is what will happen to you if you don't put your foot down at once on your husband's inventions."

Fortunately, the next morning, when I woke up, I found I had not developed any dangerous symptoms, and my dress, which had been taken away by the maidservant, was brought back to me in the morning, and it had dried all right, but when I went down to breakfast I took the opportunity of speaking plainly to Frank, and informing him that I didn't think he would ever make much money by his home shampooer. He said that it was all right only he hadn't finished it off properly, and that when it was all right it would be a great luxury, and he hoped to sell the patent to one of the big hairdressing firms for a large sum, and then he began to try and turn the matter off with a joke, and said he should write a farce for the theatres and call it *Did You Ever Shampoo Your Mother-in-Law?*

But Maud, who is a clever girl, gave him a look as much as to say that he was on dangerous ground, and he was.

I told him that I sincerely hoped his patent self-shampooer would *not* be taken up, for if it was it would be the cause of a great deal of domestic unhappiness, not to mention damage to the ceiling and the wallpaper, and I think at last he saw that I was right, for he tried another experiment with it, when Maud's Skye terrier, which had followed him to the bedroom, was with him, and the water went down the back of his own neck, right into his boots, and made him jump and dance about, and he trod on the dog's tail, and the dog, terrified, darted out of the door just as the servant was coming upstairs with a tray of jams to put away in the store cupboard, and the dog running between her feet caused her to fall down, and away went the tray, and the jam pots rolled over and fell into the hall below and smashed, and the place was a mass of strawberry jam – walls, floor, furniture and hangings, all being smothered in it.

You never saw such a terrible mess in your life, and when poor Maud rushed out and saw her lovely little home all ruined, and saw Frank standing at the top of the stairs, with a scared face, and the shampooing machine still in his hand, and the water running out of his boots, she guessed how the thing had happened, and went upstairs, and seizing that awful invention she threw it down on the ground and danced on it, and declared that her husband must choose between her and the shampooing machine – the same house couldn't hold them both.

Dear Maud certainly has a temper of her own. I can't think where she gets it, unless it is from Mr Tressider's side of the family.

Memoir X

My German Son-in-Law

I HAVE NEVER BEEN ABLE to understand why Jane, my third daughter, married a foreigner. I have no particular objection to a foreigner, but I can't say I ever anticipated being mother-in-law to a German.

You will doubtless wonder how it is that my third daughter, and not my first or second, bears my Christian name.

It was entirely due to my weakness in yielding to the wishes of Mr Tressider. Our dear son was named John after his father, at his father's request, and I never made the slightest objection, although I should infinitely have preferred a more romantic name. I am aware that several distinguished men have been named John, but after all it is a name associated with a groom or a footman.

When I go to the theatre and get there early enough to see the farce I usually find that the servant's name is John. It is always, "John, has your master come in?" or, "John, if anyone calls say that I am not at home." And in the old volumes of *Punch* which I sometimes look over in the library, John is generally the footman, especially in the pictures. Only the other day I took some of my grandchildren to an afternoon performance at the circus, Mr Tressider accompanying us for a wonder, and there was an absurd "Scene in the Arena" – I believe that is how they put it on the bills – called "A Riding Lesson". A lady comes in – she is a man dressed up, of course – and wants to be taught riding, and she has a servant with her – an utterly ridiculous person in crimson-plush breeches and a red wig – played by the clown, and he rides a horse behind her, and is called "John".

My grandchildren screamed with laughter at the antics of John, and they kept looking up at their grandpapa, slyly, and nudging each other, and I heard one whisper to the other, "It's just how grandma talks to grandpapa."

Children have the oddest ideas. Of course I never addressed Mr Tressider in the ridiculous manner that circus woman (man) did her (his) groom, but they got it into their heads, and when during the performance I turned to Mr Tressider to ask him to get up and close a door behind us which was letting in draught enough to blow all our heads into the middle of the ring, and I said "John" rather sharply, as he was looking the other way, I thought the children would have had a fit.

I don't think the name ever sounded so ridiculous to me before, and for days afterwards when I went to say "John" to my husband, I thought of that footman on horseback in crimson-plush breeches and a red wig, and I said "Mr Tressider" instead.

I wanted our first son to have a nice romantic name, something that would distinguish him from the common herd, and look well in print if he ever did anything to become famous. I have always thought that a very serious responsibility rests upon parents in giving the children the name they are to go through life with – labelling them, as it were. I wanted to call my eldest son Marmaduke, but Mr Tressider made the most absurd remarks about it, and said it sounded like the *London Journal*. It might have done, but, at any rate, it didn't sound like a circus clown. You never hear a groom or a footman called Marmaduke in a farce.

Mr Tressider said, "Let the boy have my name and my father's name, as it has been in our family for years," and as I didn't want to quarrel over our first baby on the eve of taking him to the baptismal font I yielded, and John it was.

Of course, you would have thought after that, when my eldest daughter was christened, Mr Tressider would have returned the compliment, and allowed her to be christened Jane after me; but when I mentioned the matter to him one night he said he would have her named after a sister who had died. When he told me her name was Sabina, I said: "Well, I must say I think that rather good. You didn't allow me to christen my son Marmaduke because it's *London Journal*, and yet you want my daughter to be called Sabina! If *that* is not *London Journaly* it's *Family Heraldy*, and besides, it doesn't sound English."

We had an argument about it, but eventually I yielded. I was rather weak-minded in those days, and gave way a good deal more than I did afterwards; and so my eldest daughter was named Sabina, which caused considerable confusion, as the servants until they got used to it used to call her Sab-i-na, making the "i" sound like "i". Maud, my second daughter, was christened Maud after her godmother, from whom at that time we had expectations, though she deceived us cruelly, leaving all her property to a Wesleyan chapel* in a side street off Tottenham Court Road, which she took to attending in a bath chair in her old age, after she quarrelled with us. The quarrel arose in this way. Mrs Marsham was the widow of my mother's brother, who had died and left her his house property in London, and a good deal of money besides, but she was decidedly eccentric, and though I was very fond of her and encouraged her to visit us at first, I found that as she grew older her eccentricities increased. One of the peculiarities she developed was putting things into her pocket – sugar and biscuits and anything she could take off the table without, as she thought, being observed. With all this she had a habit of finding fault with things in the house and your dress and your furniture out loud. I believe she was really thinking to herself, but it was very unpleasant, especially when there were other visitors present. For instance, she would look at you for a minute and say, "Humph, I don't think much of that dress. Too young for you, ridiculous – humph." Or, "Humph – bad dinner – no management – extravagant, bad – sorry for your poor husband – humph."

The children called Aunt Marsham "Old Humph", and hated her, but I did not allow them to show it, as at that time it was as much as understood that, having no children or relatives of her own living, she had left the bulk of her property to us.

However, one day when I was not very well, having one of my bad neuralgic headaches, and being very much put out by a housemaid who had spilt some grease on one of my beautiful steel fenders, Aunt Marsham went a little too far; she came in to five o'clock tea with myself and the girls, and as usual began putting the sugar into her pocket, and making objectionable remarks.

I had just had the books changed at Mudie's,* and some new novels were lying on the table in my little room.

Aunt Marsham caught sight of them and picked them up and looked at them, and began to mutter to herself, "I Iumph. Novels – trash – mother of a family – ought to be ashamed of yourself. Humph!"

Being out of sorts, and perhaps more irritable than usual – I mean irritable, which usually I am not – I felt indignant at being talked "at" like that before my daughters, so I said, very quietly, "Aunt Marsham, I cannot help what you think, but I must ask you not to speak of me in that way with my children in the room. It is bad enough for them to see you putting my property in your pocket. You needn't insult their mother as well."

"Eh!" exclaimed Aunt Marsham. "Jane Tressider, are you speaking to me?"

"Yes, Aunt Marsham, I am," I said. "I have put up with your rudeness for a long time just because you are an old woman, but I don't intend to put up with it any longer."

"Oh! indeed, don't you?" she said. With that she got up and walked to the door as majestically as she could with a stiff leg caught through sleeping in a damp bed when young, and when she got to the door she shook her parasol at me and said, "Never will I darken your doors again, woman. Impudent baggage. Humph!"

"Don't you call me a baggage in my own house, madam," I said, "and as to darkening my doors, I'll take care that you don't – you are welcome to the sugar you have stolen, but be good enough not to take away any umbrellas out of the stand."

I don't know what made me say it, but I felt so angry I could have said anything. I thought Aunt Marsham would have had a fit on the doormat there and then, but she gave one gasp, which seemed to relieve her, and she went down the stairs as fast as her stiff leg would carry her.

She never came again, though I wrote her a little note afterwards, and said that if I had said anything in the heat of temper, I was sorry, as I had no desire to hurt anyone's feelings.

She did not even have the courtesy to reply, but joined the chapel in the side street off Tottenham Court Road, and when she died it was found she had left all her money to the chapel and a few charities. Soon after her death, I received a small parcel with the executor's compliments. I opened it, expecting that it was some memento of Aunt Marsham, and in it I found about half a dozen lumps of sugar and a little piece of paper, on which was written in Aunt Marsham's hand, "For Jane Tressider – after my death. I return your sugar."

And that was all we ever got for christening my second daughter Maud after her Aunt Marsham – our own sugar back again.

When my third daughter was born I thought it was about time to speak plainly on the subject, and I said to my husband, "John, this child's name is Jane," and I said it in a way that didn't encourage argument, so John said, "Very well, my dear," and it *was* Jane, though since she married Mr Gutzeit I have frequently heard her addressed as "Shane".

Jane first made the acquaintance of Carl Gutzeit at the Brauns' in our terrace – our terrace is full of Germans, mostly business people, merchants and that sort of thing in the City, and we got to know a good many before we had been in the neighbourhood very long. The Misses Braun and the Misses Kroll were among Sabina's and Maud's and Jane's best friends, having been schoolfellows of theirs at the Ladies' College in our neighbourhood.

Jane is a very amiable girl, quiet and gentle, not exactly beautiful, but very pleasing looking, and she has a quiet way that is very attractive. Jane has always been the studious member of the family. From a child she was clever with her pencil and quick at foreign languages. At sixteen she spoke French and German excellently, and being so much with German girls she became quite proficient in the latter language.

I can't say that I care about hearing very much of it myself, but I have no doubt it sounds all right to people who have been brought up to it.

The girls met Mr Gutzeit frequently at the Brauns', he being a cousin of theirs, and when they came to a dance at our house they brought Mr Gutzeit with them, and we were glad of him, for he was a lovely waltzer, and young men who dance grow scarcer every day.

I spoke to him, of course, and thought he was a very amiable man. He was tall, with a fair German beard and fair German hair, and light-blue German eyes with spectacles, and was, I thought, about two- or three-and-thirty. He was very agreeable to me, and very attentive, and he talked to me in English with a strong German accent. I had only one objection to him, and that was that he was a dentist. The girls explained that he was a very high-class dentist – a surgeon dentist – and that he had a right to the title of doctor, but I said, "I don't care how clever he is or what his titles are, if he is a dentist he draws teeth, and I shall never be able to talk to him without expecting him to say: 'Lean your head back and open your mouth wide, please.'"

I couldn't understand why it was that the girls were so anxious I should like the German dentist, but I understood everything when I found he was in love with Jane, and that Jane reciprocated the feeling.

I am not going to trouble you with the details of the courtship. You may be sure that before we gave our consent to the engagement we satisfied ourselves that Mr Gutzeit was in a good position, and I must say everything was satisfactory in that respect. He had a very nice home in Bayswater, where he lived with his sister as his housekeeper, and a brass plate on his door and a red lamp over the fanlight, and carriage people came to him to have their teeth out.

Jane assured me that she loved him very much, and that she didn't in the least mind his being a German or a dentist, and so we gave our consent, and there was a good deal of the German language about our house for the next twelve months after that, and Carl and Jane *ja*'d (it sounds like yah in the German) at each other to such an extent that at last I had to request that they would converse in English – at any rate, while I was in the room. I felt that I had a right to ask that, especially as I didn't think it altogether proper for a young man to make love to your daughter in a language that her mother didn't understand.

After eighteen months of courtship Jane and Carl were married, and there was a tremendous German gathering at the wedding. Certainly the German young men are very fine, tall, military, well-built young fellows, and there is a frank look in their faces which I like exceedingly, though it is astonishing how many of them have to wear glasses.

"The happy pair" went for their honeymoon to Germany – up the Rhine first, of course – as I understand that is the regular German honeymoon, and my son John, who has travelled a great deal, tells me that on the Rhine the boats and the hotels are full of honeymoons in the season, and that the young German bridegrooms and brides spoon in public to an extent which is unknown in this country, holding each other's hands and looking up into each other's eyes and reading poetry together, utterly oblivious of the fact that they are on the deck of a public steamer or in a public hotel. After they had done the Rhine (Jane wrote me the most enthusiastic accounts of the scenery, and said it was a dream) they went to Berlin, where Mr Gutzeit's father and mother resided then, and the old people received their new daughter-in-law most heartily, and Carl's mother tried to teach her how to make a number of German dishes, but poor Jane never was much of a hand at that sort of thing, and never will be, and I for one don't think that men ought to look to their wives for their dinners. If that is their idea of marriage they had better marry their cooks and get the genuine article.

In her first letter after she arrived in Berlin, my dear Jane told me to address her as Frau Doctor Gutzeit, but I didn't. I wrote it on the envelope, but I didn't send it. The idea of my calling any child of mine a Frau was bad enough, but to call her a doctor because her husband pulled out people's teeth was too ridiculous, and I told her so in my letter, which I addressed to Mrs Carl Gutzeit.

Before Carl married Jane, I had suggested to him that it would be better that his sister should leave him, as I didn't want my child to go to his home and find another woman mistress there. That sort of thing always ends badly, and a husband's mother, or sister, or aunt always gets on better with his wife when they don't live under the same roof, and it is the same with a wife's relations. I have never unduly intruded in the home or the domestic affairs of any of my children, knowing what a prejudice there is against a mother-in-law. Carl told me that it had already been arranged that his sister should go to another brother's, who was in business in Manchester, and so when my dear child came home she was mistress at once, and I am glad to say that, in spite of her husband being a foreigner and having foreign ways and liking extraordinary things for dinner, she has managed admirably, and they got on very well together on the whole.

I should never have got on with him, even if I had been able to speak his language, and I am perfectly certain that I should never have been able to endure the sight of people driving up to my house in cabs, groaning with the toothache and going away with their hands to their jaws.

The first time I went to call upon them there were three people besides myself on the doorstep. Two of them were groaning, and one of them, a gentleman, was stamping his foot. I felt as if I had the toothache myself, and when I got in and had been shown into the dining room, where I found Jane looking the picture of happiness, I couldn't help saying: "Oh, my dear child, however can you smile like that when half a dozen poor creatures are sitting in your husband's waiting room downstairs, nearly mad with the toothache?"

Jane smiled, and said she didn't take much notice of it, but she confessed that at first it rather worried her always to meet them in the hall, groaning and screwing up their faces, but she had soon got used to it.

I didn't get used to it. I never went to that house without fancying that I was going to have the toothache. There was something in the very feel of the bell handle that made you uncomfortable in your teeth; and once, when I passed the consulting room and the door was open, I caught sight of the instruments of torture and the awful chair and the little basin on the iron stand and the glass of warm water on the table handy, and then the thing that they give you the gas with, and if it hadn't been Jane's birthday I should have turned round and fled.

A large portion of Mr Gutzeit's business, and the most profitable, was in artificial teeth, for which he had a great reputation, and he used to amuse me sometimes by telling me of the vanity of some of the old ladies and gentlemen who came to him for new sets. They always wanted them to be pearly white, and were most particular about the shape of them, and one old lady of seventy-two, after she had had a set fitted in, which she insisted on being as white as marble, stood in front of the glass for a quarter of an hour, and practised smiling so as to show them off.

He declared that after she had those teeth she was always on the broad grin, and at last got to believe that the teeth were her own, and told people that she inherited her beautiful teeth from her great-aunt, who was a Court beauty in the reign of George the Fourth.

It was not till my daughter had been married nearly a year that I accidentally discovered an extraordinary phase in her husband's character. To his wife and to us he was the most amiable man imaginable, but it seems that he was a man who never could get on with his neighbours. He was always having trouble with them, and had a kind of insane belief that they were interfering with him in some way or other. Of this phase of his character, which was quite unsuspected by any of us, and what it led to, I must tell you on another occasion. It was a source of very great alarm to me for my child's sake, as it made Carl very unpopular in the neighbourhood, especially with a lot of grooms and coachmen who lived down a mews or stable yard, which was exactly opposite his front door. Between these men and Carl there was a perpetual war waged.

But I shall come to that in due course. I did not find it out until after an event had happened which made me the grand-mamma of a German baby.

Imagine it! Think of it! If ever there was an Englishwoman I am one, but the time came when I held in my arms a dear pink little bundle of humanity, and had to stand at the font and hear an English clergyman make a wild attempt to call it Carl Gottfried Wolfgang. I certainly think they might have left out the wolf. Mr Gutzeit declared that it was a Christian name, but I couldn't see anything Christian in calling a child a wolf.

Those names made my grandchild more German than ever, and I couldn't help feeling that I was grandmother to a little foreigner. It was a beautiful baby, but it had a German look in its face, and I felt convinced it would take to spectacles at an early age, and that it would begin yah-yahing (only spelt "*ja*", so Jane informs me) at the very earliest opportunity.

Old Mr and Mrs Gutzeit came over from Berlin on a visit just before the christening, and they were at the ceremony and at the luncheon afterwards. I was introduced to them, of course, but as they couldn't speak a word of English it was rather awkward.

I spoke very loud, and with a foreign accent to make them understand, but they only shook their heads, and said something which might have been swearing by the sound of it, but which Jane translated into a very pretty compliment.

Jane told me afterwards that old Mrs Gutzeit didn't like the way the baby was dressed. She wanted it done up in a bundle, which I am told was the old-fashioned way in Germany, but I said, "Jane, your child may be a German, but you are an English mother, and don't you allow a foreigner to teach you how an infant ought to be reared. Your own mother has not brought up nine children without knowing something about it."

We asked Mr and Mrs Gutzeit to dine with us, and they came and seemed very nice people, but I was glad when they went. To carry on a conversation by shrugging your shoulders and waggling your head, and pretending to understand when you don't, and having your daughter saying every minute she says this and he says that, and then having to speak to your daughter when you wanted to speak to your visitors, and having to listen to her repeating your words in a gibberish that makes your throat dry only to listen to it is not a pleasant way of passing an evening in your own house at my time of life.

I was really glad when they went, but I had to promise through Jane that I would call and see them at Carl's house before they left. They were really a charming old couple, but why on earth didn't they learn English before they came to

London? I went once to see the baby soon after the christening, and I tried to extract a promise from my daughter that she would bring him up as English as possible. She told me that his father was equally anxious that he should be as German as possible. Thank goodness the poor child is a British-born subject, and he won't be torn from his mother's arms at an early age to be slaughtered in battle, or to have his hair cut and be made a German soldier.

The idea of the bare possibility of any grandchild of mine ever being a German soldier and eating black bread, and fighting the French, kept me awake night after night, and I wasn't relieved in my mind until Carl assured me that there was not the slightest danger of that.

I have a great respect for the German army, but never of my own free will could I bring myself, as a loyal British subject, to be the grandmother of a German soldier.

Memoir XI

The People Opposite

I NEVER SHOULD HAVE BELIEVED that a nice, quiet, amiable man like my German son-in-law, Carl Gutzeit, could have been so faddy on certain subjects as he eventually turned out to be. I read an article in one of the magazines the other day in which the writer tried to prove that everybody is mad on some particular subject, that is that everyone has a mania, though perfectly sane and sensible on every other point. I was very much interested in that article, because I have not gone through life with my eyes shut, and I must say I have noticed many instances myself of people being mad on one particular point.

I don't care to read very much about those things, because I think we are getting to know a great deal too much about ourselves. What with germs and other awful things that science is always discovering, the world is becoming a most trying place for everybody that is at all nervous.

It certainly is true that many people are eccentric, to say the least of it, on one special point. I had a relative of my own, an uncle, the nicest and kindest man in the world, and an elder of his chapel, but he has often told me that he could never bring

himself to walk about the streets, because he had such a temp-
tation to ring the bells and run away. If he was passing a house
and caught sight of the bell handle he felt that he must pull it,
and it was because he felt that it would be a disgraceful thing
if a respectable old gentleman, the father of a family, were to
be caught doing such a thing that he always took a cab or an
omnibus if he went out alone. If he went out with anyone he
always begged them to keep hold of his arm, and not on any
account to let him go near a bell handle.

I knew a lady once who was the victim of something of the
same kind, only her weakness was for ringing the alarm bell
in a railway carriage. She didn't do it, but she told me that
she never found herself alone in a compartment with one of
those alarm signals staring her in the face but she felt the most
intense desire to break the glass, set the machinery in motion,
and see what would happen. She used to get in such a state of
terror lest she should do it that the perspiration used to burst
out at every pore, and she was quite thankful when somebody
else got into the carriage or she came to her journey's end.

I believe a great deal of what is called kleptomania is very
much the same sort of thing. Respectable people are suddenly
seized with an intense longing to pick up something and hide
it and take it away, and at last the madness becomes too strong
for them and they yield. I was talking to my husband about this
one day, and he assured me that there was a well-known man
who never went to a dinner party without putting the silver
spoons and forks in his pocket, and this was so well known

that nobody took any notice at last, as his wife always searched his pockets and sent them back – the spoons and forks, not his pockets – with her compliments the next day.

We lived once, soon after I was married, next door to an old gentleman, who was a great professor of something – I never knew what – and I was told that there was no doubt about his being right in his mind, because he was a member of a great many societies, and wrote for *The Times*, but he was the terror of all the nursemaids in the neighbourhood, because he used to walk along and stop suddenly, and clasp his hands violently together and say: "Ho, oh-oh-oh!" just as if he was groaning. He couldn't help it. He knew it was ridiculous, and that it made people stare, but he couldn't stop himself doing it.

I only mention these cases as they occur to me, because, knowing them, it made me, perhaps, less astonished than I should have been when I discovered that my son-in-law, Carl Gutzeit, the dentist, was eccentric in one particular way.

He had an insane idea that the neighbours were always doing something which it was his duty to stop, and a nice character he got in consequence.

My daughter Jane didn't notice at first when he began to complain of the people opposite not drawing up the blinds evenly. She agreed with him, when he pointed out to her that one blind was halfway up, and another a quarter way up, and another three-quarters of the way up, that it didn't look well; but when she saw him sitting down in his easy chair in the dining room and staring at the blinds opposite, and declaring that they irritated him, and that he couldn't stand it, and that he should have to step across and ask the people to alter them, she laughed at him, and said, "My dear, how foolish of you to let a thing like that annoy you. Don't look at the blinds opposite." But she was worried when he declared that he couldn't help it, and began to drum his feet and twitch the corners of his mouth; and one day, when he suddenly jumped up and went across the road and knocked at the door of the people opposite, she felt quite alarmed.

When he came back he was in a towering rage, and declared that the people opposite were "animals", and that they had grossly insulted him, and told him to mind his own business, and from that moment he conceived a violent dislike to the people opposite, and always imagined they were trying to annoy him.

One day, looking out of his window, he saw that down the stable yard, the entrance to which was visible from his consulting-room windows, a coachman's wife had hung out some clothes to dry. He was across the road in a minute, and down the yard, and he ordered the coachman, who came out to him, to take them down at once, as a clothesline was an eyesore and an injury to the neighbourhood. The coachman was rude and told him to go to a place which is not on the map of Europe, and this so enraged him that he went off to his solicitor at once and took out a summons against the coachman for being a nuisance. This caused a great deal of ill feeling against him, and the coachmen and grooms down that mews made it very unpleasant for him, even going to the length of chalking upon his front door, under cover of the night, unpleasant references to his nationality such as "Dirty German", and also to his profession such as "Old Tooth Tugger", and that name was taken up; and sometimes when he went out he would hear the men across the way call out, "Old Tooth Tugger. Yah!"

Poor Jane told me that this used to make Carl go livid with rage, and sometimes when they were in a hansom cab, just starting off somewhere, she really had to clutch hold of him tight, or he would have jumped out and hit his persecutors, and then there would have been bloodshed.

When Jane told me about these things, I thought it my duty to speak plainly to Carl on the subject, and I did, but I got no thanks for my kindness, Carl getting quite excited, and declaring that there was a conspiracy in the neighbourhood to injure him in his business because he was a foreigner.

Of course, I told him that was absurd, and that he was too sensitive – and many Germans are. They are not accustomed to our rough-and-ready English ways, and they are always on their dignity, and seeing slights and insults when none are intended.

I was very worried about Carl's extraordinary mania about the conduct of his neighbours, for I was afraid that he would get into trouble, and I begged Jane to try and make him take less notice of trifles, but instead of getting better he got worse, and began to quarrel with the people next door as well as the people opposite, and he took to writing letters and sending them in next door and opposite as well. It is always a mistake to write letters, especially when you write them in a hurry and in a bad temper.

The people opposite, whose blinds had so upset Carl, had two sons, and these two sons took a delight in teasing Carl. Whenever he came to the window, they would come out onto the balcony and pretend to have the toothache, and put their hands to their faces and jump about and say "Oh!"

Of course they had a perfect right to play at having the toothache on their own balcony, but Carl was furious, and wrote a letter to their father, and sent it across, complaining that the boys were insulting him, and the father was indignant, and wrote a letter back, and told Carl that if it annoyed him to see people pretending to have the toothache, it was a much greater annoyance for the neighbours to see people who really had the toothache always going in and out of his house, and sometimes coming out and holding their jaws as if they had been broken. And he had the audacity to hint that Carl was a nuisance, and that it was lowering the neighbourhood for a man to open an artificial-tooth shop in a terrace where there were only private houses.

That didn't improve the neighbourly feeling, you may be sure, and unfortunately it was just at that time that Carl took it into his head that the people next door were annoying him. He declared that his consulting-room fire smoked when the people next door had their dining-room fire lit, and he sent in and complained, and the old gentleman next door, who was a highly respectable stockbroker, came round and desired to see Carl, and walked in and asked him how he dared send in impudent messages about his dining-room fire, and they had high words, and the old gentleman said: "I tell you what it is, sir. You're a confounded nuisance, and if you don't soon get out of the neighbourhood everybody will move. Mind your own business, such as it is, and leave your neighbours alone."

Poor Jane, who listening trembling in the next room, came in, as if by accident, at this, fearing that there might be bloodshed, and the old gentleman took up his hat and bounced out of the house; but after that Carl had another enemy, and Jane said it was really awful, and she didn't like to go out, for everybody seemed to glare at them.

I said, "My dear, if he were my husband I should put my foot down and bring him to his senses," and so I should have done, but Jane was afraid to speak plainly, for fear of hurting Carl's feelings. She was devoted to him and defended him as much as she could, declaring that except for his unfortunate mania for quarrelling with his neighbours he was the most amiable and devoted husband that a woman could possibly have, and he certainly was, but as I said to my child, "It's all very well, my dear, but he is making himself obnoxious and getting himself hated, and some fine evening his windows will be broken, and if the stones hit you, what is the use of his amiability and devotion?"

After baby Carl was born, he was a little more patient for a time, and took less notice of the things that were done to annoy him. There is no doubt that a good deal that upset him was done purposely, but really it was his own fault, and he had brought it entirely on himself by taking offence at every trifle in the first place and making himself unneighbourly. There is nothing so disagreeable as the disagreeable or litigious neighbour, as I know by experience, having once lived next door to an old lady who was perpetually sending to us and objecting to things – now to a dog of ours that used to bark in the front garden, now to the children throwing their shuttlecocks over her wall, and now to our servants beating a little square of carpet, really not much bigger than an antimacassar. And the trouble that woman gave me over a favourite cat of mine was really infamous. It was the most harmless cat in the world, but it would occasionally get over into the garden and sit on her lawn, and then she would come out and drive it away, talking at it, and calling it names which I knew she intended for me. But I was quite equal to a little argument of that sort, and when my cat came back I played the same game, and I addressed remarks to my own cat that were intended for the cat next door.

And it at last became so intolerable, that woman having the impudence to send in, whenever my girls sat down to practise, an insolent message to say that if the piano wasn't moved away from the wall, where she could hear it, she should apply to the Court of Chancery for an injunction, that I went round myself to her house, and walked in when the door was opened without waiting to ask if she was in, and then spoke my mind so plainly that she never troubled us again and moved soon afterwards.

I didn't hear much about Carl for some time after dear baby was born, because I went out of town, and Jane didn't mention her troubles in her letters to me, the dear girl not wanting to worry me, and being afraid, perhaps, that I should think Carl was a little too eccentric to be a satisfactory husband and father.

I had so many other things to worry about myself that I was rather glad not to have any bad news in her letters, and so I tried to think that Carl had seen the folly of quarrelling with his neighbours, and had settled down into a calm and sober English citizen.

I came back just before Christmas, and, as usual, all my children and their families dined with us on Christmas Day. It has always been my wish that Christmas Day should witness a family reunion beneath the roof of the old home, and as far as possible my children have gratified me in this respect, though of late years it has been rather a strain upon the capacity of our house to accommodate them all. Our Christmas Day dinner parties have, it is true, occasionally been marred by little family quarrels, but nothing serious. I think a Christmas dinner is not always a promoter of peace and goodwill, especially in a family which is inclined to indigestion and not without gouty symptoms. My girls are angels even after turkey and plum pudding and mince pies, but my boys are apt to get what we call a little "cantankerous" after dinner, and to begin chaffing each other in a way which occasionally leads to a little display of temper.

On this occasion we were all very agreeable, and everything passed off quite pleasantly, until John, unfortunately, began to chaff Carl, asking him if he had sent a Christmas card to all his neighbours.

Carl gave rather a grumpy answer, which I put down to plum pudding and mince pie not being the kind of food to which a German is brought up, but I gave John a warning look, and tried to turn the conversation.

It was no good, for the next minute John, who delights in teasing people, though he is exceedingly tetchy himself, told Carl that he ought, as it was Christmas, to put a red woollen comforter round his neck that night and go and sing outside the neighbours' houses that carol about "Goodwill to men", accompanied by a German band.

Carl's face flushed at that, and he told John to mind his own business. "That's just what your neighbours say you ought to do, old chap," said John, who had had a hot mince pie, and a cold mince pie, and would keep on eating almonds and raisins at dessert, though he knew they were poison to him.

Carl got up in a rage at that and rushed out of the room, took his hat and put on his overcoat and, before we knew what had happened, had banged the front door after him and was out in the street.

Poor Jane, the tears in her eyes, darted a withering glance at John, and exclaiming, "What do you want to upset everybody for?" ran out, and never stopping to put anything on her head rushed off after Carl, and then John, vexed to think that he had been the cause of a scene, rushed off after her, and I couldn't help speaking my mind and saying that it was abominable, and that really my sons- and daughters-in-law might manage to get through Christmas Day without quarrelling, for we might not be together many more.

Of course, as usual, Mr Tressider was not there. Immediately after dinner he had taken himself off to his den, and was having what he called a quiet half-hour to himself. I went down and found him with his pipe in his mouth and *The Times* in his hand – yesterday's *Times*, none having been delivered on Christmas Day.

"Really, John Tressider," I said, "I should think on Christmas Day you might do without reading yesterday's *Times*. If you had been in your proper place at the head of the family you might have prevented a disgraceful scene."

"Eh?" he said. "Why, what's the matter now?" I told him, and I requested him to put on his hat and overcoat and go after Carl and John at once, and order them to come back. I had no doubt they were disputing somewhere down the street, and the idea of poor Jane with no bonnet on standing listening to them, and wringing her hands, on Christmas Day, was too much for my motherly heart.

However, before I had roused Mr Tressider sufficiently to a sense of his responsibilities to get him out of his easy chair, the bell rang, and when the door was opened I heard Carl's voice in the hall, and I ran upstairs, and he and John had made it up, and come back again, but poor Jane was shivering with the cold, for a bitter east wind was blowing.

I couldn't help saying to Carl that he ought to be ashamed of himself for giving way to his temper, and dragging his poor wife out of a warm and happy home on such a bitter afternoon, but he only frowned and grunted, and went into the drawing room.

Fortunately, the little quarrel had no after-effects, and we spent the rest of the day very comfortably, with the exception of a little trouble with Augustus Walkinshaw junior, who, unobserved by everybody, had got a jar of Chinese preserved fruits in syrup – chow-chow I believe they are called – and had eaten nearly the entire contents, making his beautiful new little sailor's suit one mass of stickiness from top to toe, and when I gave him a little shake for his bad behaviour, he began to cry, and then turned a deathly white and was so sick that he had to be taken upstairs and put to bed.

On New Year's Day I had promised to lunch with Carl, and I went early, as I wanted to have a little chat with Jane before lunch. While we were talking together, the servant came up with a small package which had just been left at the house with a New Year's card stuck in under the string. It was addressed to Carl, so I said, "Send downstairs to him, my dear, and ask him to come up and let us see what is in it. Perhaps it is a New Year's gift from one of his clients or friends." "Most likely it is," said Jane, "for he has had several already, and some of them are very nice ones."

The servant asked Mr Gutzeit to come up to his wife's boudoir where we were sitting, and when he came I said, "Carl, here is another New Year's gift for you. We are both anxious to see what is inside it."

He laughed, and said that he was a lucky fellow, for he had had plenty of kind remembrances that day, which showed that, if he was unpopular with the horrid people who lived opposite and next door to him, he at least had plenty of friends elsewhere.

He began to open the package, and when he took off the brown paper there was a small wooden box inside, which was fastened down with tacks. He took out his knife, and with the big blade forced up the lid. It flew open, and instantly there leapt out into the room two huge awful sewer rats!

I gave one wild shriek and climbed up on a chair as well as I was able to, and poor Jane shrieked and jumped onto another chair, while those horrid rats ran about the room terrified, now darting into one corner, and then into another.

Carl said some dreadful word in German, and then one of the rats ran between his legs, and he was so alarmed thinking it might crawl up the leg of his trousers, that he leapt up in the air, and, catching hold of the tablecloth, dragged it off, and all the things that were on it; and in trying to save a large glass vase full of flowers, slipped up in some way, and fell with a crash on the floor. That made us shriek louder than ever, and the servants came running up, but when they saw the rats they gathered up their petticoats and fled.

Carl got up from the floor using the most dreadful language, fortunately in German, which I did not understand, but which must have shocked my daughter very much, as she did. At least I presume if you know a language thoroughly, you must recognize swearing when you hear it, and he said quite savagely: "Don't stand shrieking there, the rats are more afraid of you than you are of them."

Then he seized the poker and began banging on the floor, and saying "Sh! Sh! Sh!" and the rats, who had concealed themselves behind a curtain, ran out again and flew about the room, Carl after them with the poker.

He killed them at last, but oh, the state my poor child's lovely boudoir was in. Carl, in his rage, had banged that poker down without caring what he was doing, and he had smashed no end of things before he killed the rats.

When we were calmer, and I had got down off the chair and left off trembling, and Jane had recovered from the fit of hysterics into which the sight of her beautiful room had sent her, I went to the box and looked inside it, and there at the bottom was a card on which was written in a big sprawling hand:

"A Happy New Year to you, Old Tooth Tugger."

Carl snatched the card from my hands, and, glancing at it, exclaimed, "I knew it. It's those wretches across the road. Ah, if I had them in my country, I would shoot them like dogs – like dogs."

We persuaded him to be calm, and not to make any further trouble, because it would be impossible to prove who had done it, and for Jane's sake he consented to let the matter drop. But I am quite sure that it was the people opposite who played him that nasty, spiteful trick, for when I went to the dining-room window a little later on I saw those two fiends of boys looking across the road at our house, and grinning in the most insolent manner possible.

Still, I don't think those rats were altogether thrown away, for Carl has had much less trouble with his neighbours lately.

People who would try to break up a happy home with sewer rats will not stick at anything, and Carl has, I think, come to the determination not to do anything more to deserve their most unpleasant attentions.

Memoir XII

Two of My Grandchildren

A MOTHER-IN-LAW naturally expects to become a grand-mamma in time. Some mothers-in-law are by no means anxious to enjoy the honour. There is something in the word grandmamma that suggests old age, and it is quite comprehensible that women should be anxious to put off old age as long as possible. When a woman marries young, it is quite possible that she may have a grown-up daughter by the time she is forty, and if that daughter marries young too, she may be a grandmamma at forty-two, though she has kept her figure and doesn't look anything like her age. Then, if she has not outlived the vanity of youth, it is certainly a little trying to be addressed as "grandmamma".

I am glad to say that the word never gave me anything but pleasure, though I was by no means an old woman when little Augustus Walkinshaw conferred the title on me.

I am quite the grandmamma now, for I have ten grandchil-dren, and some of them are rapidly becoming young men and women, and I have long since settled down in the role. I don't think Mr Tressider quite liked being called grandpapa for the first time. Men, in spite of the popular idea to the contrary, are really much vainer than women.

Soon after little Augustus was born, I had occasion to say a few words to Mr Tressider with regard to his absurd habit of making jokes in the presence of comparative strangers. It was at a little garden party which I gave that he offended me by telling a lady to whom I had only just introduced him a ridiculous tale about my quarrelling with him. Coming home from the theatre in a four-wheel cab, because he wouldn't get out and see if the cabman was drunk, he declared that I said, "Then if you won't I will," and that I went to put my head out of the window to tell the cabman to stop, and put it right through the glass window, which was up, and that he had to pay the cabman four shillings for the window, and that I sat up for two hours after we got home, picking pieces of glass out of my bonnet.

What led him to tell that story was the lady making a remark about a hansom cabman who had driven her to our house, and who had been so drunk that when she got out he drove off without waiting for his fare.

The story as John Tressider told it was untrue, though it had some foundation in fact. But he told it in a way to make me appear ridiculous, which is what some men appear to take a delight in making their wives look. I didn't say anything then, merely giving him a look, but afterwards, when everybody was gone, and he was sitting alone in the garden tent, finishing up the ices, I said to him, "John Tressider, I think it is time you learnt to behave yourself properly now you are a grandfather."

"Good gracious me! Don't, Jane," he said. "The idea of reminding a man that he is a grandfather just as he is in the middle of his sixth strawberry ice."

He turned it off as a joke, but a little later on I caught him in the breakfast room looking in the glass and running his hand through his hair, which is still thick and only slightly grey. And I knew that he was thinking to himself that he didn't look a bit like a grandfather.

But he thought he would have his revenge, and after that he insisted for a long time in addressing me as "grandmamma", much to my indignation, when people were present, and when I said anything that he didn't like he would say, "Hush, hush, my dear, remember that you are a grandmother."

But we soon got over the first novelty of the situation, and my dear little grandchildren brought quite a new pleasure into my life, though at times there were moments of unpleasantness as to what their names were to be. When I selected a name that I thought I should like one of my grandchildren to bear, its father had always strong views in another direction, and of course I had to give way.

Little Augustus Walkinshaw was a very delicate child at first, but his mother made a great deal too much fuss over him, and I had to speak plainly to her on the subject, and remind her that I had brought up nine children, so that I ought to know something about it. She coddled the child too much, being afraid lest so much as a breath of fresh air should blow on him, and she was always upsetting herself about the shape of his nose.

One day I met the nurse out with little Augustus on the terrace, and the nurse was walking backwards with him, and would have run violently into a butcher's boy who was standing looking at a man repairing the church steeple with a tray of meat over his shoulder – the boy, not the man – had I not called out to her and warned her of her danger.

And when I told the girl she ought to be ashamed of herself to walk about the public streets like that with an infant in her arms, she told me it was by her mistress's orders that she did so, as the wind was cold and her mistress didn't want the baby to meet it.

I spoke to Sabina about it directly I saw her, and told her such conduct was ridiculous, and that children coddled up like that invariably grew up delicate. But it was no use. She was as fussy and as nervous as ever directly afterwards, and when little Sabina was born it was the same thing over again. It was a source of great annoyance to me, because my eldest daughter made herself a perfect slave to her babies, hardly ever trusting them out of her sight, and being in a state of painful excitement all the time she was away from home. She was always imagining that something terrible would happen to the children in her absence, and she changed her nurses so often for some fancied neglect or trifling fault that her name was never off the books of the registry office to which she went for her servants.

She got a nurse at last who suited her and who suited the children, and that nurse very soon became the mistress of the house. Both she and Augustus gave way to her – Anne her name was – in everything for fear of offending her, and Anne had only to threaten to leave in order to get everything she wanted. And then Anne, finding her power so great in the house, began to give herself airs, which was only natural.

This was after the children were four or five years old. They took to Anne, and Anne was the only one who understood them and managed them properly. When she found out how necessary my daughter considered her presence for the children's comfort and safety, she began to pretend that she should have to leave, and she would tell the children that their "Nanna" was going away from them, and then they would begin to scream and cling to her.

The idea of having a fresh nurse terrified poor Sabina so that she gave way to Anne in everything, and, in order to prevent her going out, allowed her to have her friends to see her. Once I went over to see my daughter one evening, and, hearing a good deal of laughing going on downstairs in the kitchen, I said, "Good gracious me, whatever is the matter? Have the servants got a regiment of soldiers in the kitchen?" "No, Mamma," said Sabina, "they are only Anne's friends – her father and mother and her sisters and brothers and the cook from next door and the housemaid from across the road."

I was very much astonished at my daughter allowing so many followers as that, and I did not hesitate to speak my mind on the subject, pointing out to her that I had never tolerated such a state of affairs in any house of mine. Sabina excused herself on the ground that it was Anne's birthday, and as she didn't want her to go away for the day and leave the children she had allowed her to have her friends there to tea.

I said that it was absurd, and that if she was not careful Anne would be the mistress of the house. And she very soon was. Sabina was a most devoted mother, but nervous, and always imagining that the children were going to be ill or to catch something, and that was one of the reasons she didn't like the idea of Anne's going out to see any of her friends and acquaintances, for fear she should bring home measles or scarlet fever, or something of that sort. She made her life almost a misery with her constant nervousness, and Anne naturally took advantage of it.

One day she told her mistress that her cousin to whom she was engaged had returned from sea, and she should like to have him to tea, and after that there was a sailor constantly calling and being asked to tea in the kitchen. Then Anne quarrelled with the sailor and he went away to sea, and soon afterwards Anne became of quite a serious turn of mind and commenced to attend a chapel* in the neighbourhood. That chapel was the terror of my daughter's life, for Anne suddenly became one of its most active members, and wanted to go to the evening service about four times a week after she had put the children to bed.

Sabina didn't like to refuse her for fear she should threaten to leave, so when Anne went to chapel she had to go and sit upstairs with the children herself, because if little Sabina woke up and found nobody there, she used to scream and want her "Nanna".

I remember once I had a little family dinner party on my eldest son John's birthday, and I was most anxious that all my children should be present, and at the last moment I received a long letter from Sabina begging us to excuse her, and explaining that it was quite impossible for her to come as it was a special night at Anne's chapel, and Anne had arranged to go to it, and the children couldn't possibly be left alone.

I was very indignant, and I wrote to Sabina a very severe though motherly letter, and I told her that if Anne were my servant I should very soon put a stop to this chapel business. I had no objection to servants being religious – on the contrary – but I do not consider that any servant is doing her duty in that station of life into which she has been called by wanting to go to chapel four times a week. You engage servants to work, not to go to chapel every other evening.

Anne remained with them long after their children were old enough to do without a nurse, simply because neither Augustus nor Sabina had the moral courage to tell her to go, knowing that the children, who really were very much attached to her, would make a scene. But at last she left of her own accord to marry a City missionary, and I wasn't at all sorry. There was a great deal too much "Anne" in my daughter's household to please me.

Augustus junior grew up a very clever lad, but exceedingly delicate. He grew so rapidly that he not only outgrew his clothes, but his strength, and as he was delicate, his mother and father gave way to him in everything. He developed an extraordinary taste for astronomy, and was always getting up out of bed and looking through his bedroom window at the stars, and really, for a child, he knew a great deal more than was good for him about Mars and Venus and Saturn, and the moon.

When he was about twelve his uncle John gave him a large telescope, which stood on a three-legged arrangement, and was really a very splendid instrument. At first Augustus junior had this fixed up in the garden, but as the stars and the planets didn't come out until after nightfall, and the grass was then damp with the evening dew, his poor mother was in a terrible state, as the doctor said being out in the night air was bad for him. So the telescope was fitted up in his bedroom, but the window being small, he had to lie down on the floor to look through it at the moon, not being able to get it to a proper elevation any other way.

It was bad enough for that boy to be lying on his stomach staring at Mars and Venus through an open window when he ought to have been in bed, but he insisted on his father and mother assisting at his astronomical discoveries, and so poor Sabina had to lie down on the floor and look at the moon too, and to pretend to be very much interested in Saturn's rings and Jupiter's satellites, and all that sort of thing, which I candidly confess are Greek to me.

I was not sorry to see the boy take an interest in something scientific, though I should have preferred something more useful and profitable than the stars, but I thought Sabina went a little too far in humouring him by lying down on the floor night after night and screwing up one eye and squinting with the other at the moon.

She confessed to me that she never saw anything but a mist, and that her position on the floor was not only an inelegant one for the grown-up mother of a family, but slightly painful too at times.

One evening when I was at their house I was marched upstairs by young Augustus in order to see a comet or some wonderful thing which he had discovered with his uncle John's telescope, but when I was requested to lie down flat on my stomach in order to look through the telescope at it I said that I would take Augustus' word that the comet was there and wait till it was visible to the naked eye before I gave my opinion concerning it.

Augustus was very shocked to think that his grandmamma took so little interest in the phenomena of the heavens, but I explained to him that at my time of life knowledge that could only be gained by one's lying on one's stomach, screwing up one eye and flattening the other against a small piece of glass, was a little beyond me. I appreciated his devotion to astronomical science, but I told him that the extent of mine had been limited by circumstances to looking at an eclipse of the sun through a piece of smoked glass.

After that I think he rather looked down upon his grandmamma, and he never took me into his confidence again with regard to the heavenly bodies. But I learnt from his mother that in one month he discovered three new stars that he had never seen before, and caught three separate and distinct colds, one of them being so bad that he had to be put to bed and have a mustard plaster over his chest.

And the very night he had the mustard plaster on, his poor mother, coming into his room before going to bed, was horrified to find him lying on the ground with only his nightshirt and the mustard plaster on, with his telescope, at the open window, looking at Venus. He said that he was obliged to do it, for he had suddenly remembered that that was the very night that something happened in that planet which would not happen again for a hundred years, and as he would probably not have a chance of studying the occurrence then he thought he had better not miss it now.

My poor Sabina was naturally horrified, and coaxed him into bed again and tucked him up, and the next day she wrote to John and told him that she hoped he would never wring another mother's loving heart by presenting a delicate and weak-chested boy with a telescope that wanted the window open before it could be used.

Lately my grandson, Augustus junior, has grown stronger, and though his devoted mother rejoices greatly, her joy is somewhat leavened by the fact that he has developed a taste for athletic sports and taken to cricket and bicycling. He is somewhat unfortunate in his cricket, though his schoolfellows say he is a good player. He has come home from a cricket match with a black eye from the ball striking him in the face, and once with a twisted ankle from slipping upon the grass while running.

He never announces his intention of going off to play cricket without putting his poor mother's heart in her mouth, and his bicycling adventures cause her no less uneasiness. He is, I fear, somewhat reckless. Possibly he gets looking up at the sky and studying the sun. At any rate he has a peculiar knack of coming off suddenly and doing fearful damage to his face and knees and clothes, on the roadway, not to mention the tremendous wear and tear to which he subjects his clothes. On the whole, Sabina would, I think, be happier if he would confine himself entirely to the telescope. She does know what has become of him when he is in his bedroom studying the stars, but he never goes cricketing or bicycling without causing her to have a presentiment that he will be brought home on a stretcher.

My granddaughter Sabina is of a literary turn of mind. At the age of six she commenced to write short stories on a slate, and at seven took to pen and ink, with terrible results to the tablecloths and her pinafores and her fingers.

At ten she commenced to write her autobiography and reminiscences, which were principally confined to the life and adventures of the various cats and dogs who at different times had been members of the family.

Her stories are considered "bosh" by her brother, but her father and mother think they show signs of future greatness. They are peculiar in this respect, that none of them ever contain the slightest reference to boys. The characters are entirely female, with the exception of the dogs and the cats. Even in the fairy stories which she writes there are no boys – all the fairies are young ladies, and they never under any circumstances have sweethearts or hint at any kind of love, save their love for each other and their dogs and cats. The queen of the fairies lavishes terms of endearment on a pet canary, and changes a bad dog who had killed a cat into a black beetle, but there is not so much as a he baby in the collection of tales with which my granddaughter Sabina has filled several copybooks.

The conversation of the principal characters is realistic in a sense, for it is taken from real life. Little Sabina is in the habit of dropping her father and mother's conversation into her stories, and this habit had upon one occasion very startling results.

Augustus Walkinshaw is, like all men, slightly impatient at times. One evening when little Sabina, then about ten years old, was writing a story, he, not knowing the child was in the room, lost his temper over a box of matches, having struck some half-dozen, one after the other, without getting a light for his pipe. When the seventh match sputtered out he exclaimed, "Dash the matches! I wish the man that made them was at Jericho."*

A short time afterwards little Sabina's fond and devoted mother, conversing one day with the clergyman of the parish who had called, told him how fond of writing stories her little daughter was. The clergyman begged to be allowed to see some of the child's work, and the proud mother, easily allowing herself to be persuaded, went upstairs and brought down the copybook containing her child's latest effort.

The clergyman read a page or two with great interest. Two young princesses being much troubled about a housemaid who would not come in at ten o'clock on her Sunday out, agree that if she is ever late again they will ask their fairy godmother to turn her into a toad. The girl comes in at eleven, and the princesses are so indignant that they summon their fairy godmother at once, and ask her to turn the girl into a toad. The fairy godmother instantly orders a cauldron to be brought into the drawing room for the purpose of incantation, and when sticks and logs of wood have been put under it, she takes a box of matches to set light to it. But the matches won't strike, whereupon the fairy godmother exclaims, "Dash the matches! I wish the man who made them was at Jericho."

When the clergyman got as far as that he dropped the copybook. "Dear me," he said, "what strong language for a child to put into the mouth of a fairy."

Poor Sabina took the book and read the lines, and her face turned crimson. She knew at once that the child had picked the expression up from her papa. She closed the book and didn't ask the clergyman to read any more. She was afraid that perhaps something even a little stronger might have found its way into the conversation of the fairies.

Little pitchers have large ears, and parents cannot be too careful what they say when the children are about. I once knew a little girl who, at a children's party, because a little boy trod upon her toe accidentally, made use of a remarkably strong expression, to the horror of the company, and it was all through her papa, who had the gout, saying the same thing that very morning, when the pageboy accidentally touched his foot in putting the stool for him to rest it on.

Dogs are the principal heroes of little Sabina's stories, and this arises from the fact that she and her brother, and her father and mother as well, are devoted to an absurd bull terrier, who is called "Jack". Jack is the master of the house. If he takes the easy chair, Augustus waits until he has done with it. If he settles himself down for forty winks on the drawing-room sofa no one thinks of disturbing him. He has a huge brass collar, on which his name and address are engraved, together with a fabulous reward to the person who finds him, in case he should be lost, and brings him home. When Jack goes to sleep on little Sabina's lap of an evening, she declines to go to bed until he wakes, for fear of disturbing his slumber; when Augustus junior has one of his colds, and has to keep his bed, the old cradle, which was little Sabina's, is made up as a bed for Jack and placed in young Augustus's room. Jack has his meals with the family, having his own chair and his own plate, and he has been trained to drink out of a little china mug, which was presented to him by the children on his last birthday, and has "Jack" painted on it in gold letters. Jack has a coat for the winter because his chest is delicate, and he has also a mackintosh for wet weather, and altogether he is made as much fuss with as though he was a human being.

One day he was lost, and the whole family sat down to tea and wept, and couldn't touch anything, and when he was found and brought back they all flung their arms round his neck in turn and kissed him.

And one week when Jack was really very ill with congestion of the lungs, and the veterinary surgeon said he didn't think he would recover, the whole family... But I shall have to tell you the story of the Walkinshaws and the night they thought Jack was going to die, on another occasion.

I happened to be at the house in the evening, and I couldn't help speaking my mind on the subject. Upon my word, Augustus and Sabina were quite as idiotic as my grandchildren were. I said it was absurd, though I am fond of animals myself. When I came in, they were all crying round him on a rug, and Augustus junior looked up and saw me, and said to the dog, "Jack, dear Jack, here's your dear grandma come to see you for the last time."

I am a sentimental woman myself, but my sentiment stops short at bulldogs.

Memoir XIII

Lavinia

I NEVER THOUGHT that my fourth daughter Lavinia would make the match of the family. But she did. She was always the most delicate of all the family as a child, frightening me out of my life through taking everything that was in the air, and never being really out of the doctor's hands until she was quite eighteen years old.

Yet, although she was the most delicate, she was the merriest and the most mischievous. I never knew such a child for getting into trouble in my life. Before she was seven years old she had set herself on fire playing with matches; she had fallen out of the first-floor window onto the top of the conservatory, and rolled off the roof onto the ground, fortunately without seriously injuring herself; she had got her foot stuck in an iron grating outside a shop, and had to remain there shrieking while a blacksmith or something of the sort was fetched to cut a bar; and she had fallen head over heels into a bath of hot water that was being prepared for her younger sister.

She always declared that she couldn't help these accidents, that she didn't do anything to cause them, and I am not sure but that the child was to a certain extent right.

But they happened. She was unlucky. She was unlucky in always catching any epidemic that might be about, and she was unlucky in always having an accident happen to her.

We called her "Lavinia the Unlucky" for years, and I always made up my mind that the poor child would be unlucky through life. But she was not. She was lucky in love, lucky in her marriage, and I am bound to say that she was lucky in her husband.

Charles Wigram – that is her husband's name – and Lavinia suit each other admirably. They have both calm, amiable dispositions, taking life as it comes, never worrying, and going through existence in that cool, calm, delightful manner which must be a great blessing to you when you can do so.

I can't. I never could, and I never shall. I am a highly sensitive, nervous woman, and a little thing upsets me. Most of my children take after me. Lavinia is the only exception. She is as calm and stoical as her father – as she is delicate that is a blessing. If she had been what John Tressider calls "a worrier", she would probably have died at an early age. She never worries, and so she is happily married, rich and blessed with two charming little children who inherit her extraordinary tendency to alarming accidents, and have hairbreadth escapes, colds, measles, whooping cough, mumps, rashes and any complaints that may be fashionable at the moment.

But she does not worry about her children as I used to about mine. She is a devoted mother, but she always takes it for granted that things will turn out right eventually, and pursues what the poet calls the even tenor of her way.

One day she went out into the garden of her country house and discovered her little boy, aged five, at the top of a ladder which some workmen had been using to repair the roof.

I should have shrieked and wrung my hands, and possibly have fainted.

My daughter Livinia did nothing of the kind. She just looked up and said, "Oh, you naughty boy; get onto the roof, sir, and stop there till I come."

She waited till the boy got off the top of the ladder onto the roof, which was flat at the side; then she went quietly upstairs and took him in through the attic window.

I couldn't have done such a thing to save my life – or the child's – but that is one of the blessings of having no nerves, and taking things calmly.

I think it was her perfect calmness in a moment of danger that won her her husband, though her liability to accidents had something to do with it.

She and her sister were out riding one morning with the riding master, and she trotted round a corner a little way ahead while the riding master dismounted to tighten a strap or something on her sister's horse.

Just as she got round the corner a wretch of a boy burst an air balloon with a violent bang right in front of her horse's nose, and the animal bolted. Lavinia didn't shriek, but she held on tightly, and tried all she could to pull the horse up.

But the animal never stopped till he came to his stable, and then he dashed right in, and she had to bend almost flat on his neck to prevent her brains being dashed out against a beam.

As soon as the men had come to her horse's head she slipped off and got on another horse which had just come in and was not unsaddled.

The men said, "Good gracious, miss, you are not going out again?" "Oh, yes, I am," said Lavinia. "I must ride back to my sister, who will be in a fright about me," and she rode the horse out of the yard, although she had just been bolted with, and met her sister, who was coming after her with the riding master, both pale with terror, and wondering what had happened.

It was certainly a very brave thing of her to do, and shows how coolly she takes everything. That was how she first attracted the attention of Charles Wigram, a young gentleman living in our neighbourhood. He had been out walking and had seen the horse bolting into the stable, and was astonished to see Lavinia come out again immediately on another horse, just as cool and collected as though nothing out of the ordinary way had happened.

He was an acquaintance of one of my sons at the time and had been to see him once or twice, but after that it seems he told everybody that it was the coolest thing he had ever seen in his life, and he began to pay a great deal of attention to Lavinia when he met her out at balls and parties in the neighbourhood, and eventually they became engaged.

It was an excellent match, and I was very pleased, for my dear Lavinia, with all her pluck and coolness, was not one who could have led a hard life or married a poor man. Charles Wigram was living with his mother, who was a widow, and had an excellent income, with expectations from several wealthy relatives, and very soon after he had begun to pay Lavinia attention an uncle died and left him £30,000. That, with the money he inherited from his father, gave him an assured and comfortable position, and so I felt that Lavinia had done very well indeed, and I said that her horse had bolted with her to some purpose after all. But I was always in a terrible state of anxiety while she was out riding afterwards, and I never knew a moment's peace till she came back, and if the girls were a little over their time I used to go out and stand on the doorstep and watch for them, and once, when they came back about half an hour late, they found me wringing my hands at the front garden gate, and Lavinia said that, under the circumstances, she wouldn't ride again in London.

I said that I was very sorry, but I felt so nervous and anxious that I really couldn't help it, and though, probably, they thought it very foolish of me, it was only my having a mother's loving heart and a nervous system shattered by the cares and anxieties of a large family and a husband never at home when anything went wrong.

After Lavinia and Mr Wigram were married they went to live in the country, at a charming place in Oxfordshire, which Mr Wigram had purchased, and I did not see quite so much of my daughter as I could have wished. But when they came to town they stayed with us, and it was then I had an opportunity of studying Charles Wigram's character and noting how admirably they suited each other.

I do believe that if a bombshell had suddenly burst between them while they were sitting side by side on the sofa, neither of them would have moved away in a hurry. They never hurried. They never seemed to be in a hurry. I remember once going with them to the opera, and when we came out we got mixed up in a big crowd, and our carriage came to the door, and before we could get through it was moved off again, as it was blocking the way.

I was most indignant, and began to get excited, because I saw we should probably be stuck there for another half-hour before the carriage came back again, and as it was raining we couldn't go out into the street and walk after it. But Mr Wigram and Lavinia didn't seem at all put out. He said, "Oh, it's all right; let's go and sit down till it comes back again. The people will all have driven away by then." And he coolly marched off, and sat down on one of the seats in the vestibule or hall, or whatever it is called at the opera, and pulled out an evening paper from his overcoat pocket, and began to read the "Latest City Intelligence", and Lavinia went and sat down beside him.

That made me lose my temper, and I spoke my mind, but he just looked up and said quietly, "Oh! what's the good of worrying? We shall get home sometime."

I couldn't be like that. I must worry, and I never could wait for anything a minute longer than was absolutely necessary. I daresay your calm, quiet people, who take things as they come, are much happier, but that sort of feeling has to be born in you. It never comes to you after you have been born if it isn't.

I never go on a journey without being in a state of nervous anxiety for hours before the carriage comes to the door. I fidget about the packing; I fidget for fear I should have forgotten something; I fidget for fear anything should go wrong while I am away; I get anxious and flurried if the carriage is a minute late, and I'm not easy in my mind until I'm in the train, and then I fidget all the time I am away about the house and the servants, and Mr Tressider and my children, and I keep on fidgeting till I get back home, and then I am not easy in my mind, for there is sure to be something to upset me.

Of course, I know that this is very foolish, but you can't help your nature, and my nature is to worry. My daughter Lavinia, and my son-in-law Charles Wigram, cannot help their natures, and their nature is to take things coolly.

Once when I was staying with them at their house in Oxfordshire they gave a big garden party. Nearly everybody in the neighbourhood was invited, and great preparations were made, a great many things being ordered from the confectioner's in the neighbouring town, such as ices, etc.

On the day of the garden party it poured with rain in torrents, and the wind blew a perfect hurricane. When I looked out of the window and saw the weather I said: "Oh, dear me, no one will ever come on a day like this."

Of course, I expected that my daughter and her husband would be very much upset, especially as they had made elaborate preparations for a very large number of guests. But nothing of the sort. Lavinia looked at the rain, which was coming down in torrents, and said: "No, I shouldn't think we shall have many"; and Charley laughed, and said: "If any people do come, we ought to communicate with the nearest lunatic asylum." Then he lit a cigar, and went off into the billiard room and played billiards with himself all the morning, just as if nothing unfortunate had happened.

It never left off raining all day, and in the afternoon it blew such a gale that a couple of trees were blown down in the grounds. Nobody did come, and under the circumstances it wasn't to be wondered at.

Now, I should have worked myself up into a terrible state of excitement over such a contretemps as that, but Lavinia and her husband didn't. They joked about the refreshments which were in the house, and they asked me how many ices I thought I could manage, and when the time was past, and it was certain that nobody would come, they had the ices brought in, and we all sat round the table and ate as many as we could, and the rest were sent down to the servants, and the next day the pastry and the things that wouldn't keep were distributed among the cottagers on the estate and the children at the village school. And never from the beginning to the end did the disappointed host and hostess show by the slightest sign that they were annoyed or in any way put out. They took the whole thing as coolly as though nothing particular had happened, and in the evening, after dinner, they sat and talked about the weather, and said it was a good thing for the country, for rain was very much wanted.

My son-in-law is a justice of the peace in his neighbourhood, and has to sit on the bench and try the people for stealing apples and pulling up turnips, and taking firewood and trespassing and all that sort of thing, and one day he was one of the magistrates who sentenced a very bad character to fourteen days for assaulting the landlord of the village alehouse. The fellow, who really I don't think from what I heard afterwards could have been quite right in his mind, glared at the magistrates as he was being taken away, and looking hard at Mr Wigram, against whom he had a grudge, as he had been a tenant, and ordered to leave for his bad behaviour, he said: "You wait till I come out. I'll be even with you." Whereupon Mr Wigram had the man called back and suggested that the sentence should be made more severe, as it would not do for magistrates to allow themselves to be threatened, and the fellow got a month.

Mr Wigram came home that afternoon and told his wife about it, and said: "Black Jack" (that was what the fellow was called in the neighbourhood) "threatened me today, and we gave him a month. When he comes out we shall have to keep our eyes open. I daresay he will try to get into the poultry yard or the grounds and do some mischief."

I should have been terribly alarmed if Mr Tressider had told me that he had been threatened. In fact, once something like it did happen to him, and I was in terror about it for years afterwards, and I don't even like to think of it now.

One night Mr Tressider was coming along the City Road, when a man ran out of a crowd and seized his watch and chain, and made off with them. Mr Tressider called, "Stop thief," and ran, and presently the man was seized and given to the police, and Mr Tressider went to the station and charged him, and appeared in court against him. The man was proved to be an old offender, and got twelve months, and as he was leaving the dock he said to my husband: "I'll do for you for this when I come out."

When Mr Tressider told me, I was haunted by the idea that one day he would be found murdered in the streets, or in the back garden, or that somebody would break in in the night and kill him in his bed, and that it would be this man. And I got in quite a low, nervous state about it, and about a year after that, my husband not coming home to dinner as expected, and it getting very late, and my having no telegram or message, I made up my mind that the man had come out and had "done" for him, and I went out when midnight came and no John, and went straight to the police station – trembling like an aspen leaf – and gave the inspector on duty full particulars as to my husband's appearance and the clothes he was wearing and the washing marks on his collar and socks, and his initials, and came back and sat down on a flowerpot turned upside down and sobbed violently in the front garden until I heard his footstep.

And then, upset as I was, I couldn't help speaking my mind, and I refused to listen to his excuses that he had met an old schoolfellow and they had dined and gone to the theatre together, and that he had given a cabman a note and two shillings to bring it to me, and that the cabman must have kept the two shillings and torn up the letter.

I told him it was cruel of him to leave me in such suspense, seeing that a man had just come out of prison who had sworn to "do" for him, and then I told him that I had been to the police station and given a full description of him.

He was furious at that, and absolutely had the audacity to say that I had made myself look ridiculous, and that he would be the laughing stock of the neighbourhood. Of course, women who show wifely affection always *are* ridiculous in men's eyes, but they miss us when we're gone.

It was quite a year before I gave up being anxious about John when he stayed out late, because I always began to think about the fellow who had threatened to "do" for him over the watch and chain. But it is a good many years ago now, and my husband has never been set upon in the streets or in any way violently assaulted, and so I suppose the man, when he came out of jail, thought better of it, or, perhaps, he got sent to prison again for something else before he had time to look John up.

My daughter and her husband were not quite so fortunate. About two months after the Black Jack episode, Lavinia was sitting in the dining room, which opens onto the lawn in front of the house, late one summer's evening, when she thought she saw something moving in the shadows of the trees. Charles had gone to town and wasn't expected home until the last train, and the coachman had gone to the station to meet him. The housemaid and the parlourmaid had been allowed to go to a circus, which had come to the neighbourhood, and the only persons in the house besides Lavinia were the cook, who was very fat and a great coward, and the nurse, who had gone to bed ill with a violent cold.

Lavinia, who wouldn't be frightened, I believe, if a ghost suddenly walked into her bedroom in the middle of the night, called out, "Who is there?" and, getting no answer, thought she must have made a mistake. She got up and went to the other end of the room to get a match and light the lamp, and while she was looking about for the matches she heard a sound and, turning round, she saw that the French window had been pushed to and a man was inside the room.

She hadn't had time to find the matches, and it was almost too dark to see anything but the outline of a form.

"Who are you, and what do you want?" she said, quietly.

"I'm Black Jack, and I want Mr Wigram," was the answer.

"He is not at home," she said calmly, knowing now whom she had to deal with. "Will you call again or wait till he comes in?"

The man seemed rather surprised at her calmness, so he hesitated, and came nearer towards the middle of the room.

At that moment she put her hand down on the sideboard and felt something cold against it. Then she knew what it was by the shape. It was a pistol. She picked it up quickly, and walking towards the man she said, "I don't want to harm you, but as you have no right here, and you may be going to hurt me, I shall fire this pistol straight off in your face if you don't instantly sit down in that chair," and she pointed to an armchair.

The man hesitated.

She pulled back the trigger of the pistol, and he heard the sound. He put his hand in his pocket and pulled out something that looked like a life preserver.*

"You'd better not try any of your tricks on me," he said, "or I'll—"

"Sit down, or I'll fire!"

She held the pistol up, there was light enough for him to see that she was pointing it straight at him.

He sat down in the chair.

"Now," said Lavinia, "I will tell you what I am going to do. I am going to keep you here till Mr Wigram returns, which will be in a few minutes. You can talk the matter over with him, because I don't understand the merits of the case. But as you are probably hungry, I will ring for something to be brought to you. Would you like something to eat?"

The man hesitated, but at last he said he should.

Lavinia backed to where the bell was and rang it, and the cook came.

"Cook," she said, "bring in some cold meat and pickles on a tray for this gentleman."

The cook couldn't see who it was in the dark, but she said: "Shall I light the gas, ma'am?"

"No, we don't want a light yet. Bring the tray."

Cook went out, and directly she had gone, Lavinia raised the pistol again, just to show she'd got it ready.

The cook came back presently with the tray and some beer, and Black Jack, who, I assume, was very hungry, fell to and made a good supper.

And while he was eating there was the sound of carriage wheels, and Mr Wigram drove up.

The man began to fidget in his chair.

"I think I'll go," he said, looking towards the window.

"No," said Lavinia, "if you do I shall shoot you."

Mr Wigram came in, and was very much surprised to see his wife in the dark, with a strange man in the easy chair eating cold beef and pickles.

"My dear," said Lavinia, "Black Jack called to see you, and I invited him to stay here till you came back. Get a light."

Mr Wigram, very much astonished, took a match from his pocket, struck a light and lit the gas, and Lavinia put the pistol in her pocket, still keeping hold of it with her hand, and letting Black Jack see she'd got it.

Mr Wigram entered into the spirit of the thing, and handed his cigar case to Black Jack, and made him smoke, and then began to talk to him, and to tell him what a fool he was, and the end of it was he said he was very sorry, that Mr Wigram was a real good sort, and his missus was a "plucky 'un and no mistake", and Mr Wigram promised him that if he would try and retrieve his character, not only to hold his tongue about his coming there in the way he had done, but to find him a job.

And Black Jack went away, blessing the man he had come to injure, if not to kill, and when he had gone, Lavinia said, "Charley, what do you think I kept Black Jack at bay with? This!" And she pulled out of her pocket a little toy pistol of her eldest son's – one that children fire off.

Her husband burst out laughing, and said she was a little brick.

When I heard the story, I couldn't help saying, "Well, Lavinia, you certainly are the coolest, most self-possessed young woman I ever heard of. I can't think where you get your nerves from."

And she looked up at me and laughed, and said, "Not from your side of the family, Mamma."

And I didn't contradict her.

Memoir XIV

Frank Tressider

I HAVE ALWAYS GOT ON very well with John's wife, and also with William's wife, except for that little misunderstanding which I told you about concerning the price of lamb at the dinner party. Marion understood me better afterwards, though, finding she was so sensitive, I was careful not to say anything that could possibly wound her feelings.

I know that some young wives have a foolish idea that their husbands' mothers are very terrible people, and will look down upon them as interlopers. I remember Marion, after we were better acquainted, telling me that at first she was absolutely terrified of me, having heard such wonderful accounts of my management from William, and knowing that I had a quick eye in domestic matters.

She told me that at the dinner party she was trembling all the time lest anything should go wrong or be wrong, because she felt sure that I should think it was her fault, and that William had made a mistake in marrying a girl who knew so little about housekeeping and domestic management.

But her feeling of nervousness soon passed away, and we became excellent friends, and she always came to me for my advice when she was in a difficulty either with her servants or her tradespeople. A woman who has brought up a large family must know more of the world than a young girl just beginning married life, and I think young wives are very foolish not to consult their mothers-in-law oftener than they do.

It is all very well in wealthy families or the upper circles, where the wife has nothing to do but to look pretty, smile on her husband and entertain her guests, but in middle-class homes, where it often happens young people have none too much money to spare at the outset of their married life, the wife's responsibility is a great one. A good, thoughtful, careful young wife may have much to do with the future prosperity of her husband, and a careless, extravagant wife may bring a man to ruin.

A grave responsibility rests with the mothers who bring their daughters up in ignorance of domestic matters, and without any training for the management of a household. I once heard of a young married woman who, hearing some friends conversing about a recipe for a pudding and mention the word suet, asked, "What is suet?"

Fancy what must be the fate of a man of limited means tied for life to a young woman who doesn't know what suet is! I don't blame the girl. When the story was told to me, I blamed the mother. Had I been a man and the husband of that young woman, I should have gone to her mother and spoken my mind plainly on the subject. I should have said to her: "Madam, you have neglected your duty as a mother shamefully. You have allowed your daughter to grow up to womanhood and marry an honest man, and you have kept her in the grossest ignorance. She does not even know what suet is."

The ignorance of some young women when they leave their mothers' home for their husbands' is really startling. If I hadn't known many cases myself, I should have hesitated to believe some of the stories I have heard.

Once, many years ago, when I was staying with my children at Eastbourne, we made the acquaintance of a young couple who were then on their honeymoon, and we became rather friendly. One day we were walking through the wheat fields. I said: "How splendidly the wheat is coming on," and the young bride said: "Yes; let me see. Horses eat corn, and barley is used for barley water – but what do they do with wheat?" I looked at her a minute, and I said: "Why, make bread with it." "Do they?" she said. "I always thought bread was made with flour."

I have dwelt upon the peculiarities of the wife who knows nothing that she ought to know, and has no sense of the responsibilities of married life, because my third son, Frank – a bright, handsome young fellow he was too – married just such a girl. A pretty doll, I called her, but he was infatuated and thought she was an angel upon earth. I don't wish to say a word against Laura generally. She and Frank are now in Australia expiating their folly, but I must tell the truth concerning her, as it may act as a warning to other young men who fall in love with a pretty face and don't trouble as to what is behind it.

Frank never wished to go into his father's business. I don't know how it is that young men object to their fathers' business, but they very often do, and so when he left school he was sent abroad to a German university to finish his education, with the idea of his going in for a profession later on. I should have liked him to have been a clergyman, because I think that a clergyman in a family is a great advantage. There is something so thoroughly respectable about it, and any mother may feel proud to say: "My son, the Revd Mr So-and-So." I would sooner have had a son a clergyman than have one of my daughters marry a clergyman. The clergymen girls fall in love with are generally poor curates, and I always said I never could stand a curate about the house courting one of my daughters.

But a son a clergyman is a very different thing to a son-in-law a clergyman, and so I thought I should like Frank to be the Revd Frank Tressider.

But there were never any indications of a bent for the Church in Frank's character. He himself made up his mind that he would either be a solicitor or a barrister – the latter preferred. When he went to Bonn – the German university his father sent him to – it was really undecided what he should be, but what happened there quite put an end to all our ideas of his ever being an ornament to the pulpit. Frank was always a little unsteady; I am sorry to say that he was easily led into mischief. He went to Germany with the firm intention of studying hard, but, unfortunately, there were a lot of young English and American fellows there, and he got in with them, and a nice lot of scrapes they led him into. Of course, neither his father nor I had any idea of it at the time, but while we thought he was studying hard he was going about with these young fellows to the German village festivals and dancing, and stopping out till all hours of the night, and learning to smoke and drink German beer, and play cards, and I don't know what.

We knew nothing of anything wrong till he had to write home for money – a rather large sum – and then he had to explain that he was in debt in the town, and that he had lost money gambling.

We were naturally very worried; so I said to my husband that it was his duty to go to Bonn and see what really was going on, and he did, and the result was that he did a very sensible thing. He paid what Frank owed, but he told him that he was evidently not man enough to be trusted abroad without being under proper control, and so, instead of letting him live in the town and attend the university as he had been doing, he took him to the house of a tutor in Bonn who received young Englishmen, and he put him under the tutor's absolute control, thinking that at least would stop him being out half the night and gambling.

Frank wasn't there very long before he got mixed up in an affair which led to his saying goodbye to Bonn. The young fellows at Blumberg's – Blumberg was the name of the tutor – had plenty of liberty, but they were expected to be in at ten o'clock, unless they had special permission to remain out later – which was only accorded to them when they went to a private party or a dance given by some of the English families settled in Bonn.

One night there was what is called a *kermesse** at Poppelsdorf – a village close to Bonn – and all the fellows at Blumberg's made up their minds they would go. They asked permission, which was refused, and so, when they went out that evening, instead of coming back at ten they went off to the *kermesse* and coolly walked back at twelve o'clock at night.

Mr Blumberg was in a furious rage, and so he did a very unwise thing. He said Frank was the ringleader, and when Frank went up to his room the next evening to dress to go out, Mr Blumberg came upstairs and locked the door from the outside, and said, "Now, my fine fellow, you can stop there for your impudence yesterday."

Frank laughed at first, and went to the window, which was on the third floor, and opened it, and waited till the other fellows went out, and then he called to them and told them what had happened, and they went to a lot of other young fellows in the town and told them that old Blumberg had locked Frank in his room.

When it was dusk, Frank – who had been sitting smoking and thinking what he should do – looked out of the window, and he happened to see a friend of his go by – a young American named Lathrop. Instantly he had an idea. He signalled to Lathrop to stop, and then he wrote on a piece of paper, "Can I stay at your rooms if I get out?"

He wrote it for fear Mr Blumberg should be in a room below and hear him. The young American nodded his head, and then Frank wrote on another piece of paper, "Come back at midnight."

At midnight everything in Bonn is very quiet, and there is not a soul about.

At twelve o'clock Mr Lathrop came back, and a lot of other English fellows with him, who were anxious to see what Frank was going to do. Frank was ready for them. He had taken the sheets off his bed and tied them together, and then he wheeled the bed up against the window, and made one end of the sheets fast to the leg of it, and then threw the sheets out of the window to see how far they would reach. They were a long way from the ground, so he pulled them in again, and tore them right down the centre, making the two lengths four, and these he knotted together. When he threw them out they fell within four feet of the ground; so throwing out his hat and overcoat, and a handbag with some linen and things in it, he got out of the window, and began to lower himself down the sheets, amid the encouraging exclamations of his friends below.

But just as he got to the bottom the front door opened, and out darted Mr Blumberg, who had heard the noise, and had peeped out of his own window, and taken in the situation at a glance.

Mr Blumberg seized Frank and began to get excited in German. Frank dropped to the ground, and, I regret to say, in the excitement of the moment, hit Mr Blumberg on the nose and got clear of him. But the noise had attracted the attention of a gendarme who was passing the end of the street, and he ran up, and Mr Blumberg called to him to arrest Frank, which he tried to do, but Frank, who was a strong young fellow, hit and kicked and struggled till he got free; then all the others got in the way of Blumberg and the gendarme, and Frank and his friend Lathrop ran off as fast as their heels could carry them.

But they were in a bit of a fix.

It would not do for them to stop in the town, as all the places where Frank was likely to be would be searched.

So they ran on till they got outside the town, and then went along the Coblenz Road till they came to a village, and then they knocked at a cottage door and a frightened girl came down with only a petticoat and a shawl on, and asked them what they wanted.

They said they were Englishmen on a walking tour, and had missed their way, and wanted shelter for the night, and, after a little parley, the girl called her father, a labourer, and he agreed to let the young gentlemen have an empty room, and there they passed the night on some straw.

In the morning, Frank told me, they had to wash in a pail of water and dry themselves with the straw, which was very romantic, but could not have been very comfortable. And then they paid liberally for the accommodation, and set out again.

They hesitated for a long time which way they should go, but at last they made for the Rhine, and took a small boat across to Koenigswinter, on the other side, and then they made their way up to the top of the Petersberg, a mountain which lies behind the Drachenfels. On the top of the Petersberg was a little hotel, and there they made up their minds they would stop for a bit.

It was out of the season, so there was hardly anybody there, and they stopped for a day or two, Mr Lathrop going down quietly into the town to see how things were going on. He couldn't hear that anything had been done by Mr Blumberg, but all the English fellows were talking about it, and as soon as they knew where Frank was, some of them came up to see him, and they played cards in the evening.

But it began to grow rather monotonous on the top of that mountain, so one day Frank thought he would venture down, and he went to dine with some of his fellow students at the Rheinischer Hof in the town.

While they were in the middle of dinner, in walked a gendarme and Mr Blumberg, and the gendarme told Frank that he was to consider himself in custody for assaulting the police, and marched him off to the *Rathaus*,* where a magistrate heard the charge, and fined him fifty thalers. Fifty thalers was about seven pounds ten, and Frank was what he elegantly called "stone broke", and he had to borrow the money of a friend, and wire home for some to be sent him. But Mr Blumberg had written to Mr Tressider previously to say that Frank had run away, and so when we got his telegram, I said to my husband, "That boy had better come home," and Mr Tressider sent him the money and sufficient for his fare, and told him to come back at once – and he did.

I should not have alluded to these early escapades of Frank's, but that they had a great influence on his later life, for it was while he was at Bonn that he met the young lady whom he afterwards married. There were a good many English families settled in Bonn at the time, because living was cheap then on the Rhine, and Bonn was a favourite place with the English. These English families used to give small and early dances, and the young English fellows studying there were frequently invited. It was at a dance at the house of Colonel Willings, a gentleman with eleven daughters, who was retrenching at Bonn, that Frank first met Mrs Helston and her daughter. Laura Helston was a very handsome girl, but her mother was a fashionable invalid – one of those ladies of unlimited pretension and a limited income who find it necessary to live abroad for the benefit of their health. Mrs Helston, who had been left a widow when her daughter was twelve years of age, sold off everything after her husband's death, and finding that he had left very little behind him, having been compelled by her extravagance to live beyond his means, she moved about on the Continent from pension to pension making many friends and acquaintances by her agreeable manners, but certainly thinking a great deal more about her own comfort than her daughter's future. A young woman who passes her life from the age of twelve to the age of twenty in foreign boarding houses is perhaps not to be blamed if she fails to grow up thoroughly domesticated, and I always took this into consideration when Laura Helston, afterwards Laura Tressider, annoyed me.

Frank met the Helstons, as I have told you, at a dance given by Colonel Willings, and, boy-like, fell in love with Laura, and managed to see a good deal of her. When he had to leave Bonn, it was the idea of not seeing her again that grieved him, and it seems that these foolish young people went for a walk by the Rhine one day just before he left, and entered into a secret engagement. Miss Helston promised to write to Frank, and let him know all her movements, so that they could correspond with each other, and Frank vowed that his heart should never hold any other woman's image, and as soon as he was old enough he would claim her as his bride.

I used to wonder after Frank came home how it was so many foreign letters came for him in a female handwriting, and why he never said anything about them, but I have never been one to be unduly inquisitive as to my sons' correspondence, and I did not attach any serious importance to the matter.

Mr Tressider gave Frank a severe lecture on his folly, and told him that he would have to turn over a new leaf if he wanted to make a position in life for himself, and Frank professed to be genuinely penitent and thoroughly ashamed of himself, and declared that it was his intention to settle down and to begin seriously to prepare himself for the profession of the law, which he wished to adopt.

We were quite agreeable to his being a lawyer, and after a year's study in London, during which time he certainly seemed very steady and worked very hard, Frank was articled to our family solicitor, Mr Benjamin Jones, of Lincoln's Inn Fields.

But when he got to the law, Frank didn't like the law. He stuck to it for a time, but I could see that the boy wasn't happy in his mind, and one evening when we were alone I asked him what was the matter, and then he said he was afraid that he had made a mistake, and that he should never take kindly to the law, and that he was sure he was only wasting his time in going to Mr Jones's. He said that Lincoln's Inn Fields themselves were enough to drive anybody melancholy mad, and that a lawyer's office was utterly unsuited to a man of poetical temperament.

Of course I was very much worried, because I saw that Frank was likely to be a rolling stone, but I talked the matter over with his father, and the next day Mr Tressider called on Mr Jones, and the result of that interview satisfied him that Frank would never do any good at the law, and Mr Jones agreed to release him from his articles.

But before the matter was settled, we asked Frank what he proposed to do, as it was not likely that we could let him lead a lazy life at home. He would have to be something.

To our great surprise he had a plan of his own already formed. A fellow student of his at Bonn was a young Frenchman, and the young Frenchman's father had a business in Paris, and they wanted a young Englishman speaking French and German to act as a kind of secretary, and Frank's friend had written to him to ask him if he knew of anyone.

Frank, it seems, thought that the post would suit him, and he told his father that he was sure it would be a good thing for him, as he would get a lot of business experience which would one day be useful to him, and he couldn't do any harm in trying it for a year, as the salary was a very liberal one.

Mr Tressider was a little astonished, because Frank had always railed so against business, but after enquiring in the City as to the status of the Paris firm and finding it to be a house of high standing, he consented to the new departure, being rather relieved in his mind, I think, at the idea of Frank beginning to do something for his own living.

The moment the matter was arranged, Frank became quite jubilant. I never saw such a sudden change in a lad. He was quite eager to be off, and a week after his father had given his consent he had shaken the dust of Lincoln's Inn Fields from his feet, and, with his trunks filled with new suits, had taken his departure for Paris.

We received a long letter from him very soon afterwards, in which he said that he was very happy, and that he liked his post immensely, and he thought he should do well and learn a business, which might be a great thing for him later on.

I shook my head over the letter, because I knew Frank by this time, and had often tried to make him see the truth of the old proverb: "Unstable as water thou shalt not excel."*

I quite expected that after the first novelty of the change had worn off Frank would begin to grumble again, and that his letters would be a little less high-spirited.

But I was mistaken. The months went on, and Frank continued to write in the same strain, and I began to congratulate myself on having discovered Frank's antipathy to the law, and having been the means of giving him a chance to embrace a commercial career.

Poor, silly mother that I was. I little knew the truth. Afterwards, when I found it out, I quite understood Master Frank's hatred of Lincoln's Inn and his eagerness to get to Paris.

That girl and her mother were there!

Mrs Helston, having wandered about Germany for a year, and undergone a course of treatment for her imaginary ailments, had decided to spend six months in Paris, and Frank had been duly apprised of the fact by the young lady.

Of course he was happy, and of course he was contented – for a time. But it wasn't the secretaryship he was in love with. It was Laura Helston. He hadn't gone to Paris to make his fortune, but to be near his sweetheart – it was my using my influence with his father to let him go to Paris that gave me the only daughter-in-law who ever caused me any really serious annoyance.

I do not think when you hear the way in which she treated me that you will think I was in any way to blame for what happened.

It is, perhaps, just as well Mrs Frank Tressider is in Australia now.

It enables me to speak my mind concerning her with greater freedom than I could have done had she been within visiting distance.

Memoir XV

Mrs Frank's Mother

FRANK TRESSIDER AND HIS WIFE are in Australia now. I told you that they were before I said very much about them. If they had still been in England, I should not have been able to speak my mind so plainly as the love of truth – which has always been one of my distinguishing characteristics – requires that I should.

I do not wish to speak unkindly of my son Frank. Many a time my mother's heart has gone out to him, and many a time my eyes have filled with tears at Christmas time when I looked around the table and saw the break which his absence makes in our little family circle. Perhaps little family circle is hardly the word for it. It is rather a large family circle now that the children have begun to grow up to a dining age, and we have some difficulty with the chairs; and one of my servants actually left me on account of the plates, saying that there was too much washing up and she didn't engage for a hotel, but a private family.

Really, servants are most trying, and are rapidly becoming the mistresses in some families; not in mine, because I would rather beg my bread from door to door than be dictated to as to what I am to do in my own house.

I am sure the questions that some girls put to you when they come about a situation would never have been allowed even at the Inquisition. You can imagine my feelings at being asked by a young woman in a fashionable hat one day if I kept much company. I looked at the girl for a moment, and then I said, quietly, "Oh, no, none at all. The master blacks his own boots, and we have an invalid chair to carry the housemaid up- and downstairs in. Good morning."

The girl turned red, and got up and said, "My fare, please."

I said, "Your what?"

"My fare. You promised me my fare one way if I came to see you."

"Yes, I did, but I did it under the impression that you were a servant looking for a place. You are evidently a young lady, and have made a mistake in coming here."

"You'll have to give me my fare, ma'am. I live at Islington, and you can't expect me to be out of pocket."

"Oh, certainly not," I said. "If you will be good enough to go downstairs and sit in the drawing room you will find an album there with the portraits of all my family in it. You can amuse yourself with that while I order the carriage to come round for you."

"I don't want your carriage," said the girl. "I want my fare."

"You will have the carriage or nothing," I said. "You don't get any money out of me."

"I'll county-court you for this, see if I don't," she said.

"If you do, you'll lose. I am quite ready to send you home in the carriage, and that is all you can expect. The money I promised was for your 'bus; if you have my carriage, you can't claim for a 'bus. Please yourself."

The girl saw she had her match, so she gave me a spiteful look, said I was no lady, flounced out of the room and went out of the front door, banging it after her violently.

But I must not begin writing my experiences of servants, or my pen will run away with me. It is not as a mother, but as a mother-in-law that I am endeavouring to do my duty by society in these pages.

Talking of pages, we had one once – but only one. It was Mr Tressider's idea. He thought it would look well to have a page to open the door, and the boy would be able to do all the boots and knives instead of our having the coachman in to do them, because the coachman was always grumbling, and, of course, man-like, Mr Tressider always took the coachman's part.

I was willing for one thing, and that was it would keep the coachman out of the house. I don't care for coachmen and grooms coming into the house too much. They get chattering with the female servants, and that is how half the gossip is carried about the neighbourhood.

Some day if I can find time I will write the history of a neighbourhood as servants tell it. I think it would very much astonish the neighbourhood. I know what is said, and the extraordinary tales that go about, through my maid, who has been with me many years, and amuses me sometimes by telling me the stories she hears in the kitchen and the servants' hall at the boarding house in the country where I occasionally stay for the benefit of my health, which unfortunately of late years has necessitated my being away from home a great deal, especially in the winter, which as one grows older gets more and more unendurable in London. In fact, it is hard to say what portion of the year *is* endurable in London nowadays, for the seasons are all alike.

We tried that page. He was a very nice-looking boy, but, oh, dear me, never were appearances more deceitful.

Although he was only seventeen, he conceived a wild attachment for the cook, who was thirty-six if she was a day, although she always declared she was only twenty-eight. Cook was cold to him, having a private in the Guards* who was going to marry her as soon as she had saved up enough money to make a home, and of course, at the same time, disliking to allow herself to be made ridiculous by walking out with a bit of a boy like that.

It was some time before I found out what was the matter, because my stupid housemaid sympathized with the boy, being of a romantic turn of mind herself, and given to fiction of the penny-novelette order, and so did the parlourmaid, because she hated the cook through a little misunderstanding about an umbrella, cook having borrowed hers one Sunday without her leave, and left it in an omnibus, and through that the poor girl went out to meet her young man one Sunday with a new hat with ostrich feathers in it and no umbrella, and the rain coming on, the feathers came to dreadful grief and hung down and dripped all the bright-blue colour down her face, which made her look such an object that when the young man met her he burst out laughing, and the match was broken off in consequence. The parlourmaid was in a great state about it for a long time, and would frequently reproach the cook with having taken her umbrella and broken her heart.

This was the position of affairs when James (his name was Alphonso, but we could not possibly call him that) began to behave in a very extraordinary way, owing to his addresses being rejected by the cook.

I noticed after James had been with us about six weeks that he seemed to be very absent-minded and strange in his manner, but I never suspected the truth. He would wait at table sometimes and hand you the potatoes, and when you had taken one still stick at your elbow staring into vacancy and holding the vegetable dish towards you.

And when he was not handing anything round he would stand behind my chair and sigh in such an unearthly manner that once or twice I turned round quite startled, feeling as if a ghost were behind me.

One day I was seriously alarmed by the housemaid rushing upstairs and saying: "Oh, ma'am, do come, ma'am. Please, ma'am, James is rolling about on the kitchen floor in the dreadfullest agony, and I'm afraid he is going to die."

I went downstairs at once, thinking the boy was ill, and there he lay on the hearthrug in front of the kitchen fire groaning and pressing his hand to his stomach.

"What is it? What's the matter?" I said, thinking perhaps he had been eating something that had disagreed with him.

But he didn't answer, and then the housemaid began to cry, and said, "I think you'd better ask cook, ma'am."

I looked round, but cook wasn't there. So I said, "Where is she? What does she know about it?" and the housemaid said, "She's locked herself in the larder, ma'am."

I began to think they were all mad, so I went to the larder, and finding the door locked, I rattled it and said: "Cook, are you there? Whatever is the meaning of this nonsense?"

Cook only groaned, and said: "Don't say he's dead; oh, don't say he's dead."

"Dead? Fiddlesticks!" I said. "I can't think what's the matter with you all. Come out at once."

She came out wiping her eyes with her apron and trembling, and I said: "Now, what's the meaning of all this?" but before she could answer, James had got up off the hearthrug, and he came and said: "I'm better now, ma'am; I think it was some tinned lobster that I had for breakfast, some I bought with my own money."

"Yes, ma'am," said cook, "I expect that's what it was, but, oh, dear, he looked so awful I thought he was going to die, and I never could abear to see anybody die, not even a kitten, let alone a human being, ma'am."

I wasn't altogether satisfied with the explanation, but I knew that cheap tinned lobster does occasionally make people feel as if they had been poisoned, so I told the boy he had better go to a chemist's and get something, and if he didn't feel better he could go and lie down.

After that I didn't hear anything more, and I had almost forgotten the circumstance when one day the cook herself came rushing up to me, wringing her hands, and exclaiming: "Oh, ma'am, James has gone and locked himself in the boot cupboard with a rope, and he's left a note on the kitchen table to say he's hanging himself to the hook in the ceiling, and he isn't to be cut down till he's quite dead."

"Good gracious!" I exclaimed. "Whatever does all this mean? I must get to the bottom of it."

Off I went downstairs as fast as I could, and there I found the parlourmaid and the housemaid kneeling down outside the boot-cupboard door, which was locked from the inside, and sobbing and calling through the keyhole to James not to hang himself, but to think of his mother!

I pulled them aside and banged at the door.

"James, are you there?" I said. All the answer I got was a groan, so I said to one of the girls, "Go and get a policeman."

That must have frightened my lord, for presently he opened the door, and there he stood in the middle of the little room with a cord fastened to a hook in the ceiling and a noose at the end of it and a chair underneath it.

I ran in and seized him by the shoulders and shook him.

"Now then," I said, "what is the meaning of this business?"

He didn't answer. He only looked at me in a stupid sort of way and gurgled.

"Please, ma'am," said the parlourmaid, "it's all cook's fault. She encouraged the poor boy and then broke his heart."

"Oh, you owdacious hussy," screamed cook. "How dare you say I encouraged him? James, tell the truth. Did I ever encourage you?"

"No, Maud," said the boy, "you never did. If you had things might have been different."

"You stupid boy," I said. "Do you mean to say that you were going to hang yourself over cook?"

"Yes, ma'am, I was, but I humbly beg your pardon for thinking of doing it in your house. If you'll look over it I'll leave now, ma'am, and go and do it somewhere else."

I said that it wasn't likely I was going to let him leave my house with the deliberate intention of committing suicide, and that it was my duty to send at once for a policeman and to give him into custody.

The cook and the housemaid and the parlourmaid all began to sob and cry at that, and begged me not to ruin his young life, which of course I had no intention of doing; so I said if he would give me his solemn promise not to get up to any of his ridiculous tricks again, I would send for his mother and let her take him home, instead of a policeman taking him before the magistrate.

He agreed to that, so I told him to go and sit on a chair in the hall, where I could see what he was about, and I sent the housemaid off with a note to his mother.

While he was sitting in the hall, I kept him pretty well under my eye, but I was glad when his mother came, because it was very inconvenient my having to keep getting up and going out of my little room, and peering over the banisters to see if James was attempting to commit suicide in any way again.

When his mother came, I had her up to my room and told her what had happened, and the poor woman cried, and said she was very sorry but she was afraid Alphonso wasn't quite right in his head, his father having been in a lunatic asylum some years, and one of his brothers being now at Earlswood.*

I was very sorry for the poor woman, but naturally very indignant at such a family history having been kept back from me when I engaged the boy, and I couldn't help speaking my mind plainly on the subject, telling the poor woman that if she allowed her boy to go out to service again with insanity in his blood, as there undoubtedly must be, she might find herself charged with murder through being an accessory before the fact, or whatever the Old Bailey name for that sort of thing is.

She promised she would keep the boy at home for a time and look after him, and so I gave her a month's wages which were due, and I was very glad to see the back of Master James, our first and last page, I can assure you.

"No more male servants living in the house for me," I said to John Tressider that evening, "and if Spink" (that was the coachman) "doesn't care to clean the boots, we'll put them outside the front door at night when we go to bed, and get a bootblack to do them the first thing in the morning."

But it didn't have to come to that, for Spink expressed his willingness to do them again, saying he was willing to do "anything to oblige the missis".

Yes, I daresay there was a lot of obliging the missis about Spink. I have no doubt if the truth were known Mr Tressider raised his wages on the quiet and got him to do the boots so that I shouldn't say again that he was afraid of his own coachman. My experience may be unusual, but I have generally found that men know nothing about the management of servants, and that a clever man can twist his master round his little finger. It would take a clever female servant to twist me.

But my reminiscences of servants have led me a long way from my son Frank and his wife. I told you in my last memoir how he threw up the law and went to Paris to be secretary to the head of a firm there, and how he wrote home and said that he was quite happy and the place suited him. Laura Helston and her mother were in Paris. That, as you have doubtless guessed, was at the bottom of everything.

While he was there, Frank became engaged to Miss Helston, with her mother's consent, but said nothing about it until he came home for a fortnight's holiday, and then he coolly informed us that he was going to be married in Paris, and invited me and his father to the wedding.

Of course, I asked for a little further explanation and when I found the young lady had spent her life in boarding houses with her mother, I said: "Well, I don't think much of that as a training for a wife, Frank. What can she know of household management?"

"Oh, Mother," he said proudly, "I don't want my wife to cook or mend linen, or that sort of thing. I'm not going to marry a domestic servant, but a lady."

Well, he married his lady, and, as I expected, she got tired of Paris, or her mother did, and the next thing we heard was that Frank was coming back to London, having been offered the London agency of the Paris firm, and that Mrs Helston was coming with them.

He wrote to his brother William and asked him to get him a furnished house at a moderate rent, and William got them really a pretty place near Westbourne Park, and I myself took a great deal of trouble in going over the place, and seeing to many things, such as the plate and linen, and at Frank's own request I went to a registry office and engaged a cook and a housemaid for them, and sent them up to the place after getting an excellent character with them, so that they might have everything in readiness when Frank and his wife and mother-in-law arrived.

I was a little bit anxious about the mother-in-law living in the same house with them. When a wife's mother lives with her and her husband there is generally trouble.

I thought I would not seem to interfere in any way, so I didn't go to the house on the day they arrived from Paris, but made a formal call on my new daughter-in-law and her mother the next day.

My first impression was not favourable. Mrs Frank Tressider was a very stylish and a very good-looking young woman, but her mother was a very shallow and a very arrogant person indeed. I haven't patience with humbug. I daresay the word may appear strong for one mother-in-law to apply to another, but if ever there was a humbug it was Mrs Helston.

The woman was one mass of artificiality and sham and pretence, and we very soon agreed to differ. I hadn't patience with her affectation and her grand airs, and I soon let her see that she wasn't going to come the lady over me. Scratch the Russian, they say, and you'll find the Tartar. I am not a Russian but it doesn't take much scratching to find the Tartar in me. Directly Mrs Helston put on her fine airs and began to talk as if she were quite a distinguished member of society, and to find fault with the house William had taken, and to say she detested English servants, they were so common and to use a lot of French words, I spoke my mind pretty plainly. I told her that I didn't talk French, not having kept it up since I left school, and I should prefer our conversation to be carried on in English and I said no doubt she felt it strange to have a whole house to live in after having had only a bedroom in a boarding house, and I was sure I could quite understand her not liking our English servants after being accustomed to the sort of foreign servants one finds in cheap foreign pensions.

I had not the slightest desire to be rude, but I could not sit down and let my son's mother-in-law ride roughshod over me as if she had been guilty of an act of great condescension in allowing her daughter to marry my son.* Really, if Miss Helston had been a great heiress, or the last scioness (is it scioness in the female?) of a noble house, that woman could not have given herself greater airs.

I might, perhaps, have been a little more patient under the infliction then, but when I knew that she had not given her daughter a penny (having, no doubt, no more than she could do with herself), and that the late Mr Helston, though he occupied at one time a very good position, came to London as an office boy, and very likely didn't even know his grandfather's name, it was a little more than flesh and blood could stand.

I went to that house, I assure you, with the full intention of making myself as agreeable as I possibly could, and I can be very agreeable when I like; though some of my children may not think so, other people have not failed to notice the wonderful control I frequently exercise over a sorely tried temper, and I had not been in the house five minutes before that woman ruffled my feathers very considerably the wrong way. My own impression is that she did it on purpose. She felt that if it was to be war between us, she had a foewoman worthy of her steel, and she probably had her own reasons for not wishing me to see more of Frank's domestic interior than she could possibly help. She had the poor boy completely at her mercy, and she was mistress in that house. There is no doubt about it, she was afraid of me. She trembled for her influence over my boy. She could hoodwink and deceive him, but she couldn't hoodwink and deceive me.

As Frank's wife was in the room during our conversation, I said as little as possible, but what I did say was to the point, and, though it wasn't interlarded with a lot of French words, I flatter myself that my lady understood it.

I was glad when the time came for me to go, but when I thought it all over on my way home I felt very low-spirited, for I could not help thinking it was not a happy married life for my son. The girl was under the complete control of her mother, and the mother was evidently going to be the mistress of my son's house. When Frank came to see me, I didn't say very much, not wishing to hurt his feelings or to make mischief, but I couldn't help saying: "My dear boy, I shouldn't have Mrs Helston as part of my family more than I could help. The Marriage Service says that a woman shall leave all other and cleave unto her husband. It doesn't say she shall take her mother with her."

Frank laughed, and said: "Oh, Mrs Helston's all right. She has queer notions about some things, through having lived so long abroad, but I can't very well turn her out. You see, she's such an invalid."

"An invalid!" I thought to myself. "Yes, I could be an invalid like that if I wanted to. It's a fine thing to be waited on hand and foot, and always to have your own way, because you've persuaded yourself and everybody else that you're in delicate health."

I am quite sure that when I and Frank's wife fell out it was entirely owing to her mother's influence, but of that I shall have to tell you in another memoir.

Memoir XVI

Frank and Laura

B EING A WOMAN who has not gone through the world with her eyes shut, I have long ago come to the conclusion that the best wives do not always get the best husbands, and vice versa. There are, of course, many English homes in which the ideal of married life is attained – where husband and wife really are one, and the children grow up honouring and respecting, as well as loving their parents. To enter such a home is indeed a privilege. There one sees family life, as we understand it in this country, at its very best. Such ideal homes as these occur occasionally in all classes, but perhaps more frequently among the middle classes than among the upper or lower classes.

I am the last person in the world to dwell with too much emphasis on the unhappiness of married life, though it is useless to deny that there is a great deal of it about, and I fancy nowadays it is on the increase. It is not reasonable to expect that all marriages shall turn out happy ones – certainly not now that young men and women rush into matrimony without sufficient means on the one side and sufficient domestic experience on the other.

In my youthful days a young fellow never expected to marry until he had made something like a position for himself. Now the young men marry first and expect to make the position afterwards.

It is very much the same with the young women. In the old days a girl was carefully trained in the art of domestic management, and was able to manage a household before she had one of her own. Now she waits till she has a household of her own before she attempts to learn how to manage it.

It is a very beautiful theory that adversity brings people closer together, and that troubles only increase the strength of family ties, but it doesn't always work out in practice. Many a young couple who would have gone on loving each other to the end of their days become estranged through the troubles and difficulties which crop up early in their married career, troubles and difficulties which are entirely due to their own folly in getting married before they were fitted to undertake the responsibilities of married life.

I sometimes come upon a church where there is a wedding going on, and although I do not mix myself up with the grinning crowd outside, I usually wait if I can and see the bride and bridegroom come out. At the poorer class of weddings the rice is thrown as the young couple leave the church, generally in a four-wheel cab, and I like to see the happy smile upon the young fellow's face and the loving look in the young girl's eyes as she takes her husband's arm for the first time. The expression of their faces generally alters under the shower of rice, which is not the nicest thing in the world to have thrown in your eyes, and they make rather an undignified bolt for the cab, and put up the window as quickly as they can.

But I forget all the fun, all the horseplay, and all the sentiment which accompany these poor little weddings, and I say to myself, "I wonder if these two young people have the slightest thought of the serious step they have just taken. I wonder if they know that they have the making or the marring of each other's lives in their hands." It is to me always a very solemn thought. Young people can make each other's lives a blessing or a curse. They have crossed the river and burnt their boats today. What are they going to do on the other side? Make it for each other happiness or misery?

My son Frank and Laura Helston meant, I have not the slightest doubt, to make each other thoroughly happy when they married. They were as romantic when they stood side by side at the altar as they were when they plighted their troth on the banks of the beautiful Rhine.

But they were both getting married under what I call false pretences. Frank had no settled position, and Laura no domestic experience. They were ships putting to sea without any provision for stormy weather. They were fair-weather sailors on the ocean of matrimony, who would be quite out of their element if it began to blow a gale. Unfortunately, it is generally the ship which is least fitted to encounter heavy weather which is steered with the least amount of caution. It is your inexpert swimmer who is most reckless in getting beyond his depth.

I am dwelling perhaps rather too seriously on this phase of the great marriage question, but, you see, it has come home to me very severely indeed. My son Frank's whole career was shipwrecked by his injudicious marriage, and though his wife never put herself out of the way to be agreeable to me, I confess she might have done very much better had she married a man of more solid character. They were the last people in the world who ought to have come together, and so they came.

They got married on Frank's income, which was £400 a year, and they took a furnished house and brought an extravagant, selfish woman to live with them who installed herself as mistress of the home at once, and, instead of trying to make it a happy one, did all in her power to foster discontent all round.

I have told you of my first interview with Mrs Helston, and you may be sure that, after I found out what she was, I did not go out of my way to seek another.

I didn't mind the woman trying to impress me with a sense of the intense superiority of the Helstons to the Tressiders – I could afford to laugh at that – but I was rather annoyed to find by a few hints which she threw out that Frank had deceived her with regard to his prospects. I am pretty quick at putting two and two together, and it was clear to me that Mrs Helston, in allowing Frank to marry her daughter, had built upon my husband doing a good deal more for his son than it was reasonable he should do, remembering what a large family he had to provide for.

Frank had had his chances and neglected them. He might have been in the business had he chosen, but he didn't choose. He might have been a solicitor or a barrister, but he wouldn't take the trouble to qualify for either. He had chosen his own line, and I thought myself he was very lucky to be getting £400 a year. It wasn't reasonable to expect Mr Tressider to make him a big allowance, or to give him a large sum of money to enable him to launch out into a style of living which he would be unable to keep up by his own exertions.

Mrs Helston evidently didn't mean to sacrifice any portion of her income for her daughter's benefit. In fact she told me as much. But, instead of setting the young people a good example and instilling principles of economy into them, she was constantly urging Frank to launch out beyond his means, and telling her daughter that she had thrown herself away on a "clerk".

There is no doubt that Mrs Helston was very much disappointed in her daughter's marriage. It would have suited my lady if Laura had married a rich man with a good position in society. It would have enabled her to "cut a dash", as the common saying is, and there was nothing that suited Mrs Helston so well as cutting a dash at other people's expense.

It was not long before the evil influences of Mrs Helston began to tell on Frank, and one evening he came round to see his father, and told him pretty plainly that he wanted money. Unfortunately he didn't put it in a nice way. He tried to make out that he had been very badly used, and that his father ought on his marriage to have given him a big allowance in order to enable him to keep up a decent establishment.

My husband told me afterwards what had occurred at the interview, and I said it was all nonsense. When we married we began very quietly, and we didn't try to run before we could walk. Frank already had £200 a year from his father for doing nothing, and that with the £400 he earned ought to be enough for him, but I suggested to my husband that the most sensible thing to do would be for him to give Frank his furniture if he took a small house of his own. That would be giving him a fair start in housekeeping, and would save him the expense of living in a furnished place, which always comes very expensive.

Mr Tressider was quite agreeable to this, and so he went to Frank and told him what he could do, but he pointed out it would not be fair for him to give Frank a larger yearly allowance without he did the same for the others, and he couldn't afford that. Frank jumped at the offer, and he and Laura and Mrs Helston started house-hunting at once.

But from what I heard afterwards the person who had to be pleased was Mrs Helston. She objected to this place and she objected to that, and at last selected a pokey little bit of a house which hadn't a single convenience, and was as dark as a cupboard, because it was in what she called an aristocratic neighbourhood. When Frank's wife called on me and told me what they thought of taking, I spoke my mind pretty plainly, and pointed out there were plenty of nice, roomy houses with nice gardens to be had at half the rent they were going to pay, if they went to look for them in a cheaper neighbourhood – such as Camberwell or Islington, or Camden Road or Holloway.

"Oh, dear me," said Laura. "The idea of our living at Camberwell or Holloway; Mamma would not hear of it for a moment."

"Really," I said, "I didn't know that my husband was going to furnish a house for your mamma."

"Oh," she said, bridling up, "you are always throwing my mamma in my face."

"Nothing of the sort," I said. "I am the last person in the world to throw anything in the face of my son's wife. Certainly not her own mother. But I repeat, that where your mamma wants to live is a matter which only concerns herself. Frank is looking for a house for himself and you."

"Very well," she said, "then under the circumstances I can't see why you should want to interfere. You are not going to live in it."

The speech was not quite so rude as that, but that is what it amounted to, and so I contented myself with shrugging my shoulders and saying that, for the future, I would take care and not express my opinion at all, but naturally, as a mother, I didn't like seeing my boy going headlong to ruin.

I don't know how our interview might have ended, but fortunately Sabina came in with the two little Walkinshaws, so the subject was dropped, and very soon afterwards Laura left.

They took the house in spite of me, and I was never so much as consulted once about furnishing it, though my taste, I have been told by many good judges, is excellent.

Mrs Helston, if you please, took the entire control of the decoration and furnishing upon herself, and a nice gimcrack, theatrical-looking affair she made of it. Everything for show and nothing for comfort. There was not the slightest attempt at interference on her part when the bills came in. She allowed them to be forwarded to my husband without even taking the trouble to check the items or look over the charges.

The bills came to a good deal more than Mr Tressider had bargained for, but he had said that he would pay them, so he thought he might as well do it with a good grace; but he agreed with me that there was a good deal too much "mother-in-law" about Frank's domestic arrangements.

Soon after they were in the house and settled down, we received an invitation to dine with them. I didn't want to go, but I felt it was my duty. I knew that some of Mrs Helston's friends would be there, and I said to my husband, "We had better go – if we don't, people will imagine perhaps that we are not good enough for her grand acquaintances to meet. There is no knowing what that woman would say to account for our absence."

We went and I was absolutely horrified. The dinner was magnificent, but the extravagance was alarming. I was quite sure that nothing had been done at home, and my husband told me that the wines were all of the choicest vintages. Everything had, as usual, been left to Mrs Helston, and a pretty penny it must have cost Frank. It was an absurd dinner for a young man in his position to give. It was the sort of dinner, as my husband said as we drove home that evening, which could only be paid for in the bankruptcy court – a shilling in the pound.

Laura had a dress on which might have done very well for a duchess or the wife of a City Croesus,* and she had the impudence to tell me that it had been made in Paris, and that she intended to have all her "frocks" made there.

I held up my hands in horror and said, "My dear, you have surely made a mistake about your husband's income. It is £600 a year – not £600 a week."

She only laughed and said, "Nonsense; Frank is a good deal better off than you think. We shall astonish you by and by."

They did astonish me, for soon afterwards she came to call on me in a brougham. I happened to be looking out of the window, and saw it stop at my door, and I wondered who it could be. The horse was a beautiful creature, a high stepper, and the coachman was in a smart livery and had a cockade on his hat.

When Laura stepped out of that brougham dressed like a duchess, you might have knocked me down with a feather.

I couldn't of course imagine that it was her brougham, so I said to her: "Whoever lent you that beautiful carriage?"

"No one," she said, with something that looked very like a sneer on her lips. "It is my own; Frank gave it me for my birthday."

"He must be going mad!" I exclaimed. "How on earth is he to pay for it or keep it up with his income?"

"Oh," she said, "he is making money very fast now. He made £2,000 last week."

That sent me into a cold perspiration. I guessed at once that he was betting, or gambling on the Stock Exchange, and I knew how that always ends.

But Laura commenced to explain. Frank, it seems, had gone into partnership with a friend of Mrs Helston, who was something in the City, and they had started as company promoters.

I didn't quite understand what a company promoter was, but I felt very unhappy about it, for I couldn't think that a young man like Frank could make £2,000 in a week if everything was all right.

Directly my husband came home I told him all about it, and he was as astonished as I was. He didn't even know that Frank had given up his situation, and he shook his head gravely over the company promoting, and said he should make enquiries about it in the City the next day.

He did, and found out that Frank had joined a Mr Smith, a gentleman with anything but a first-class reputation in the City, and that the firm was Smith & Co., Frank being the Co., and that they were engaged in bringing out public companies: gold mines, and trifles of that sort.

I said to my husband: "Is it all right?" and he looked as if it wasn't, but he told me that the only company that they had floated up to now had gone off well, but he didn't care about

Smith altogether, and he should have to see Frank and give him a word of warning.

I could see that Mr Tressider was rather worried about it. He told me that company promoting was all right, as long as the company promoted was a genuine affair, but that a good many companies were brought out which were little better than swindles, and he was afraid Frank might get mixed up with something that wouldn't be altogether creditable.

My husband went to the offices of Smith & Co. next day, and found Frank in a luxuriously furnished apartment, smoking a big cigar and talking to a gentleman who was a mass of fur-lined overcoat, and positively glistened with diamond rings. That was Smith.

Frank introduced his father, and they had a little conversation, and Frank went out to lunch with his father.

He was quite cock-a-hoop, and when his father asked him why he had taken such a step as this without consulting him, and had, in fact, kept the whole thing a secret from the family, Frank said he didn't want to say anything till he had seen how things turned out, but now, as he was on the high road to fortune, he didn't mind everybody knowing it.

Then he quite took his father's breath away by the easy-going manner in which he talked of millions of pounds and the schemes that he and Smith had in hand. Mr Tressider said that to hear him talk you would have thought that all the gold and diamonds in the world were modestly waiting round the corner until Frank chose to introduce them to the British public.

As soon as my husband could get a word in, he asked Frank if he had any knowledge himself of the value of these wonderful mines and properties.

"No," he said, "but Smith has, and we are in with some of the sharpest men in London."

"Well, my boy," said his father, "take care they are not too sharp for you. I tell you candidly I don't care for the business you are mixed up in. You have no experience and no commercial status, and I can't think if these things are so good that you would be taken into them by a man like Smith."

"Oh, Smith's a rattling good fellow," said Frank. "He introduces me to all his friends and clients as the son of Mr Tressider, the well-known City merchant, and he says that if I can induce you to be a director of some of our companies he will be very happy to give you the chance. We've got some grand things coming on, governor, and if you've got a few thousand to spare you can make a pot of money. I made two thousand last week, you know, in one coup. I tell you what, governor, you've got a lot of City friends; if you can get them to be directors to one or two things we are bringing out, you'll be doing me a good turn."

Mr Tressider asked what the companies were, and Frank showed him the prospectuses of some. There was a company for building a Winter Palace and Eiffel Tower in the Sandwich Islands,* a company for acquiring a gold mine in Madagascar, a company for erecting permanent Punch and Judy shows at the corners of the principal streets of the United Kingdom, and a company for utilizing the street fire alarms as automatic machines for delivering ham and beef sandwiches by putting a penny in the slot.

I don't understand much about City matters, so I cannot remember or explain all that Mr Tressider told me, and I may have got some of these companies wrong, but I know that he came home with a very long face and said that he was afraid it would end badly.

It didn't begin badly, for Frank drove up one afternoon to call on me with a phaeton and pair, and Laura came to our ball really quite a diamond show, and they took a house in one of the best squares, and entertained on quite a magnificent scale.

I used sometimes to rub my eyes, and ask myself if I was dreaming, or if this young fellow who was living at the rate of twenty thousand a year could be my son Frank.

But Mr Tressider never cared to talk about it, and after a time he avoided the subject altogether, and I could see that he had something on his mind. I know that on several occasions he went to Frank, and tried to induce him to sober down and get out of the business he was in, but it was all to no good, and at last the crash came.

I don't want to dwell on it, because it was very painful to all of us. There were long articles in the newspapers about bubble companies, and one day I learnt that Smith & Co. were bankrupt, and that Frank had not only lost every shilling he had in the world, but had been made liable for more money than he could ever hope to pay.

I know that he would never have made such mad haste to get wealth but for the ambition of his mother-in-law and the selfish extravagance of his wife. He was more sinned against than sinning. He was the dupe of Smith, who was glad to have the son of a well-known and respected London merchant associated with him when he started again, after a year or two of enforced retirement from the City.

Every shilling of Frank's legal liability was discharged. Mr Tressider declared that for the honour of his own name that would have to be done, even if he impoverished himself. Fortunately the amount my husband had to make up was not very great, as the shares held by Frank in companies which had turned out well when sold, together with the realization of all his property and his wife's diamonds, nearly covered the amount for which he could be made legally responsible. When his estate was wound up he was absolutely penniless, and in debt to his father some thousands of pounds, but he escaped the taint of bankruptcy.

Mrs Helston, when the crash came, found that the state of her health demanded her immediate presence at Carlsbad,* where she was ordered to take a course of waters, but Laura, for the first time since I had known her – as my youngest son Tommy would say – turned up trumps. Her husband told her that he would have to begin life again, and begin it as far away from everyone who knew of his past career as possible. He had been offered a good berth in Australia, and he intended to take it. She put off all her fine airs at once, and told him that she would go with him and do all in her power to help him to retrieve the past.

And I believe she has honestly kept her word, for Frank always speaks of her in his letters in the most affectionate terms.

Frank and his wife are in Australia now, but I hope at no distant day to have them both back among us – and this time without Frank's mother-in-law.

Memoir XVII

The Peacock's Feathers

T HERE ARE A GREAT MANY PEOPLE who laugh at what they call "old women's superstitions"; such as sitting down thirteen to dinner, walking under a ladder, seeing the new moon through glass, opening an umbrella in the house and peacock's feathers. I am not particularly superstitious myself, but there are two things which I would not do, and which nothing would ever persuade me to do, and that is to sit down thirteen, or to have a peacock's feather in the house.

One day we were talking about superstitions, at a family birthday dinner party, and we nearly all agreed about the thirteen being the sort of thing that none of us would care to risk (the subject came up through our narrowly escaping being thirteen, one of the party not arriving till the very last moment, when everybody had given him up), but we were by no means agreed about peacock's feathers.

Marion, my second son William's wife, who paints very well and is certainly artistic in her ideas and makes her rooms look charming, and at a very small outlay, would not agree that there was any harm in peacock's feathers, and William, like a dutiful husband (it is a pity there are not more husbands with a similar weakness), supported her arguments.

"It is absurd to pretend that peacock's feathers are unlucky," said Marion. "If they were, they would not be used so much for decorative purposes. At any rate, I am going to have them in my house, for I have seen a lovely pair of peacock's-feather fans that a friend of mine has had sent her to sell for a clergyman's widow she knows in the country, and I am going to buy them and put them over my drawing-room mantelshelf."

We all shook our heads and said that bad luck would very likely come of it, and John, my eldest son, told a terrible tale about a gentleman who picked up a peacock's feather in the street and brought it home, and the next day slipped over a dustpan the housemaid had left on the stairs and broke his leg.

"Yes," said William, "but that only proves that it is unlucky to leave dustpans on the stairs, and there I agree with you."

"Ah, but that wasn't all that happened," John went on. "That very same afternoon the wife of the man with the broken leg was curling her front hair with the curling tongs, when the nurse in the next room, who had the baby in her arms, sat down on a chair without noticing that the cat was asleep in it, and when the cat yelled she was so frightened that she jumped and shrieked, and that caused the lady to turn round suddenly, being horrified, and she put the tongs right against her cheek and burned it, which was a dreadful disfigurement. What do you say to that?"

William shrugged his shoulders. "Only that women who value their hair oughtn't to curl it with hot irons, they burn the life out of the hair, and that nurses should look before they sit down. The accident was due to the tongs and the cat, not to the peacock's feather. Did anything else happen?"

"Oh, yes; that same evening the housemaid smelt the gas very strongly as she was going upstairs with her taper, and thinking it might be in the little back drawing room, opened the door and went in, and there was a dreadful explosion; the window was blown out and bits of the ceiling came down, and the ornaments on the mantelshelf were shivered, and only one thing was left untouched upon it!"

"And that was?"

"The peacock's feather, which the lady had put there when her husband gave it to her. Now, what do you say?"

"That the housemaid must have been a very careless girl not to turn the gas off in the drawing room the night before when it was turned off at the meter. That piece of bad luck was due to the housemaid, not to the peacock's feather."

"Of course, you can argue that way about everything," I said, "but it doesn't alter the fact that all those accidents were very bad luck, and that they happened after a peacock's feather had been brought into the house. If I were you, Marion, I would let somebody else run the risk of those fans."

Marion smiled, and said that as a matter of fact somebody else would be running the risk, for as they were staying in apartments in town (they were living in the country at this time), the peacock's feathers would be on probation at the apartments first.

By and by the conversation took a turn; nothing more was said about peacock's feathers, and I very soon forgot all about the subject.

A week afterwards I went to see Marion at the apartments she was staying in, and the first things I noticed were the peacock's-feather fans stuck up at the side of the looking glass.

"Oh, then you have bought them?" I said.

"Oh, yes," she answered. "I bought them the next day, and they have been here ever since, and nothing dreadful has happened to anybody yet. On the contrary, they have brought me a piece of good luck."

"Indeed!"

"Yes. You know the bother I have had in trying to get a good housemaid to come back with us."

I nodded my head, as William had previously told me the trouble they were in about servants. The housemaid they had had for some time, a very nice girl indeed, had left them to get married, and they found it difficult to get a really first-class girl to take her place on account of their living in a very quiet country spot, so far from the nearest station that William had to drive there every morning, and have a fly to meet him at night and take him back again. Marion didn't like the local girls because they were not smart enough for her, and the London girls all objected because it was so dull for them on their Sundays out, and all their friends would be cut off from them.

I told Marion that I had heard of her trouble, and thoroughly sympathized with her in her difficulties.

"Then you will be glad to hear that my difficulties are over," she said, "and it is entirely owing to those peacock's feathers. After I had bought them, the lady asked me if I knew of anyone who wanted a good housemaid, as the clergyman's widow who had sent her the feathers with some other things to sell had also asked her if she knew anyone who wanted a servant. She was giving up housekeeping, and was anxious to find a place for her housemaid, Mary Jones.

"I jumped at the idea at once, Mother, you may be sure," said Marion. "If the girl was a good servant, my difficulties were over. Having lived in the country, she wouldn't object to live there again, and I should be saved the trouble of looking up references and all that sort of thing, as my friend's recommendation would, of course, be sufficient.

"I asked her to write and enquire of the clergyman's widow why Mary Jones was leaving, and to make the usual enquiries, and if the answers were satisfactory I said I would engage the girl at once, and she could come to me as soon as I went back home. The enquiries were made – the answers were most satisfactory. I have evidently secured an excellent servant in Mary Jones, and I owe it to these peacock's feathers."

"I am sure I congratulate you, my dear Marion," I said, "but my experience has taught me not to believe in perfect treasures till I have found them out for myself."

Marion went back home in a few days to St Albans (their house was in rather a lonely part, about two miles and a half from the town), and Mary Jones, the new housemaid, so highly recommended by the clergyman's widow, duly arrived, and, I judged from the references to her in Marion's letters, gave every satisfaction. And the peacock's feathers were duly installed in the new house also, for in the first letter Marion wrote me after their arrival there was a little postscript at the bottom: "P.S. The peacock's-feather fans are in the place of honour in the drawing room, and we are *still* in the best of health and spirits."

About a month afterwards I went down to St Albans to stay for a few days with William and his wife, and I had an opportunity of seeing Mary Jones and judging what she was like for myself. My first impression was decidedly favourable. She was a tall, refined-looking girl with a very quiet voice and very quiet ways. She had, I thought, rather a sad look, but that is much better than the simpering expression which some servants have, and there was no doubt about her being thoroughly up to her work. Marion and William were delighted with her, and she got on very well indeed with the other servants.

"Does she grumble about the loneliness of the place?" I said.

"Oh, no; not at all. She goes to church when it is her Sunday out, and twice she has asked me for an evening on a week-day to go to St Albans. She tells me she likes the place very much, and we hope she will stay. She is the best servant we have ever had, and good servants make such a difference to one's comfort."

During the whole of my stay I never saw any reason to alter my opinion of Mary Jones, and I returned to town convinced that my daughter-in-law had every right to congratulate herself on having secured a perfect treasure, and confessing that she owed her good luck to her determination to secure those peacock's feathers.

Not very long afterwards, being with some ladies, the conversation turned on the subject of servants, and I mentioned the good fortune my daughter-in-law had had, and eventually I mentioned the girl's name.

One of the ladies seemed rather struck by it, for she asked me if she was a tall, refined-looking girl.

"Yes," I said, "she is."

"Do you know how your daughter-in-law got her?"

"Yes. She was recommended by a friend of hers, who knew her former mistress."

"Was her former mistress a Mrs Hesketh?"

"I don't know the name, but she was a clergyman's widow."

"She *is* the same Mary Jones," exclaimed the lady.

"You know her, then? I hope you know nothing against her," I said, beginning to feel slightly uneasy.

"No, poor girl, nothing at all. On the contrary, everything I have heard was in her favour, but she was connected with a terrible affair. Don't you know how the Revd Mr Hesketh met his death?"

"I know nothing about the Heskeths," I said. "I did not even know the name of the girl's former mistress. But pray tell me all about it."

"I will tell you all I can, but I don't think, if I were you, I would let your daughter-in-law know. It is evident that Mrs Hesketh said nothing because she felt it might hinder the girl from getting a situation, and some people would probably be against having a girl who had been mixed up in such an affair."

"Pray tell me about it at once," I said. "You begin to make me feel quite uncomfortable."

"The Revd Mr Hesketh," said the lady, "was an old gentleman about sixty years of age, and he was reputed to be of peculiar habits, and to have a great deal of money in the house, and also valuable old-fashioned jewellery which he had been in the habit of collecting. He had once lost money in a bank failure, and after that it was popularly supposed that he kept his money somewhere in the house, only investing it in securities when it reached a certain sum.

"He lived in a pretty, old-fashioned house in the country with his wife and two servants – an old woman who had been in his service as cook ever since he was married, and a housemaid who had been taken by him as a little girl when she left the local school to go out to service. When this girl grew up, she fell in love with a young man employed on a farm close by. He went out to America, saved money and wrote for his sweetheart to come out and marry him, and she went. The Heskeths were sorry to part with her because they liked her, and also because they disliked strange faces about them. However, they had to get another servant in her place, and in some way Mary Jones was recommended to them. Mrs Hesketh, who told me the story herself when I met her recently at Bath, where she is staying, poor old lady, for her health, told me that her references were excellent, and that during the twelve months she was in her service a more excellent or more devoted servant it would have been impossible to have.

"It was after Mary had been with her about two months that the terrible affair happened which cost the poor old gentleman his life.

"One winter night the whole household had retired rather early – about ten o'clock – and Mr Hesketh was fast asleep, when his wife called to him and shook him by the shoulder to wake him up.

"As he awoke he heard the clock in the hall strike twelve.

"'Stephen,' his wife said, 'listen; do you hear a noise downstairs?'

"'I heard the clock strike.'

"'No – hush – now, can you hear anything?'

"Mr Hesketh sat up in bed and listened. Sounds, as if someone was moving about in the house below, were distinctly audible.

"'What can it be?' exclaimed his wife. 'Oh! Stephen, do you think anyone can have broken in?'

"'Absurd – there are no burglars about, my dear. It's most likely the cat. At any rate, I'll go down and see.'

"He got up, put on his dressing gown and went out into the hall. As he did so, to his astonishment he saw Mary Jones standing on the stairs just below him, and she was nearly fully dressed.

"'Mary,' he exclaimed, 'is that you? What on earth are you walking about the house at this time of night for?'

"The girl turned a white face to her master, and held up her finger. 'Hush, sir!' she said. 'They'll hear you.'

"'Hear me – who?'

"'I heard a sound, sir, and I came down to see what it was. There are men in the house. Oh, don't go in, sir, pray don't; they'll kill you.'

"But the thought that someone had broken into his house and was robbing him of his treasures was too much for the old gentleman. He pushed by the girl and rushed down the stairs.

"But he was an old man, and feeble, and in his excitement he made a false step and fell heavily to the ground. When his wife, alarmed at his long absence, came out trembling on the staircase, she found him lying at the foot of the stairs, and poor Mary Jones bathing his forehead with cold water. The noise in the rooms had ceased. The thieves had taken what they wanted and escaped through the ground-floor windows into the garden, and got away. Mr Hesketh never recovered the shock of the fall, and died a month afterwards."

"Dear me!" I said. "What a painful thing, but the girl seems to have acted very bravely in going down, and she was quite right to try and stop her master from risking his life."

"Yes, Mrs Hesketh felt that, and when she broke up her home and sold everything off, she did what she could to get the girl another situation. It was probably to spare the poor girl being asked about the painful affair, or reminded of it, that she said nothing in her letter to your daughter of the circumstances under which Mary was leaving her. I shouldn't tell your daughter if I were you. Ladies, especially young ladies, don't care for people about them who have been associated with tragedies."

I felt that the lady was right, and so I made up my mind to say nothing about it to Marion, and I did not, but I determined to tell William all about it the first time I saw him.

He and Marion were coming to dine with us in a week, and that, I thought, would be a good opportunity to get a few words alone with him and tell him the strange story of Mary Jones.

William and his wife came to dinner, but I had no opportunity to speak to William alone, and they left early to catch the last train which would take them home.

The next afternoon, to my utter astonishment, about four o'clock William arrived with Marion, and they both looked terribly ill and worried.

"Good gracious," I said, "whatever is the matter?"

"Everything's the matter," said William. "A most dreadful thing has happened, and I want you to let Marion stay here with you for a day or two. She's too frightened to stay at our place now. When we got home last night about midnight, we rang and knocked and we could make no one hear."

"A burglary!" I exclaimed. "Don't say there has been a burglary."

Why I said that I don't know, but it came into my head suddenly, thinking of Mary Jones and her story.

William looked at me quite astonished. "Yes," he said, "there has been a burglary."

"Go on, go on," I said, "did they get much?"

"A great deal more than we care to lose. All the silver, all the wife's jewellery except the few things she had on, and about twenty pounds in gold that she had saved up and kept in a corner of a drawer, and a lot of valuable things as well. But we only found that out afterwards. What bothered us at first was why neither of the servants came to the door. 'They must have fallen asleep,' I said to Marion, so I knocked louder than ever.

"Our flyman who had brought us home had driven away, and there we were stuck outside in the dark and the wet, for it had begun to rain, and Marion began to get very frightened.

"At last I thought I would go round to the side and see if I could knock at any of the windows and make the girls hear. To my surprise I found that the shutters were not shut at the side, as they ought to have been, and a window was half open.

"'This is terribly careless,' I said to myself. 'Whatever can have happened to the servants?'

"I climbed up by holding on to the sill, got in through the window, and then I saw something was the matter. I ran into the dining room and found it all in confusion, and all the things gone from the sideboard. I opened the front door and let Marion in at once. 'Don't be frightened,' I said. 'The place has been robbed. I hope no harm has come to the girls.'

"Marion wanted to faint, but I persuaded her not to, but to help me to get a light and look about the place, which was in darkness. She stood at the top of the stairs, while I went down to the kitchen.

"'Mary,' I shouted, 'Mary, where are you?' I heard a groan.

"'Good heavens!' I thought. 'The girl has been hurt.' I listened to hear where the groan came from.

"'Where are you?' I shouted.

"'Here, master, here,' said a feeble voice, which I recognized as cook's.

"It came from the coal cellar.

"I ran to it and found it locked on the outside.

"I turned the key and poor cook came out pale and trembling.

"'Oh, sir,' she said, 'have they gone?'

"'Gone – who?'

"The burglars! Oh, sir, it was Mary Jones that let 'em in, sir. They locked me in the cellar because I began to scream, and I suppose they've stripped the place.'

"'Mary Jones let them in?' I said. 'What do you mean?'

"'I don't know, sir, but tonight, just as it was dark, three men drove up in a cart. Mary had asked me to go on an errand for her, but after I got out I thought it wasn't right to leave her alone and I came back, and I just got to the door as she was letting the men in. I saw her let one in, and I saw they knew her by the way they spoke, but they saw me and dragged me in, and because I screamed they pushed me in the coal cellar and locked me in. I heard 'em moving about the house. Oh, sir, have they took much?'

"That was the cook's narrative, my dear mother," said William, "and it turned out to be true – the place had been stripped, and Mary Jones, who must have been in league with the men, finding cook had discovered her secret, had put her box onto the cart, and gone off with them and our silver and Marion's jewellery. Whoever would have thought that girl could have been in league with burglars?"

As soon as I had heard a few more details from William, I told him the story I heard from the lady who had met Mrs Hesketh, and we all agreed that there was no doubt the nice, refined, innocent-looking girl was in league with the robbers there, and had let them in and told them previously where everything was.

"My dear," I said, "I see it all now. When the poor old gentleman saw her on the stairs, she was keeping guard for the thieves, and she tried to stop him going down, and called out to give them warning that he was coming, the wretch."

"It's very dreadful," said Marion, the tears in her eyes. "I shall never trust anybody again, and I shall be afraid to live in the country. There's no doubt Mary let the men know in some way that we should both be in town till late at night. She knew we were coming to dine with you yesterday nearly a week ago."

Marion stayed with us for a week while William was busy at St Albans with the police, endeavouring to trace the men and recover his property. The police found people who had seen the men pass in the cart late at night, and they had a woman with them, but all trace of them was lost about a mile beyond St Albans. The London police, who were communicated with, said they thought they knew the gang who had done the job, and when they heard about Mary Jones they made inquiries about the other robbery, and by that means they eventually got a clue which enabled them to lay their hands on one man, but though they convicted him of having a lot of stolen property in his possession, they never brought either of the robberies home to him. Of Mary Jones nothing more was ever heard. It is quite possible that she may be "a perfect treasure" at this moment in some quiet family in some other part of the country.

I don't often speak of the robbery to Marion (who lives in town now, William having decided to give up the country), because it is a sore point with her, but I couldn't resist one day asking her if she still had the peacock's-feather fans, which were the means of introducing her to Mary Jones.

"No, indeed," she said, "I burned them long ago. I felt as if we should never have anything but bad luck as long as they were in my possession."

Certainly there would never have been any Mary Jones in their home, and consequently no robbery, but for those peacock's feathers.

Memoir XVIII

And Last

I N LOOKING OVER THE NOTES which I have made during a series of years with the intention of some day writing my experiences as a mother-in-law, I have been compelled to discard a great deal that would have been useful to me in proving how much mothers-in-law have to put up with, and how very grossly they are maligned both on the stage and in fiction.

It is all very well to speak plainly as long as you can do it within four walls, but when it comes to speaking your mind plainly in print, there are a great many things which you have to consider. That is the great disadvantage which writers who only write the truth and don't draw upon their imaginations labour under. You can never tell the truth without offending somebody or other, and as these memoirs chiefly concern members of my own family circle, I naturally am anxious to avoid offending them.

I had no idea when I commenced these memoirs of the many difficulties which would be mine before I completed my task. I never could have imagined for a moment that people would be so thin-skinned.

I cannot say that I am surprised at Mr Tressider saying that I have held him up to ridicule and made him the laughing stock of the City, because I am not surprised at anything Mr Tressider says. But I will not attempt to deny that I was really grieved and hurt when Augustus Walkinshaw wrote me a long letter and declared that I had made his life intolerable to him, because everywhere that he went, since the commencement of the publication of these memoirs, his friends had indulged in ribald remarks at his expense, and my own daughter, Sabina, actually so far forgot herself as to allow her eyes to flash fire when she told me that she thought it was very unkind of me to try and make out that she was afraid to give her own servants notice and that she made herself a slave to her children.

These memoirs have acted like a bombshell flung into the middle of a domestic circle, and Maud's husband has gone so far as to declare that he shall write a memoir of a son-in-law, and have his revenge.

What a terrible thing it is that a little wholesome truth should be so unpalatable.

Of course, in most instances, our discussions on the subject have not gone beyond a few words, but my German son-in-law has behaved in the most ridiculous fashion, and had the temerity to talk about an action for libel. My feelings can be more easily imagined than described, when one fine morning I received a letter from him informing me that if I made any further public reference to his private affairs, or his domestic circumstances, he would, much as he should regret having to do so, place the matter in the hands of his solicitor.

I was very indignant when I received that letter, and I said that if he had anything to object to, the least he could have done would have been to have told me in a polite and friendly manner. I took the letter to my husband, and I said: "John Tressider, this is what comes of harbouring a foreigner in one's bosom."

John Tressider looked up at me and said: "I assure you, my dear, I never harboured a foreigner in my bosom in my life. What do you mean?"

"Don't be absurd," I said. "Read that letter."

He read it, and when he had finished it, I said: "What do you think of it?"

He hummed and ha'd in his usual aggravating way, and said that on the whole he couldn't say he was altogether surprised.

"I see," I said. "You are going to sit with folded arms, and allow a poor, weak woman to be trampled underfoot. If I had a husband who had an ounce of proper pride in his composition, Carl Gutzeit would never have dared to send me such a letter as this. It is an outrage on the sanctity of home. It is an attack on the deepest instincts of humanity. When one's own daughter's husband can threaten one with the law, and one's own husband takes his side, it is time that women of independent spirit asserted the rights of their downtrodden sex."

"Oh, nonsense, my dear," said Mr Tressider. "If you will come down off your stilts and look at the matter from a common-sense point of view, you will see that the best thing you can do is to acknowledge the letter, treat it as a little burst of ill temper on Carl's part, and assure him that you hadn't the slightest intention of hurting his feelings."

"What!" I exclaimed indignantly. "Do you expect me to apologize to *him*?"

"Well, you needn't exactly apologize. Smooth him down, my dear; smooth him down."

"Smooth him down, indeed," I said. "I should like to see myself doing it. No; I'll go round this very day and tell him what I think of him, and point out to him that, so far from being offended with me for what I *have* said, he ought to be grateful for what I have *not* said. I'll give him another memoir all to himself."

And I certainly should have done so, but for the fact that Jane came round to me that afternoon and told me that she was worried about her youngest boy, who at the age of five had developed the most uncontrollable temper, and thought nothing of throwing his bread and milk at the wall, spoonful by spoonful, if anything was done that didn't particularly please him, and had even gone to the length of violently hurling his toys through the open nursery window one after another because he wasn't allowed to have the cat in his bath with him.

"My dear Jane," I said, "that child takes after his father. It is the German blood in him." And then I gave vent to my feelings on the subject of Carl's letter to me.

Poor Jane was quite upset. She declared that Carl had only done it for a joke, and that he had the highest respect for me, and was constantly saying that he thought my children got all their cleverness and their domesticated habits from me, and eventually, to pacify her, I agreed to think no more of the matter. Only before she left she asked me to promise that I would not make another memoir of Carl, and I was weak enough to do so.

A few days afterwards I went to call on Sabina and see the children, not having been to see them for some time, as they lived some distance off, and when I arrived I guessed by the manner of Augustus junior that something was wrong. He gave me anything but the cordial greeting I had a right to expect from a grandchild, and he put his hands in his pockets and walked out of the room.

"Whatever is the matter with the boy?" I said.

"I'm afraid he's offended," said Sabina. "He is very sensitive, and the boys at his school have been chaffing him about his 'mamma and his telescope'. I hope, Mamma dear, you will excuse me saying it, but I do think you might have left the dear children out of your memoirs. One's own family ought to be sacred."

"Sabina," I said, getting up off the sofa and walking about the room, for I felt great difficulty in keeping myself calm, "are you attempting to teach me my duty as a mother?"

"No, Mamma, certainly not. I was only speaking as a mother myself. Of course, I know you didn't mean to hurt my children's feelings, but—"

"Say no more, Sabina. I never was appreciated by my own children, and I never shall be. I am sure I have said nothing unkind about anyone, and only that which is strictly true. And as to Augustus junior's objecting to being written about and behaving in this absurd way, it is ridiculous. Some of our greatest men and women are written about every day, and even Her Majesty the Queen has had every incident of her childhood described over and over again. Why, only the other day, in a high-class magazine, there was a long article on the Prince of Wales as a little boy, and all his childish pranks were included, and the story about the eldest son of the present Emperor of Germany, who objected to be washed, and how his papa punished him, has been printed in dozens of newspapers; so I am sure if the Prince of Wales and the Crown Prince of Germany don't object to be written about, Master Augustus Walkinshaw need not."

"My dear mother, I hope you are not going to take what I said too seriously."

"Oh, no, my dear, certainly not, but I cannot help feeling hurt that my motive should be so misinterpreted. However, as you are all so very much on your dignity, I will take care never to allude to a Walkinshaw again in my memoirs. I will even abstain from mentioning your dog Jack. He might take offence, and put up his back and growl at me the next time I call."

I was naturally a little put out by the incident, but I thought it as well not to dwell on it, and turned the conversation. But when I got home and turned to my notes I could not help feeling that I had earned very little thanks for sacrificing some of the most interesting material which I had done rather than hurt anybody's feelings. And all the thanks I received was to hear that I had made capital out of the members of my own family.

This is where the gross injustice comes in. For years past – I might say for centuries past – mothers-in-law have been held up to scorn and contempt by every little whippersnapper who can spell. They have been painted in the blackest colours, as scandalmongers, mischief-makers, fomenters of family discord, and unwelcome guests in the households of their children, and directly one of the tribe takes up her pen to defend her order, she is told that "the family" is sacred.

It is a great pity that the men who have devoted so much time – which might have been a great deal more profitably spent – to decrying the mothers of their own wives, have not practised themselves what they are so ready to preach to others.

I suppose I should be violating family confidences if I were to dwell upon the folly of young people taking houses without consulting their parents, who must have more experience in such matters. It's all very well to say that where your daughter lives or where your son lives is no concern of yours after they are married, but it is only a woman who has brought up a family who knows how important it is to go into a house with your eyes open.

I should like some day to write my experiences of the "eligible villas" and "the desirable residences" which are so many traps for unwary young married couples. I am sure I should be doing a public service if I were to narrate the experiences of my own sons and daughters in this respect, and these experiences would act as a warning and prevent many young people from rushing rashly into "pretty places" and "well-appointed houses" which are so many whited sepulchres, but the victims of their own rashness would doubtless reproach me and say that I was holding them up to ridicule, or, as my eldest son, John, elegantly puts it, "giving them away".

The result of my eldest son taking a house, which I begged and entreated him to beware of, would be a most useful contribution to domestic history, but I hesitate now to tell the truth about it for fear of being reproached.

When he told me he was going to take that house, I said to him: "John, it is on clay. It is in a swamp. You'll have rheumatism for the rest of your life if you take that place, and you'll repent it as long as you live." But he would have it, and a pretty penny it cost him before he got out of it. It looked beautiful outside, and the rooms were large, and the landlord had stuck a lot of new paper on the walls – high-art paper he called it. Yes, I know that high-art paper. It's stuck on to hide the dampness of the walls. It is wonderful how a pretty paper and an early English doorway blind young house-hunters to every imperfection. Bait your hook with something Queen Anne outside and a high-art paper inside, and you are pretty certain to catch a tenant. You should see some of the high-art papers after they've been on six months, and the big patches of damp have come through them, but it's too late then. Your romantic young couple have taken a seven years' repairing lease, and they haven't as a rule very much money to spare for repapering and redecorating the walls. The bulk of their income has generally gone on the roof.

That's about the last place your young couple trouble about before they go in, but it's generally the first place they *have* to trouble about after they are in. I have seen some "charming residences" that had roofs which were only useful for one purpose, and that was to save having a shower bath in the house.

One of my sons-in-law I really thought at one time would have gone insane, and it was all owing to an eligible residence with a couple of rose trees stuck in the front garden and a cheap wooden balcony run up round the second-floor windows. "It looked so picturesque," he said. "So artistic, you know," and in spite of my pointing out that it lay low, was on a clay soil, and that it had evidently been run up in a hurry, he took a long lease of it.

My daughter and her husband entered into possession during one of those delightful summers when it rains straight off for three weeks at a time, and a fire is not only a luxury but an absolute necessity.

They had spent a good deal of money in wallpapers and dados and greeny-yellowy drapery, and certainly the place looked a perfect little picture when they had finished it. But it wasn't a picture long. The roof was the first trouble, and when the wet began to come in and drip through the ceilings and run down the walls and the papers began to peel off, they had a local builder in to see what was the matter. He said a few slates were loose at one of the corners, and he put the slates right. But a few days afterwards the rain came in at another corner, so they sent for the builder and had that reslated. When the rain still came in, and ruin was rapidly spreading over the ceilings and walls, my son-in-law grew desperate, and told the builder he was a bungler, and that he should not pay his bill, but the man said: "It's no use going on at me, sir; you told me to patch, and we patched, but patching's no use, the whole roof is old and crumbling to pieces; the lead is gone wrong, and the slates are broken. You must have an entirely new roof."

And a new roof he had to have before he had been in the house six months. When it was finished he said: "Thank goodness, that's done. It has been an expensive job, but we shan't have any more worry." They didn't have any more worry with the roof, but my daughter had a bad sore throat, and so did the servants, and everybody in the house, with the exception of my son-in-law, was taken ill and had to go to bed.

The doctor who was called in shook his head at the symptoms and said, "My dear sir, I'm afraid you'll never be well in this house until it is redrained. The last family who were here were never well. It will be much cheaper in the long run for you to have the place thoroughly redrained."

Poor boy. When he told me about it, his face was almost white with rage, and he said he felt that if he met the man who had let him the house he should do him an injury. But he had to do all the redraining himself and send his wife and the servants away while it was done, and I think if an earthquake had come and swallowed that "eligible villa" up on the spot he would not have been at all sorry.

When the drainage was all right again and the bill paid – and a nice heavy bill it was – he felt a little better, and said: "Well, it's done; now we're all right overhead and underground there ought to be an end to our troubles."

But there wasn't. When they came back, it was the end of October, and they had to have fires all over the house, and there wasn't a chimney that wouldn't have tried the patience of Job when everything else had failed.

The moment you made a fire anywhere, it filled all the rest of the rooms with smoke. And when you had lit it there was only one possible way in which you could remain in the room while it was burning, and that was by having the door and the windows wide open all the time.

The fireplaces in the dining room and in the drawing room were the worst. You either had to sit without a fire, or have a fire and sit and let your head be blown off with the draught.

I shall never forget calling one day and finding my poor children sitting down to lunch in the dining room. My daughter had on her bonnet and sealskin jacket, and a large travelling rug over her knees, and my son-in-law had on his ulster and a railway-travelling cap pulled down well over his ears.

I was naturally a little astonished, and I said, "Dear me, are you just going out?"

"Going out," said my son-in-law, "no; this is how we have to sit all day long now we have fires. Don't you see, the window has to be left wide open, or we should be suffocated with the smoke."

Poor fellow, he made a gallant effort to stop the chimneys smoking. He had the grates altered, he had patent cowls put on, he made the roof of his house resemble a steam circus, and the view from the distance of a dozen tall cowls all whirling violently round was positively alarming. But he never quite got rid of the smoke, and at last, in despair, they gave up burning coal in the dining room and drawing room, and in the bedroom, but had asbestos fires instead, and used gas, which is a very good thing in one way, but not, I should imagine, particularly healthy.

My poor daughter was quite heartbroken at the continual worry and expense of their "charming villa residence", and she tried to persuade her husband to let it. But these eligible villa residences are rather harder to let than they are to take. People came to see the place, but there was always something wrong which they noticed at once. There was one lady who came to look over it, and would, I believe, have taken it, but, unfortunately, just as she was on the point of deciding and giving the name of her solicitors, to whom the agreement was to be sent, the housemaid rushed upstairs and burst into the drawing room, and exclaimed, "Oh, ma'am, do come at once, ma'am; the kitchen wall's a-bulgin' in, and cook thinks the house is settling down rapid with the damp."

The lady didn't give the name of her solicitors. She left in a hurry, promising to write, which she did that very night, saying that on mature consideration she had decided the house wouldn't suit her.

Eventually the landlord was induced to take two years' rent and release them, and as my son-in-law had laid out considerably over a thousand pounds on the property in two years, the landlord didn't do badly.

Alas! how many a young couple have commenced married life with a "charming villa residence" as a millstone round their necks. And all because they would not take the advice of people with more experience than themselves. You would not catch *me* being taken in by a Queen Anne balcony or a high-art wallpaper.

I have alluded to this subject because the choice of a villa residence made by her married children has a good deal to do with a mother-in-law's peace of mind and happiness.

And so does the choice of servants. A son-in-law with a good cook is always much more amenable to reason than a son-in-law whose digestion is perpetually being upset by ill-prepared and badly cooked meals. Young people don't know how much the cook has to do with the course of true love after marriage.

There is always a great difficulty in thinking of something to give to a bride as a wedding present, because so many people hit on the same thing, and some young wives start housekeeping with ten silver biscuit boxes, twelve cases of dessert knives and forks, six pairs of fish-carvers, twenty paper knives and half a dozen sets of Tennyson's poems. There is a nice present that nobody has ever given yet, and which would be the most useful present of all – a really good cook.

I could give instances of the mischief a bad cook has caused among the members of my own family, but after my recent experiences I hesitate to do so. I do not wish our little family reunion to be marred by any ill feeling entertained towards me by my supersensitive sons- and daughters-in-law, and grandchildren.

I have during the course of these memoirs omitted much that would have thrown considerable light upon the domestic questions of the day, because I did not want to say anything which might be considered a breach of family confidence, but I can honestly say that every word I have written here is true, and is founded on my own actual experiences. I have dealt with facts, and have in no single instance indulged in fiction. Doubtless in doing this I have lost a certain amount of effect, but, as I told you when I began these memoirs, I am not a professional writer. I am simply a mother-in-law and it is as a mother-in-law who has had large experience, and who does not hesitate to speak her mind plainly, that I have humbly attempted in these pages to throw a little sidelight upon certain phases of family life which are either neglected by historians or represented in totally false colours by novelists and the writers of romance.

And with this explanation I have the honour to sign myself the reader's obliged and obedient servant,

Jane Tressider.

Notes

p. 5, *Shoolbred's, or Whiteley's, or Marshall & Snelgrove's*:
The names of real London department stores in the nine-
teenth century. James Shoolbred & Co. was located on
Tottenham Court Road. William Whiteley's original depart-
ment store, which was destroyed by fire in 1887, was on
Westbourne Grove in Notting Hill. It reopened in nearby
Bayswater in the early twentieth century. Marshall &
Snelgrove, now part of Debenhams, was on Oxford Street.

p. 11, *the Stores*: The Army & Navy Co-operative Society,
founded in 1871, which supplied groceries and other goods
to its subscribers.

p. 13, *Punch*: Weekly satirical magazine, established in 1841.

p. 25, *Jew's harps*: A jew's harp is a small musical instrument
shaped like a lyre, which is held in the mouth and plucked
with the finger.

p. 29, *battledore and shuttlecock*: An early form of
badminton.

p. 39, *the Pretender*: Either James Stuart (1688–1766), known
as the Old Pretender, or his son Charles Edward Stuart
(1720–88), known as the Young Pretender (or popularly as
Bonnie Prince Charlie). The former was the son of James II
(1633–1701), who was banished from the throne in 1688

due to his Catholicism. Supporters of the deposed house of Stuart, known as Jacobites, rose in rebellion in 1745, but were comprehensively defeated at the Battle of Culloden the following year. Lord Walkinshaw was presumably a proponent of this uprising.

p. 54, *Mother Red Cap*: An inn in Camden Town, north London.

p. 67, *"What's in a name?"*: From *Romeo and Juliet*, Act II, Sc. 2: "What's in a name? That which we call a rose / By any other name would smell as sweet..."

p. 73, *Condy's Fluid*: A disinfectant.

p. 75, *hearing death-watches*: That is, death-watch beetles, whose ticking mating call was once believed to portend death.

p. 76, *"grateful and comforting"*: A slogan from an advertisement for Epps's Cocoa in the late nineteenth century.

p. 81, *erysipelas*: A bacterial infection of the skin, also known as St Anthony's fire.

p. 82, *riding her to Banbury Cross*: Presumably meaning that the child was sitting on Mr Tressider's back while he sang the nursery rhyme 'Ride a Cock Horse to Banbury Cross'.

p. 83, *verdigris*: The green rust formed on brass or copper by atmospheric oxidation.

p. 99, *Mansion House*: The official residence of the Lord Mayor of London, used for ceremonial functions of the City of London.

p. 102, *tipsy cake*: A dessert consisting of sponge cake soaked in brandy and sherry.

p. 105, *Evil is wrought... broken without meaning it*: From 'The Lady's Dream' by the English poet Thomas Hood (1799–1845).

p. 105, *Bluebeard... the King in the Arabian Nights*: Bluebeard is a nobleman who murders several wives in succession in the story by the French writer of folk tales Charles Perrault (1628–1703). In the story that frames the collection of Middle Eastern and Indian tales known as the *Arabian Nights* or the *Thousand and One Nights*, the Persian king Shahryar, on discovering his wife's infidelity, has her executed, and thereafter marries a succession of virgins, executing each after the wedding night in order to prevent her from being unfaithful to him.

p. 111, *on the knifeboard of a Favorite 'bus*: The fleet of dark-green "Favorite" omnibuses (likely named after an inn in the Holloway area that was the hub of the vehicles' routes) was run by the company E. & J. Wilson. The "knifeboard" was the name of the long bench on the roof deck.

p. 115, *"Who ever loved that loved not at first sight?"*: From the mythological poem *Hero and Leander*, originally published in 1598, by the English dramatist and poet Christopher Marlowe (1564–93).

p. 118, *Empress Eugénie*: Eugénie, Comtesse de Teba (1826–1920), wife of Napoleon III and Empress of France 1853–70.

p. 123, *Come into the garden... here at the gate alone*: A famous lyric from *Maud* (1855), a long poem in the form of a dramatic monologue by Alfred, Lord Tennyson (1809–92), whose narrator, like Mr Johnson, is in an unbalanced mental state.

p. 144, *Wesleyan chapel*: That is, a Methodist chapel. The dissenting Methodist Church was founded in the late eighteenth century by the brothers John (1703–91) and Charles Wesley (1707–88).

p. 145, *Mudie's*: A chain of lending libraries in nineteenth-century England named after its founder, Charles Edward Mudie (1818–90). The original London branch was on New Oxford Street.

p. 176, *to attend a chapel*: The point being that Anne belongs to a Nonconformist Protestant denomination, most likely the Methodists.

p. 182, *at Jericho*: That is, in hell. The expression "Go to Jericho!" was the equivalent of "Go to hell!"

p. 198, *life preserver*: A kind of club, otherwise known as a blackjack.

p. 206, *kermesse*: Actually a Dutch word meaning literally "church mass" and denoting a local fair or carnival.

p. 209, *Rathaus*: "Town hall" (German).

p. 213, *Unstable as water thou shalt not excel*: From Genesis 49:4 in the King James Bible.

p. 218, *the Guards*: The household division of the British army, that is, the troops employed to protect the king or queen.

p. 223, *Earlswood*: The Royal Earlswood Hospital, an asylum in Redhill, Surrey.

p. 227, *allowing her daughter to marry my son*: The word "my" has been added for this edition. It was missing in the 1892 text.

p. 237, *Croesus*: The last king of Lydia (*c*.560–546 BC), proverbial for his fabulous wealth.

p. 240, *the Sandwich Islands*: Hawaii.

p. 242, *Carlsbad*: Karlovy Vary, known in English as Carlsbad, is a spa city in what is today the Czech Republic (then Bohemia). It was a popular tourist destination in the nineteenth century.

ALMA CLASSICS

ALMA CLASSICS aims to publish mainstream and lesser-known European classics in an innovative and striking way, while employing the highest editorial and production standards. By way of a unique approach the range offers much more, both visually and textually, than readers have come to expect from contemporary classics publishing.

❧

To order any of our titles and for up-to-date information about our current and forthcoming publications, please visit our website at:

www.almaclassics.com